The Hostess With the Ghostess

The Hostess With the Ghostess

A Haunted Guesthouse Mystery

E. J. Copperman

CROOKED
LANE

NEW YORK

Published in the United States by Crooked Lane Books, an imprint of The Quick Brown Fox & Company LLC.

Crooked Lane Books and its logo are trademarks of The Quick Brown Fox & Company LLC.

Library of Congress Catalog-in-Publication data available upon request.

ISBN (paperback): 978-1-68331-917-7
ISBN (hardcover): 978-1-68331-450-9
ISBN (ePub): 978-1-68331-451-6
ISBN (ePDF): 978-1-68331-452-3

Cover illustration by Dominick Finelle
Book design by Jennifer Canzone

Printed in the United States.

www.crookedlanebooks.com

Crooked Lane Books
34 West 27th St., 10th Floor
New York, NY 10001

Hardcover Edition: January 2018
Paperback Edition: December 2018

10 9 8 7 6 5 4 3 2 1

Cast of Characters

Alison Kerby . . . . Innkeeper, ghost whisperer, reluctant detective

Melissa Kerby. . . . . Alison's thirteen-year-old daughter

Loretta Kerby. . . . . Alison's mom

Jack Kerby . . . . Alison's dad, now a ghost

Paul Harrison. . . . . Deceased but not completely gone detective

Maxie Malone . . . . Ghost interior designer and poltergeist

Phyllis Coates. . . . . Editor, publisher, staff of the *Harbor Haven Chronicle*

Detective Lieutenant
Anita McElone . . . . Chief of detectives, Harbor Haven Police Department

Everett Sandheim. . . . . Maxie's ghost husband, ex-military man

Vanessa and Eduardo DiSica. . . Alison's guests

Abigail Lesniak . . . . A guest with a request

Gregory Lewis . . . . Guest; Abigail's request

Penny Desmond . . . . Alison's guest

Keith Barent Johnson. . . . . . Deceased rich guy

Adrian Van Doren Johnson . . . Keith's wife

CAST OF CHARACTERS

Cassidy Van Doren . . . . Adrian's daughter; Keith's
stepdaughter

Braden and Erika Johnson . . . . Keith's children from a previous
marriage

Hunter Evans . . . . Keith's business partner

Robin Witherspoon . . . . Owner of Cranbury Bog,
a bed-and-breakfast

Tom Zink . . . . a visiting businessman

Chapter 1

"Something's missing." I was sitting on a barstool next to the center island in my kitchen, having a conversation with five other people, two of whom were alive. More on that shortly. "It's just not going over."

My daughter Melissa, one of the people who (thank goodness) is still breathing, frowned. She brushed her front teeth over her lower lip, which she calls "scratching," and let out a long breath.

"The spook shows just don't have the same energy," she said. "But I'm not sure how much the guests care." Liss had managed to become a teenager a mere five months earlier without actually becoming exasperating—no small feat.

And she had a point. My guests, lovely people that they were, didn't seem to care anymore if objects flew by their heads or strange substances dripped down my walls. It just wasn't as much fun as it used to be. But they were still coming to the place with the big sign at the front door that read,

"Haunted Guesthouse." So the whole ghost thing was probably still a draw, I thought.

Perhaps I should explain.

Four years ago, after freeing myself from Melissa's father (whom I "affectionately" call the Swine whenever he's not around, which is almost always) and settling a lawsuit (the details of which you're better off not knowing), I returned to my hometown of Harbor Haven, New Jersey. I found a fairly dilapidated, enormous Victorian home on the beach, put tons of work and pretty much all my money into making it much less dilapidated, and opened it to those who would like to vacation on the deservedly famous Jersey Shore.

This is where the story gets a little weird. During the renovations, I suffered a blow to the head—never mind why, because it just gets me annoyed to remember—and woke up with the ability to see and hear ghosts. Apparently this is something that runs among the women in my family. My mother and Melissa always had the knack but hadn't told me because they didn't want me to feel bad. Like I was going to feel bad about it.

Anyway, once the stars cleared from my eyes, I could see two ghosts inhabiting (some would say "haunting," but that's something of an overstatement) my new house. Their names were Paul Harrison and Maxie Malone. We discovered how they were murdered, by whom, and why, but that didn't seem to "complete their business" on this plane of existence. Instead they just hung around the house all day. After a while the whole ghost thing kind of loses its novelty. For them too.

Paul had been starting a private investigation firm when he stopped being as alive as he once was and wanted to keep his admittedly transparent hand in the business. It seems that among other things, infinity can get a bit tedious if you don't have an area of interest, and Paul didn't want to take up philately. Problem was, the vast majority of living people couldn't see or hear him, and at the time he couldn't leave the boundaries of my property, so under normal circumstances—if you can call anything about this normal—he would have been able to solve only mysteries that took place in my house. The prospects were somewhat limiting.

Instead he proposed a solution: I should sit for the private investigator examination, obtain a license from the state of New Jersey, and become his "eyes, ears, and legs" among the community of those still drawing breath, particularly the ones more than a thousand yards from my living room. He found it somewhat surprising when I balked at his suggestion, given my total lack of interest or experience in the whole investigating area.

Hang on. There's more. Almost at the same moment, I was approached by a company called Senior Plus Tours, a company that offered unique experiences for those over the age of fifty-five who wanted a "value-added" component to their vacations. Word had gotten out that my house had some not-so-living people in it, and apparently there are those who think that's a *good* thing and want to interact with ghosts while on vacation. It seems the Haunted Mansion at Disney World just isn't a big enough kick for some.

The tour group would guarantee me a certain number of guests most weeks, a stream of revenue I couldn't afford to pass up, but the promise of a supernatural experience had to be guaranteed. So knowing when I am over a barrel, I agreed to Paul's investigator plan on the condition that he and Maxie would make their presence blatantly obvious a couple of times a day by putting on what we at the Haunted Guesthouse have come to call (affectionately, to be sure) "spook shows." A deal was quickly struck when Paul convinced Maxie to participate. Maxie, who was a twenty-six-year-old budding interior designer when she and Paul were deprived of life, can be a tad difficult to deal with, but somehow Paul obtained her agreement, and she has missed very few spook shows in the past four years.

So the fact that the latest round of ghostly entertainments was falling flat couldn't be blamed entirely on Maxie. She was, in fact, now in the kitchen with me, Melissa, my mother (rounding out the alive people in the room), my deceased but still beloved father, and Maxie's equally nonliving new husband, Everett. Maxie met Everett on one of our investigations, and they had married, sort of, in a ceremony at the guesthouse four months earlier.

If I couldn't blame Maxie for the problem—which is generally my first choice—we had to define exactly what was missing from the spook shows, and in this case, that was pretty easy.

"It's Paul," my mother said. "I don't like to say it, but Paul is the problem here."

Melissa looked down at the floor to avoid eye contact around the room, but she nodded just a little. In fact, everyone gathered in the kitchen had roughly the same reaction to what Mom had said—except Maxie, who sort of grinned a little because she loves it when the source of everyone's consternation is not her. It's so rare.

"You can't blame the guy for not being here," my father said finally. "You told him that you were done with the deal, baby girl."

"I'm not blaming him," I pointed out. "Mom is."

"Alison," my mother admonished.

What Dad had said was true. Since I'd discovered Paul and Maxie in the house when I was remodeling it, Paul had been unable to travel past the limits of my property. But four months ago, through the use of some crazy gadget he'd slapped together out of discarded electronics, Paul had used a bolt of lightning—no, really—to free himself of that limitation. I'd told him I was no longer interested in the whole investigation thing, which was a lie only in the aspect that I had *never* been interested in it, and freed him from his spook show obligations. He'd taken off not long after to see the world (travel being somewhat cheaper when nobody knows you're on the plane), and we had not heard from him since.

I understood the impulse, but not a text message or a postcard in four months? I was a little disappointed and just slightly offended, but not really. Paul and I had become close friends. In the way that one is close to a person who isn't any longer alive but still talks to you on a day-to-day basis. My life is slightly complicated.

Unfortunately, since his departure, I'd discovered that a good number of the guests my house attracted were still drawn to it for the promise of some supernatural contact. Maxie had agreed to keep the spook shows going because she likes to have leverage over me. Occasionally Everett would fill in for Paul because he'd seen the routines many times before while visiting Maxie. Other times Dad would take up the slack, but he was a handyman when he was alive, not a showman, and he was occasionally distracted by a slight crack in the ceiling plaster or a nail that was sticking out of the molding around the library door. He couldn't stop himself from repairing the issue, and although the guests thought a flying hammer was sort of interesting, it didn't really have the same pizzazz as the stuff Paul used to do. It wasn't any one particular stunt—Paul wasn't the most creative of performers—but he brought a zeal that was lacking these days in a way you couldn't exactly put your finger on.

The guests, who this week in June numbered five, had shown enthusiasm over the first couple of shows when they'd arrived on Tuesday. Now it was Thursday, and attendance was on the down side. It could mean they were exploring the area, sightseeing and shopping, but that hadn't been the pattern the first four years we'd been open, and my concern was what had led to this emergency meeting in my kitchen.

"Maybe I could add things they'd find interesting." Everett had been a mentally ill homeless man when I knew him alive. Now that he was a ghost, he'd reverted to a previous version of himself, when he was a military man in his twenties. That was the man Maxie had fallen in love with, and he is always trying to be useful. "I could do drills with my rifle. I've done it before."

"I don't know," I said. I stood up and walked to the fridge because that's what I do when I'm thinking. And when I'm not thinking. "I don't blame you, Everett, and I'm really grateful you and Dad are filling in. Maybe it's just the idea of the shows that isn't fresh and right anymore. Maybe we need some other kind of ghost thing to do. I don't like to scare people, but—"

I heard something like shoes scraping on the hardwood floor in the den, just outside the kitchen, and turned even as I reached for the orange juice. Was that one of the guests? I don't serve food at the guesthouse, and they tend not to come into the kitchen, although I never suggest they shouldn't.

"But what?" Maxie wanted to know.

I ignored her, which had become my default reaction. "Can I help you?" I called out into the den, but there was no answer. I put the orange juice back and closed the fridge.

My mother saw my face, which must have been registering concern, and said, "Jack." My father, with more than a lifetime of experience with her, understood exactly and floated (sort of—it's more propulsive than that but not at all like walking) toward the swinging door that separates the kitchen and the den.

Before he could get there, though, the door opened, and I gasped a little. For part of a second, I thought the answer to the very problem we had been discussing was solved. The tall, thin frame; the light-brown hair, just a little tousled from indifferent care; the almost completely transparent body . . .

"Paul?" Melissa said. Then she shook her head, having realized as I had that this was not our absent friend.

But whoever this ghost was looked up at the name. "You know Paul?" he said with a bit of a British accent. Paul Harrison was Canadian and had been born in England, but his accent was more Toronto than Manchester. This was clearly not him, although there were similarities.

This man was older than Paul, for one thing. I'd say he was in his late forties, whereas Paul was thirty-two years old forever. And he—the new ghost—didn't have Paul's signature goatee, which he'd stroke when thinking about a case. This guy was clean shaven. Paul always wore jeans and a succession of turtleneck sweaters. This man was in a business suit.

"We know Paul," I told him even as I felt Maxie and Everett close ranks behind me. They are serious about protection, and we didn't know this ghost's intentions yet. "I guess you do too."

The ghost nodded somberly. "I am his brother," he said.

I hate to admit it, but my first thought was, *I wonder if he'd do some spook shows.*

Chapter 2

It took a moment to shake off that feeling. "You're Paul's brother?" I said, despite having clearly heard him make that exact statement. Sometimes you just need a second.

"Yes." Well, that was informative.

Maxie hopped over my head to hover in front of me. It was a welcome gesture, seeing as how the other way she would have reached that position would have been to walk through me, and I'm not crazy about that. "How do we know?" she asked.

That seemed to puzzle the new ghost. He stopped moving forward and regarded her through a pair of glasses he produced from his breast pocket. You wouldn't think a dead person would need spectacles, but we'd actually met one who'd been blind, so throw the rulebook out the window and welcome to my corner of the next life.

"How do you know what?" he asked.

"How do we know you're really Paul's brother?"

The ghost considered that. "Because I am." It was clear we were going to get tons of information out of this guy.

"Come in," Melissa said, gesturing to the new ghost, who was still partially stuck in the door. A guest in the den wouldn't have seen him but might have noticed attention in that area. Best not to take chances. "I'm Melissa Kerby, and this is my mom, my grandmother, and my grandfather." She gestured as she went. "Our friends are Maxie and Everett. Who are you?"

That girl has a future in diplomacy if she doesn't decide to become a federal prosecutor or president of the United States. Or all three, now that I think of it.

The ghost moved all the way into the kitchen and smiled at Melissa in a friendly way, which is all I ask. He did not bow exactly but held up his head and then lowered it in more than a nod and less than a salaam. "I am Richard Harrison," he said. "It is very nice to meet you."

"It's nice to meet you, Mr. Harrison," my mother said. "I'm Loretta, and this is Jack." I guess she didn't want Richard to be calling them Grandma and Grandpa, which was reasonable.

"You can all see me," he said in wonder. "How is that possible?"

"It's a family thing," Mom told him. "Did you come here looking for Paul?"

But before he could answer, Maxie, who is not easily charmed, folded her arms. "You haven't answered me," she said. "How do we know you're really Paul's brother?"

"I'm told we look alike," Richard said.

"A lot of guys look like you, pal," Maxie said. "It's nothing special."

"Maxie," Everett said. Even though Maxie usually defers to him on issues of polite discourse, she shook her head.

"Anybody could come in here and say he's Paul's brother," she said.

"Why would they?" Melissa asked.

That took some of the wind out of Maxie's sails. She stopped to think. But she wouldn't let Richard off the hook that easily. "How did you know to look for him here?" she asked.

Richard shook his head slightly, seemingly to himself. "I'm not sure," he said. "I've only been . . . like this . . . for a little while, and I don't really understand it. But I've been hearing voices of other—"

"Ghosts," Maxie said flatly. She doesn't mind the word when it's not used in relation to her.

Richard nodded. "Yes. And I sort of . . . talked back with my mind." Paul also has this ability, which I call talking on the Ghosternet. "A voice—not Paul's—suggested that I look for him here. I was in the area anyway, so I found my way here. I gather from the way you all have reacted that my brother is not here."

"No," I answered. "He hasn't been here for a few months now. How did you . . . what brought you to this state of existence, Richard?"

"Excuse me?"

"You're a relatively young man. I assume you didn't revert to a younger age, because Paul was only in his thirties. How did you die?" Sometimes you have to be blunt.

Richard did not react well; he looked at the ceiling as if it held some existential answer to his situation. "I think we should focus on the issue, which is finding my brother."

Richard Harrison did not appear to be the kind of man who would let his emotions overwhelm him, but he said he had been dead for about a week, and that's not a transition you get over quickly. Paul himself had once told me he'd been stuck in what would become my house for a couple of months after dying here before he'd totally accepted the fact that he was no longer on the same plane of existence as before.

In Richard's case, though, the outpouring of emotion was relegated to a slight widening of the eyes and a very quick intake of breath, which was then let out slowly. "I see," he said. "Would you know where he might have gone?"

Paul had not been specific about his plans other than to "see the world" now that he had the time, so I couldn't tell Richard anything about his brother's whereabouts and told him so. "I'm sorry," I said. "We haven't heard a word from him since he left."

"Is that unusual?" Richard asked.

"I don't know. He's never left before."

Melissa stood up and walked toward Richard, stepping around Everett. Maxie's husband (because that's how they were referring to each other now) was standing guard a bit to my right, not really seeming like he thought there was much danger in the area. He did not hold his military rifle, which was just as well because what good would it have done? It wasn't like Everett could threaten to kill Richard. They were both deceased. Takes the sting out of threats.

"How can we help you, Mr. Harrison?" she asked.

Richard looked just a little stunned. He'd clearly pictured this moment differently and was readjusting his reactions. "I don't know," he said.

"Maybe we can think of something together," Dad suggested. He has never stopped fixing things. It bothers him when there's a problem he can't solve. "You've known him all your life. Where would your brother go?"

Richard's face didn't exactly darken—it would have needed more color to do that—but it did sort of harden into a blank expression. "I honestly wouldn't know," he said. "We have not been very close for some time."

"Well, Paul's been dead for five years," Maxie helpfully mentioned.

"Yes, but before that," Richard told her with very little inflection.

There was a brief awkward silence in the room. As usual, my thirteen-year-old daughter took the reins and became the most responsible adult in the room.

"Well, we'll have to find him," she said simply.

Everyone turned toward Melissa. Richard, who had appeared in my kitchen less than five minutes before, looked down at her but without the condescension so many adults have for children. "How will we do that?" he asked. He wasn't humoring her; Liss has a way of making you believe in her.

"You know Paul was a private investigator, right?" she asked Richard, who nodded with a questioning look on his face. "Well, he taught my mom how to be a detective, and she'll just do what Paul would do if he were searching for a missing person." Liss turned toward me and apparently didn't notice the look of complete panic on my face. "Right, Mom?"

"Sure," I said. But my teeth were tightly clenched.

#

With five guests (a couple and three singles, which was slightly unusual—I usually don't get that many singles) in the house taking up four rooms and Richard not needing much in the way of accommodations, it was agreed he would take up residence in one of the empty second-floor guest rooms for the duration of our search for his missing dead brother. And our best hope was that the deceased Paul would hear something about Richard's search on the Ghosternet and get in touch somehow.

That's what life is like in my house. If you call that living.

Once Richard was ensconced and told that we would need some privacy for a strategy session that he might find upsetting (although to be honest, Richard was dead for a week and already acting like the CEO of a medium-sized investment firm, so his emotional fragility was assumed rather than observed), we regulars at the guesthouse reconvened in the kitchen, the only room on the ground floor that would accommodate all of us even if only three were visible to the general public.

My first order of business, this being a meeting with no written agenda, was to look at my daughter and ask in as calm a tone as I could muster, "You really think I can find a missing dead man? Why are you raising Richard's hopes, Liss?"

She lowered her eyebrows and didn't make eye contact. "I didn't want to make him sad," she said. "He's been through a lot."

"Such a sweet girl," my mother volunteered. Mom has spent her life dedicated to the proposition that I could never do anything wrong (other than marrying the Swine, but she's forgiven me), and that principle has been extended to one other person for the past thirteen years.

"Do you think there was something a little guarded about that guy?" My father, examining the ceiling near the kitchen door by rising up to get close, actually stuck his head through the plaster and then came back out. "I felt like there was something he wasn't telling you."

My father is—or was, depending on one's perspective—a very trusting man, so that was something of an extreme statement from him. Mom and I exchanged a glance of concern. "What do you mean, Jack?" she asked Dad.

"He just shows up here and says he's looking for Paul," Dad answered. Then he put his head through the kitchen door, and his body twisted up. No doubt he was making an assessment of a serious hole in the ceiling just above the doorway on the den side, where a bullet had dislodged a lot of plaster and done some damage to a beam some months back. Dad never tires of measuring and examining. He leaves nothing to chance in a repair. His face reappeared on our side of the door. "But he says he and Paul weren't close, and I don't even know if he showed up here after Paul and Maxie ended up in this house. For a funeral?" Ghosts don't like the word *died*. I figure you have to be sensitive to their preferences.

"Not every family is close," Mom said. "Besides, you weren't here when that happened, Jack." My father had spent some time avoiding my house because he felt guilty about . . . it's a long story.

"Maybe Paul didn't like him," Maxie said. "He didn't talk about his brother much. I didn't even know his name before today."

Everett doesn't talk a lot. He prefers to stand back and observe, participating only when he feels he has something to contribute. He was floating in the "at-ease" position, not tense but never really relaxed.

"Maybe they had some kind of falling out in life and now Richard wants to make amends," he suggested.

"I don't think that's it," Dad said. "But I could be wrong."

"We're getting off the topic," I reminded everyone. "How are we going to find Paul?"

There was no immediate response, but I heard a car pulling around the side of the house and into the back, where there is parking space. I looked out the back door. In June the sun doesn't go down until well after eight, so I'd forgotten how late it was.

My husband was home.

Josh Kaplan and I had been married four months earlier at the exact same moment as Maxie and Everett, except that the justice of the peace who married us—who also runs the local gas station and auto repair—could actually see and hear us, and not so much them. Josh and I had known each other, technically, since we were kids but hadn't been in touch in a long time before we'd reconnected a couple of years before. I was still getting used to the idea of being a wife and having a husband, but it wasn't an unpleasant adjustment at all. I smiled every time he walked through the door.

Mom and Melissa looked toward the door. Dad was busy determining the integrity of the ceiling, Everett wouldn't turn his head unless necessary, and Maxie was Maxie. She probably hadn't heard the car door shut or the footsteps on the gravel outside because neither of those was the sound of her name.

Josh opened the back door and stood in the doorway a moment. He looked at me first because he is a great husband and then at Melissa because they actually like each other a lot. It's not unusual for Mom to be around because she and Liss often cook dinner for us, so he wasn't surprised to see her either, but he also knows what house he lives in. Then he walked over and kissed me with his "there are people watching" kiss, which is very warm and makes promises to be kept later. When we separated, Josh being careful not to rub his work clothes against me, he headed toward the center island but did not sit on the barstools.

"Who else is here?" he asked, looking up at the ceiling as if that was going to help. Josh can't see or hear the ghosts, not even my father, whom he's known longer than he's known me. We actually met at the paint store in Asbury Park that Josh's grandfather Sy owned, Madison Paints—which he sold to Josh decades later—and played together while Dad got supplies and contractor gossip from Sy.

I gave Josh the rundown, and Liss filled him in on the drama with Richard and the spot we were in, largely thanks to her promise. She is a lovely person and only wants to help, so I couldn't even be grumpy about that, which put something of a damper on my day. If you can't be grumpy, what's the point of being from New Jersey?

Josh sat down carefully on one of the barstools. Because of the paint store, he comes home often covered in dust, smudges of wallboard compound, and flecks of paint. Normally his first move on arriving home is toward the shower, but this was a situation and he didn't want to take the time just yet.

"So how are you going to look for Paul?" he asked.

There was a small tap at the kitchen door before I could answer, which was lucky since I had no idea how to find Paul on my own. If I'd had Paul to consult . . . well, then the whole enterprise would have been pointless.

"Yes?" I called toward the door.

As I'd suspected, one of my guests was standing outside the swinging door. "Alison," called Vanessa DiSica, who with her husband, Eduardo, had been occupying the downstairs guest room, my largest, since Tuesday. "I don't want to bother you."

I stood and walked to the door. I didn't want to push it open for fear of hitting Vanessa in the face but got close enough to speak in a normal tone. "No trouble at all," I said. "Come in."

Vanessa pushed the door toward me gingerly, no doubt concerned as I had been, but I stood back far enough that the door wouldn't hit anyone but Dad, who wouldn't notice. She walked into the kitchen and nodded hello to Melissa and Josh. She hadn't seen my mother before, so introductions were made. No sense mentioning the three dead people in the room; even in a haunted guesthouse, it tends to dampen a civilian's mood. Except the ones who find it exciting.

"How can I help you, Vanessa?" I asked.

"I heard some noises right above our room," she answered. "Now, I realize this is a busy hotel"—there was no point in explaining the difference between a hotel and a guesthouse because she probably didn't care and was just using the most familiar word—"but this sounded a little weird."

My mind immediately did a mental inventory of who would be in the room directly above the one Vanessa and Eduardo were sharing, and the answer didn't really thrill me.

"There's nobody in that room," Maxie said. Maxie, wary of strangers, usually keeps away from the guests except during spook shows and stays very aware of where everyone is housed so she can avoid them.

"How were the sounds strange?" I asked, not acknowledging Maxie, although I had reached the same conclusion as she had—there was no guest in that room. My first thought had been that it was Richard moving something around, but his designated area (not that he needed much in the way of space) was at the opposite end of the house.

"I don't know," Vanessa answered, which was of no help whatsoever. "It sounded like . . . stretching."

Melissa and I exchanged a look. "Stretching?" she asked. It seemed a reasonable question at the time.

Vanessa nodded. "I can't be more helpful than that. You know, like if you had a really big elastic band or one of those colored strips they use for exercising and you pulled it really hard? It sounded like that."

"Well, let's check it out," I said. I stood and picked up a flashlight from one of the drawers in the island. I have no idea what I thought I was going to do with that; the electrical power was on all over the house.

Josh didn't say anything, but he was right behind me as I walked out of the kitchen and toward the front room, where the stairs to the second floor are located. There was no point in telling Melissa not to follow, so he was watching out for her as well. Anything within driving distance of danger gets Josh quiet and focused; he was in protection mode. My mother, I noticed, stayed behind in the kitchen, which was actually exactly what I wanted her to do. No doubt Maxie was through the ceiling—literally—and on her way to the room in question as we approached.

When we reached the stairway, which is directly to the right of the door to Vanessa's room, I stopped and listened. "Do you hear it now?" I asked Vanessa, who was clearly not going to follow us upstairs and was huddled in her doorway. Again, that was fine with me.

She shook her head. "But it was real, I promise."

"I have no doubt of that, Vanessa," I assured her. "Just wait right here."

She did not argue.

Sure enough, I saw Maxie floating across the hallway at the top of the stairs and making her way into the room in question, which was at the far left side of the upper corridor. That gave me a little confidence, but I still let Josh lead the charge up the stairs and kept Melissa behind me. I love Josh dearly, but if he wants to protect the little woman against something unknown, I'm not going to argue with him.

We didn't exactly rush up the stairs. Once at the landing, the three of us made a left turn and walked to the door in question. Josh reached over and turned the knob, but I was well aware that the door, leading to a room that was not currently occupied, would be locked. I have a skeleton key for the house that I'm never without, so I fished it out of my pocket, pushed it into the lock, and turned the key.

Maxie hadn't come out, which was odd. It's a small room. If there were something scary inside, she'd have come out to warn us. If there wasn't, she'd come out to laugh at me for being such a coward. Maxie and I have an interesting relationship.

The door opened into the room, so I just let go of the knob and let it swing open. My father keeps all the hinges oiled, so there was no ominous creak. Dad is a wizard with WD-40.

Josh didn't give me the chance to go inside first and really hadn't had to worry about much protest on my part. I wasn't scared, exactly. You get used to hearing noises in an old house, and when you're inured with the idea of ghosts floating around willy-nilly, the expectation for odd noises rises a bit. But there was something about the stretching noise—which I hadn't heard—that was a little off, and in my house when something's a little off, that can mean pretty much anything.

Josh walked inside, and I saw his head swivel from one side to the other. He turned and looked at me in the doorway. "I don't see anything," he said. "Doesn't mean nothing's here." He stood to one side, leaving me a path because he was clearly convinced there wasn't any danger present in the room.

As it turned out, that was accurate depending on your definition of the word *danger*. Maxie was hovering around the ceiling, not zipping around and around the perimeter like she would have been if she were angry or excited. She looked down at me, and her mouth flattened out.

"Nothing," she said. "No stretching stuff I can see."

Melissa was literally pushing at my back, and since Maxie had given the room her seal of approval, I let my daughter squeeze by me. She stood as close to the center of the room as she could (the bed took up much of the floor space) and then looked up. "Weird," she said.

"What?" I asked. I didn't see anything but Maxie in the direction Liss was looking.

"I smell something," my daughter answered. "Do you?"

"I can't," Maxie told her, although she wasn't the one Melissa had been asking. Maxie hates it when anything isn't about her.

Now I try very hard not to breathe in very strongly. Melissa adopted a little ghost dog a while back, and although Lester is very sweet and loving and transparent, he still manages to qualify for my allergies. I'm on three antihistamines daily and I still need to stay away from Lester. We were only one floor away from him, assuming he was staying up in Melissa's attic bedroom like he was supposed to. But puppies—and Lester will always be a puppy—don't always do what they're supposed to.

I took a sniff anyway and immediately sneezed. "I'm not getting anything," I told Liss when I recovered.

"I think I am," Josh told us. "Sort of a burning rubber kind of smell, Melissa?"

"Is that it?" she asked. "Could be. Fits in with stretching."

"Swell," I said. "Now I don't know what was going on in this room *and* I have to air it out to make it habitable for the next guest." I walked to the window and opened it. The room is too small to have a ceiling fan or I would have turned it on.

"What do you think could have caused that?" Josh said to me.

The whole thing was starting to make me weary. "I don't know," I admitted. "But I know who would have an idea."

"Who?" Liss asked.

"Paul."

Chapter 3

"I want to take out a personal ad," I said.

Phyllis Coates, editor, publisher, and janitorial staff for the *Harbor Haven Chronicle*, looked at me, and the only word that came to my mind was *askance*. "I thought you got married."

"I did," I told her with an emphatic nod. "It's not *that* kind of personal ad."

"Of course not." Phyllis had a desktop computer displaying the front page she was composing and a laptop open on the only semiclean area of her massive desk, which was piled almost to the ceiling with papers. Phyllis believes in technology in the sense that she can't disprove it exists. "So what kind of personal ad is it? Or is that too personal?"

I looked around futilely for a place to sit. There is one chair in Phyllis's office, and it contains Phyllis. "That's very amusing," I told her. "You should write for a living. This ad's the kind you post when you're hoping to connect with somebody but you don't know where he is, so you hope he sees it and get in touch with you."

"What is this, 1944?" asked my friend. "You going to meet him under the big clock in Grand Central Terminal after the war is over?" Phyllis has a sense of romance, I'm sure, but it is buried under twenty years of working for the *New York Daily News* followed by taking over the *Chronicle* and treating it like a real newspaper. "You don't have an e-mail address, a Facebook page, a cell phone number? Nothing?"

"He's not that kind of a friend," I said.

"The kind who's alive in the twenty-first century?"

Well, if you want to get technical . . . "I don't have any contact information. You going to take my money for the ad or not?"

"I'll take the ad, but I'm not taking your money." Phyllis punched a few keys and looked at me. "You're family, and this is a stupid ad. What do you want it to say?"

I repressed my desire to challenge her use of the word *stupid* and moved on. I am an adult. "I can't just fill out a form?" I asked.

"Nope. We haven't had an ad like this in years. Maybe never. Don't have a form for it. Tell me what you want to say." Phyllis is a reporter because she is a natural snoop and she found a way to make it pay for her. She certainly had a form on file for a classified ad; she just wanted to hear me say the words in mine so she could find something out.

Good luck to her with what I was going to say. "Okay, write this: To Casper, All is forgiven. Brother Richard is waiting. Please come home ASAP. A. K."

I finished, and Phyllis looked at me for a long moment. "How do I spell 'Casper'?" she asked.

"With an *e*, like the friendly ghost."

Phyllis has heard the stories about my house and knows about the sign I hung right by my entrance, but she's a news-woman and does not rely on anything except that which she can prove to be true. She needs two reliable sources to print that I have ghosts in my house, and to be fair, she's never really looked for them. So she didn't bat an eyelid and said, "Uh-huh."

"Thanks." I stood and picked up my summer tote bag, which makes me look like a tourist so that no real tourists ask me questions. It's bad business, but it speeds up my day immeasurably.

"What makes you think your friend is going to be reading a local paper if you have no idea where he is?" Phyllis asked me before I could escape her tiny office. "Why not go to a paper with an international circulation, or at least one that goes across the country?"

"Two reasons," I said.

"Besides that you knew I wouldn't charge you," Phyllis said.

"One reason," I allowed. "My friend used to live here in town, and he'll be checking the *Chronicle* online just to keep up. He's really predictable in some ways."

"I'll get it out on the website in five minutes. Does your husband know you're taking out personal ads to lure men back to town?" she asked.

"It was his idea." I figured I'd leave her with that, because it was true and because I wasn't crazy about the innuendo.

Phyllis didn't stare at me; she doesn't believe in letting on when she's surprised. But I saw her move toward her computer and start typing when I left the office. As I headed down the street to my car, a tourist asked me if I could direct her to a good souvenir store—a real one, "not a tourist trap."

The tote bag doesn't always work.

#

Placing the ad for Paul's attention was clearly a long shot, but this was a situation that required me to try every lamebrain idea I might have, even if my husband got it first. So in the interest of flailing out in every direction, my next stop was to Madame Lorraine, the local medium.

I know, I know. I can see and hear ghosts, so what did I need with a medium? It's a fair question, but the fact is that I can only communicate with those spirits in my presence. For example, I noticed a lovely older man floating just above Madame Lorraine's walk-in storefront on Ocean Avenue. He was actually dressed as a doorman for a ritzy apartment building and tipped his cap to me as I walked in. He seemed very surprised when I waved at him and nodded my head. I was sorry I didn't have any change to tip him with.

What I needed was someone in touch with dead people who might have some Ghosternet access. Free Die-Fi, if you will. The only ghost I knew like that was Paul, and maybe in six months, Richard. Neither of those was going to be helpful today.

Madame Lorraine had apparently not opened for the day yet because her door was locked. I thought a serious medium should have known I was coming, but who was I to tell a woman how to do her business? Luckily there was a buzzer next to the door, and I pushed the button.

"What?" came a voice through the squawk box.

Customer service. I took a note for my own hospitality enterprise and pushed the button as I spoke. "Madame Lorraine? It's Alison Kerby." I figured my ghost-related reputation had surely made its way to the madame. Maybe she'd give me a break on the fee out of professional courtesy. What? Stranger things have happened.

"So?" Seriously, this woman's skill in making a new customer feel welcome was unparalleled, just not in the way she probably hoped.

"So may I come in for a moment?"

The voice on the other end sounded so thoroughly weary and disgusted with the prospect that it was something of a shock that she said, "Yeah. Gimme a minute." But it was only a few seconds before the buzzer sounded and I pushed the glass door of Madame Lorraine's establishment open and entered.

I'd seen her around town before, so it was no surprise that Madame Lorraine was a trim, somewhat dusty-looking woman in her fifties with a single gray braid going down from the nape of her neck to the small of her back. The shawl around her shoulders, no doubt hand-crocheted by someone who was not Madame Lorraine, was a nice touch.

"So what do you want?"

I guessed my hostess did not act this way with most paying customers, but every entrepreneur had her own style. "I'm hoping you can get me in touch with a friend who has gone on to the next world," I said.

"You mean a dead person?" Madame Lorraine was walking around turning on lights (dim) and straightening pillows (worn).

"Yes, I guess I do."

"Then why'd you say it like that? 'Gone on to the next world'?"

"I don't know. I thought you'd like it."

"You were wrong." The room was now set up as I assumed Madame Lorraine wanted it, and she walked to the far side of the table at its center, with five chairs around it in addition to the one she plopped herself into. "I thought you could talk to ghosts yourself. What do you need me for?"

So that was it. Madame Lorraine didn't like me horning in on her territory, even though I wasn't. No sense getting into that with her. Maybe I could be humble and get her on my side. "I can talk to ghosts who are in the room with me, the ones I can see," I told her. "I can't contact the ones out of my sight line. I was hoping you might be able to do that for me."

"You're one of those debunkers, aren't you?" Madame Lorraine looked me in the eye like a lion tamer. She didn't have a chair and a whip, but the effect was there.

"I'm a what?" I honestly had no idea what she meant.

"Don't play dumb with me," she said.

"I'm not playing. I really am dumb. What are you talking about?"

"You come to places like mine and you look for ways that I'm cheating or something." Madame Lorraine looked positively distraught. "Houdini used to do it all the time, walk in and debunk people. Well, I'm a real sensitive. So do your worst! You won't find anything here to debunk!" She folded her arms defiantly.

I took a moment and then pointed at the chair opposite hers. "May I sit down?" I asked.

Madame Lorraine's eyes narrowed, trying to figure out what devious ploy I might be implementing. "Sure."

I took the seat and lowered my voice to a confidential, hopeful tone. "Madame Lorraine," I said, "I'm not trying to disprove anything here. I don't want to defame you."

"De*bunk*."

"Right. Sorry. Debunk. I'm not doing that. I need to get in touch with a friend who is a ghost, and I can't do it myself. Will you please help me?"

She stared at me for a long moment, and her eyes softened. "*Man*, you're good," she said.

The only way to deal with someone who has already decided on her own reality is to completely ignore it and keep on plowing through. "His name is Paul Harrison, and he could be pretty much anywhere," I told Madame Lorraine. "Any chance you might be able to get in touch with him?"

"Geography is not a factor for me," she answered. "The departed are reachable through the power of sensitivity."

I had no idea what that meant, but it was clear Madame Lorraine was now on my side, or at least was considering my request as she would that of anyone who walked through her door. "Is there anything I can tell you that will help?" I asked her.

She blew a puff of air out one side of her mouth in derision. "It's not what you can tell me," she said. "It's what *I* can tell *you*."

I refrained from asking what she could tell me. At this point, the less I talked, the better off I would be. I did my very best to look entranced and nodded a bit in her direction to literally bow to her authority.

It seemed to work; Madame Lorraine closed her eyes with great theatricality and leaned her head back on the chair. She did not make "ghostly" sounds, for which I was grateful. She breathed in deeply and let the breath out slowly a number of times, to the point that I was afraid she might actually fall asleep before I could get any information.

Then suddenly her demeanor changed, although her eyes did not open. She sat up straight in the chair and seemed to be staring at me through her eyelids; the effect was one of intimidation and wonder, if such a thing is possible.

"Paul Harrison was a seeker of truth," she intoned. That was true if you looked at it from a certain perspective; Paul was a private investigator who was generally seeking truth, but then so few people actually search for lies when they can avoid them. "You loved him, and you have some unfinished business."

Now, don't get me wrong. I liked Paul just fine, and he was a good friend whom I missed on a daily basis, but "loved" would be something of a stretch. As for "unfinished business," I figured that was boilerplate for anyone Madame Lorraine might be favoring with her shtick. But I said nothing because I still held out hope she might be able to get a message to Paul through the Living section of the Ghoster-net's Craigslist.

"Paul Harrison left you in a moment of stress," Madame Lorraine continued. Now, that was open to interpretation. Paul had been trying an experiment with electricity while a man was about to shoot at me; that was true. But he hadn't left until days later, having stuck around for my wedding to Josh. Madame Lorraine's batting average was lowering.

"He was searching for a new level," she said. Again, that might have been a general comment she used all the time, but it was true that Paul had been trying to evolve into the next level of existence and thought this experiment would propel him into it. So it was possible Madame Lorraine had some insight—or that I was stretching my disbelief. Either way, I let her go on.

"He has been a wanderer, roaming the Earth with no definite destination. He feels spurned and alienated, and he searches for the warmth he knew."

She was back to the "loved" thing, I thought, and that was clearly the wrong road. I almost stopped her right there, but she held up a hand, palm out, like she was trying to get me to stop crossing the street until a truck went by.

"He seeks his brother," Madame Lorraine said.

Damn, she was good!

Chapter 4

Madame Lorraine had come out of what she called her "heightened state" a few moments later and told me she'd gotten a very strong impression that Paul was looking for his younger brother. Richard was his older brother, so I was once again skeptical, but when I told Ms. Lorraine that, she simply said it had been hazy where she was and she hadn't gotten a good look.

Okay.

She promised she would try to narrow down Paul's location and give me an idea of where to look for him. I asked her to try to get across the message that his brother—whose name I did not disclose to the madame—was where Paul used to stay and that he should come back as soon as he could. Then I paid Madame Lorraine the fee she asked, which I thought was a pretty hefty sum for five minutes of theatrics. But then again, I was someone who sees ghosts asking someone who claimed to communicate with them for help. It wasn't exactly the usual business relationship.

I drove back to the guesthouse wondering if I'd just been taken for a ride. Granted, I hadn't exactly gambled the mortgage money on Madame Lorraine, but I don't like the feeling that someone had seen me as a sucker and played me. I decided not to believe that Madame Lorraine was a real medium. That would teach her.

Didn't make me feel better about my $35, but it was something.

By the time I got my ancient Volvo wagon to my driveway, I had come to the conclusion that the morning (post–spook show, which had been slightly less lackluster) had been a waste of time. Paul wasn't necessarily going to read the *Chronicle* if he was in Mumbai or even Indianapolis, and Madame Lorraine couldn't contact him even if she could write "Surrender Paul" in the sky with her broom smoke. I'd been deluding myself. I needed to act less like an innkeeper and more like a private investigator if I wanted to find my missing friend soon.

So I sort of slumped into the kitchen through my back door. Melissa was at school, winding down the year by gearing up for a standardized test. Josh was at Madison Paints with his grandfather Sy, who in his midnineties still showed up three days a week. Mom and Dad had of course gone home the night before and weren't coming back today unless I called, which I had no intention of doing. Everett still spends some days at the local gas station, the Fuel Pit, where he died. He thinks of it as standing guard at his post and will not be dissuaded. Maxie thinks it's cute and will sometimes go and try to distract her husband but had chosen not to do so today.

That meant Maxie and three of my guests would be in the house. Richard had not made an appearance that morning before I'd left, leaving me to wonder what he might have been doing and where he might have been doing it. But on entering the house, I didn't hear anyone at all, which is unusual. I walked through the kitchen, putting my tote bag on the center island, and into the den.

It's the largest room in the house, really meant to be a formal dining room, which I've used it for twice in four years. The rest of the time, I use the den as a central gathering area where guests can relax, read a book, do some knitting, or take a nap on one of the sofas if they feel like it. Most of a vacation down the shore is about relaxing, particularly for my Senior Plus Tours guests. The ghosts are just an added attraction.

At the moment it held just one person, and he wouldn't have been visible to the average visitor. Richard was floating with his back to me, staring into the fireplace that wasn't lit, largely because it was a seventy-degree day, and besides, the fireplace didn't work. That was something I had meant to start work on before a beam in the ceiling had been shot and immediately got to the top of the priority list.

Apparently I hadn't made much noise walking in because Richard didn't turn to look at me. He just kept staring into that empty space where a fire might have been in the early twentieth century.

"Something I can help you with, Richard?" I asked.

I thought I'd made an effort to keep my voice gentle, but clearly Richard would have disagreed because he spun around as if pounced upon by some wild beast, hands up defensively and eyes wide. He corrected himself after a moment and said, "Excuse me, Alison. I was startled."

"If that's startled, I'd hate to see you when you're panicking," I said.

He actually adjusted the jacket he was wearing to look more formal. "My apologies. I didn't mean to give you the wrong impression. I was simply thinking very deeply and didn't hear you walk in."

"What are you thinking about?" I asked.

"I'm sorry?" He definitely understood the words I was saying, so I could only figure he was buying himself time. I didn't respond. "I . . . I was thinking about finding Paul."

There had been something fishy about this since I'd met Richard the night before, and after spending the morning in futile pursuits, I didn't have the patience to indulge him again. "I don't think you were," I said.

"I'm sorry?" he repeated.

"You heard me. I don't think you were that worried about finding Paul. You're not worried about Paul; nothing can happen to him anymore. And you never came looking for him when he was alive as far as I know. So there's another reason you're looking for him, and for some reason you don't want to tell me what it is."

Richard floated there and stared at me for a long moment. I got the impression he was the kind of man that other people didn't talk to disrespectfully very often. I didn't think I had exactly done that, but I had been blunt, and some people mistake the two.

"You're right," he said finally. His body—or whatever substance it is that makes up the physical form of a ghost—seemed to sag. He floated over to an easy chair and pretended to sit in it, missing by three inches and sinking into the seat. "I'm ashamed of myself and didn't want to confess to anyone but Paul because he never judges."

That was true. Paul is accepting of facts only. He draws no conclusions other than what can be proved. So he doesn't make opinions about a person's character except by what the person does or does not do.

"I'm not interested in judging you," I said quietly. "But if you need help, I would like to try."

Richard closed his eyes. I don't know if that makes a difference for a ghost; I could still sort of see a hint of his eye when he did it. I've asked Paul about that and he's been vague, saying it's a state of mind, which doesn't help at all.

As Richard seemed to gather his thoughts, I saw Maxie float down from the ceiling, wearing her usual sprayed-on jeans and black T-shirt, this one bearing the legend "I'll Bet You Do." She opened her mouth, no doubt about to make some hilarious (in her view) observation, but I put my finger to my lips for fear of breaking the mood and making Richard clam up again. She looked irritated but said nothing and floated down behind his chair. I assumed Richard hadn't seen her.

He opened his eyes again and made the noise ghosts make that sounds like letting out a breath but, obviously, isn't. "I've been working for a New York firm," he said.

That was the big revelation? "What kind of firm?" I asked, not adding why it being based in New York City was some kind of humiliation.

"A law firm," Richard said, as if that should have been clear. "I am a criminal defense attorney, and I was asked by a very prestigious law firm in Manhattan to consult on a case for them. So I have been in the area for nine weeks."

Again, I didn't see anything especially scandalous about the information I was being given. "It's not like I expected you to drop in," I said.

His eyes narrowed like a person does when someone speaks to them in an unfamiliar language. "I wouldn't have imagined you did," he said.

That wasn't getting us anywhere, so I tried to move things forward as Maxie, a skeptical look on her face, rose up and maneuvered herself to get a better look than she could from behind the chair. Still she was not in Richard's line of sight, and she made no sound that would alert him to her presence.

"So how does that turn into you being a ghost now in my house looking for your brother, who was one of the original ghosts in my house?" I asked. Sometimes it just comes out like that.

"I will explain," Richard said. He put a little emphasis on the word *explain*, seeming to imply that I had somehow been keeping him from doing so. Personally I didn't think I had. "The case I was working on involved a young woman who had been accused of killing her stepfather. The prosecution said that she had drowned him in his bathtub."

"Ugh," Maxie said. Richard started again and looked up to see her just to his right and four feet in the air. "That's pretty gross."

"Thanks, Maxie," I said.

She looked at me without guile. "You're welcome."

"How long have you been here?" Richard said, sputtering a bit. In another age, he would have made a great British duke or viscount or something. In a movie he would have been played by David Niven.

"At least five years," Maxie said. It was accurate, but it wasn't much help.

"Tell me about the case," I said to Richard, since this thread of conversation wasn't getting us anywhere. "What's it got to do with you looking for Paul?"

"Don't you see? Paul was a private investigator. He can help me discover what actually happened in the case of Cassidy Van Doren."

"That's the girl who put her dad underwater?" Maxie asked.

"I don't believe she did," Richard told her. "I believe the police arrested the wrong person for the murder."

"Why do you think that?" I asked, thinking of what Paul would ask. "What proof do you have to back up that statement?"

"There is extensive physical evidence," Richard insisted. "And I got to know Cassidy over the time I spent on the case. I do not believe her to be emotionally capable of murder. She disagreed with her stepfather, but she did not hate him."

"You weren't there when he was alive," I pointed out.

"That is true, but a person does not change. I know Cassidy. Cassidy did not kill that man."

The way he said *that man* gave me a strong impression I was hoping to disprove. "Richard," I said slowly, "were you in love with Cassidy Van Doren?"

Richard straightened himself to the point you'd have thought there was a pool cue up his back. "I believe I still am," he said.

"Oh, boy," Maxie said.

"This is going to be a long story," I said. "I'm getting myself a cup of coffee."

#

I needed to sit back and be prepared to listen to a story that I probably didn't want to hear. So I poured myself some coffee from an urn I have on a cart in the den. Melissa and I wheel that out in the morning so the guests can have coffee or tea as they like. It's the closest I come to offering food in the guest-house. This is not a B and B. It's just a B.

The quietest space in the house, even when the den is empty, is the little room off the hallway from the den to the movie room that I use as a library. We have more than a thousand books on the shelves and three chairs, each with a side table, a lamp, and bookmarks. We do not dog-ear in the guest-house. So that's where I headed, dragging ghosts behind me like a train on a wedding dress (which, in the interest of full disclosure, I did not wear either time).

I settled myself into a nicely stuffed chair by the window, prompting Richard to take up a position about halfway between the floor and the ceiling, just to the left of the door. Maxie, more used to the surroundings, did her usual thing of getting horizontal like she's on Cleopatra's barge, hovering just under the crown molding.

"Okay," I said to Richard, "tell me what happened."

"I had been working on Cassidy's defense and had just made a breakthrough," Richard began. "The case was com-plex. Cassidy had a very difficult relationship with her step-father, Keith Barent Johnson, and they had been publicly estranged for some months. So when she was found in the bathroom next to his drowned body in the tub, suspicion had naturally gravitated toward her."

"Naturally," I echoed. It meant nothing but was a verbal form of punctuation. It gave him a moment to compose himself, although Richard did not need it. He was born composed, like a Mozart prelude.

"What breakthrough?" Maxie asked. "The girl's in the bathroom while her stepdad is all, you know, taking a bath? He drowns? What breakthrough could you make?"

"Keith Johnson was not taking a bath when he drowned," Richard said, shaking his head to emphasize the point. "He was fully clothed when Cassidy discovered his body."

Wait. "Discovered?" I said. "That's the story? She discovered his body after he was already dead?"

Richard nodded. It showed his neck worked in both directions. "It is not simply the story. It is what happened. Keith Johnson was a man over six feet tall weighing more than two hundred pounds. Cassidy could never have lifted him into a bathtub on her own, and he would no doubt have been able to overpower her if she'd threatened him."

"That seems like your defense right there," I pointed out.

"I thought so myself," Richard said. "The previous attorney thought we needed to prove that Cassidy had no motive to kill Keith because he said the prosecution would be able to disprove my argument."

"That she couldn't lift a two-hundred-pound guy?" Maxie asked. "How big is this Cassidy Van Doren?"

"She stands five foot three and weighs one hundred eighteen pounds," Richard said. "She lacks the upper-body strength to lift that much weight, particularly if the person involved was struggling against being put in the water, as the physical evidence suggests."

Just at that moment, I saw a small head (attached to a small body) appear in the library doorway. Abigail Lesniak, one of the Senior Plus Tours guests, had looked into the room, and while the conversation had been largely inaudible from her perspective, it was entirely possible she'd heard me speak to someone who wasn't there.

That's the advantage of advertising as a haunted guest-house. The guests don't even blink when something like that happens.

"Am I interrupting?" Abby asked from the doorway. She was a little shy of eighty and very slight but always cheerful, a quality I would like very much to learn at some point in my life. It would be such an asset in the accommodation business.

"Not at all, Abby," I said. "Come on in. Is there something I can do for you?"

"This is an intrusion," Richard protested. "I have important information to impart."

"I was just looking for a good book to take with me today," Abby answered, not having heard Richard at all. I have developed impeccable ghost-ignoring skills, so she never knew there had been any protest to her entering. "I'm going to sit on the boardwalk, and I thought I'd like to take a novel with me."

"By all means," I said. "Take your time."

Abby walked into the room tentatively, holding her arms a little higher than a person walking normally might. "I don't want to upset anyone who's here," she said, looking at the ceiling. In this case, she was correct in pointing her gaze upward for Maxie, but her direction was way off. Everybody looks up when they think ghosts are in the room. They can be anywhere, people. Trust me.

"You're not upsetting anyone," I told her. "Feel free."

"I disagree," Richard said. "I would like to proceed."

"So who's stopping you?" Maxie asked him.

Richard started to respond, rose about a foot higher, looked down at Abby, and nodded slightly. "Good point." He turned his attention back toward me. "As I was saying, it was almost impossible to prove physically that Cassidy could have placed Keith in the tub, or that she could have held him underwater long enough to drown him."

I gave Maxie a glance Abby couldn't see to signal to her that she should do my talking for me. It's not so much that I *can't* talk to the ghosts in front of my guests (try saying that three times fast!) because they are aware Maxie and sometimes Everett are there, but it becomes a distraction, and having a conversation the guest can only half hear seems sort of rude.

"So you're saying the lawyer you were working with was actually trying to set her up for the murder?" Maxie said. I knew I was in trouble when a green visor appeared on her head; Maxie was doing her 1940s noir woman, a character she thinks sounds tough but went out with Gloria Grahame.

"I was wondering if I might talk to you about Mr. Lewis," Abby said. Gregory Lewis was one of the other singles visiting this week, a quiet widower in his late sixties who had not said much but appeared to enjoy the spook shows the most of the current crop.

"I don't know what to think," Richard told Maxie as I listened to Abigail. "I have no evidence that anything was untoward, but I know the defense should have been more vigorous, and I don't know why it wasn't. When I tried to suggest there was another possibility and we should explore the idea, I was told the investigators were on it and I'd be informed when and if they found anything."

"What about Mr. Lewis?" I asked Abby. "Is he doing something to bother you?" The groups of guests are put together randomly based on who books a tour for which week. You get who you get, basically, and that means not everyone always gets along. There have been outright arguments and guests who refused to be in a room at the same time. I don't have gray hairs yet, but give me a couple of weeks.

"Oh, no!" Abby said, horrified she'd given me the wrong impression. "He hasn't said or done anything wrong at all! I don't want you to think that!"

Okay, so I wouldn't think that. "Then what would you like to know?" I asked.

"But they never told you anything," Maxie prompted Richard.

"No. I attempted to contact the lead investigator, but he never returned a call or an e-mail."

"Do you know if he's looking for anyone?" Abby asked.

Looking for anyone? Was someone else missing? How many people did I have to find now? "I don't understand," I said with great honesty.

"Sounds fishy to me," Maxie said, which threw me until I realized she was talking to Richard.

"I was wondering if you knew whether Mr. Lewis was . . . interested in anyone."

Aha. So that was it—Abby was searching for romance and had set her sights on Gregory Lewis. "I'm sorry, Abby, but I don't really have any idea. It's not the kind of thing I usually ask my guests."

That was true, and it would have been even truer with Mr. Lewis. He wasn't effusive and didn't ask me much of anything at all. He was a very average-looking man, but apparently Abby had seen something in him she found interesting.

"To me as well," said Richard. "And after what happened to me, I believe there is a more urgent concern." He looked at me. "That's why it's very important that we find Paul. We need an investigator."

"She has a private eye license, remember?" Maxie said while indicating me, which I could have done without.

"Oh, dear," Abby said. She frowned, lost in thought, then brightened up again. "Perhaps there is something you can do for me, in that case."

"I was aware of that," Richard said. He didn't avert his gaze from me even as I dealt with Abby. "I'm sure you understand I would like to discuss this with my brother. I don't mean to offend, but it's not just Keith's murder I'm concerned about." He hadn't offended; I would gladly dump the case on Paul if I could muster the investigational skills to find Paul.

"What can I do for you, Abby?" I asked.

"You can ask Mr. Lewis if he finds me attractive."

"What other murder is there, Rich?" Maxie wanted to know.

"There's mine," Richard said.

Chapter 5

I had tried very hard to convince Abigail Lesniak that it wasn't within an innkeeper's purview to arrange romantic liaisons between her guests, but Abby looked so sad and seemed so hopeful about Gregory Lewis that, while I stopped short of promising to fix them up on a date, I did reluctantly agree to try to gauge his interest surreptitiously. In other words, I'd do my best to find ways to put off having to act on it for three more days and hope it all blew over.

I always have a plan. It's not always a *good* plan, but it's a plan.

Abby was placated and off to do some souvenir shopping for her nephew, who she said was twenty-eight. Luckily she did not ask me for a recommendation in that area. I'd probably have sent her to the vape shop near the boardwalk.

Now I could turn my attention to Richard. "Your murder?" I said. "Somebody killed you too?"

"That is my best assessment," Paul's brother said. "My memory of my last day is still fairly hazy. Will that improve?" He looked at Maxie.

"Yeah, but it'll take time. A week, maybe two. With me, it took around four months. But you do get it all back eventually." Maxie has a way of being lighthearted and ominous at the same time.

"That is not a great help now."

"No," I agreed. "Tell us what you do remember."

Richard's face got a little dreamier as he thought back to the time when he was alive. I noticed he shared a trait with his brother: when he wasn't thinking about his posture, he tended to tilt a little bit to the left.

"I was in my hotel room in New Brunswick," he began, and I immediately cut him off.

"I thought you said the law firm you were working with was in New York."

Richard focused a little bit more and became slightly more vertical. "Yes, it is. But the murder case was in Middlesex County here in New Jersey. I was staying in a hotel on Livingston Avenue while the case was being heard in the county courthouse a couple of blocks away."

"So Cassidy was charged here in Jersey, and that's where Keith Johnson was murdered?" I knew that was the only possible explanation, but it changed my perspective on the matter severely, and I was adjusting.

"Yes. Johnson died in a bed-and-breakfast in Cranbury Township. He lived in Upper Saddle River and had an apartment on the Upper East Side." Clearly Keith Johnson had been a very upper kind of guy.

"Have you tried to connect with him?" Maxie asked. "You said you could make a little contact with other ghosts. Did you try to find Keith Johnson and ask him what happened?"

I thought Maxie was getting a little off the track, since we were now discussing Richard's murder, about which I had heard nothing, as opposed to Keith's, of which I had heard nothing I liked. But Richard's eyes widened a bit, and he raised an index finger.

"That hadn't occurred to me," he said. "I will try." He closed his eyes.

"Not now, Richard," I said. This could take hours. "Tell us about what happened to you in the hotel in New Brunswick."

Richard opened his eyes again and nodded; yes, he had strayed from the topic. "Sorry. As I said, I do not remember much. I was working at my desk on a laptop computer I carried with me."

That reminded me of something, and I said, "Maxie." She looked over at me and I pointed at the ceiling. Maxie keeps a laptop—which sadly is newer than mine, and she's been dead five years—in Melissa's room. When we investigate cases, she is in charge of Internet research and has shown a real affinity for it. She understood immediately what I meant, nodded, and rose up through the library ceiling.

"Please go on," I told Richard.

"Well, all I remember is hearing a sound behind me and starting to turn, but then there was just pain in the back of my head, and the next thing I knew, I was in the hotel room, but there was police tape on the door and all my belongings had been removed. It took a while for me to understand what had happened to me. Three days later, I thought of Paul and found a map in the hotel lobby that started me in this direction. Once I realized I could jump into a vehicle heading in a certain direction and speed up my trip, it did not take long to get here."

That added up with the process of ghostification as I understood it. The person making the transition spends a few days essentially unconscious, with no memory of life or understanding of his present state. Once he realizes he's dead, there's a period of disbelief, and then with eternity staring him in the face, he begins to adjust. Some do better than others. Richard sounded like he'd become a ghost with almost no trauma at all. I guessed he was lying.

Maxie floated down from the ceiling wearing a long trench coat. Ghosts, we have discovered, can carry solid objects through walls and such by hiding them in the clothing they're wearing. So when Maxie made it through the ceiling and the trench coat vanished, it was clear to see she'd brought her laptop with her, and it was already open and running. Mine would have still been sputtering to remember what functioning was like.

"Cassidy Van Doren was charged with first-degree murder eight months ago after her stepfather, Keith Johnson, was found drowned in the bathtub of a bed-and-breakfast in Cranbury Township," she read off her screen. Maxie doesn't worry about pleasantries.

"Skip to the parts we don't know," I said.

Maxie scowled. She expects everyone to be astounded at her amazing Internet skills, when in fact at this stage of an investigation, she had probably just Googled Cassidy's name like anyone else would have done. "You're no fun anymore," she said.

"I never was." I pointed at the laptop.

"Okay, okay. She's currently out awaiting trial." Maxie looked up.

"We don't do cash bail anymore in New Jersey," Richard said.

"Even so. And she's living near here, in Rumson."

I whistled. "Cassidy's not doing so bad for herself." Bruce Springsteen used to live in Rumson. In New Jersey, that's as close to a royal address as you can get.

"The family has a good deal of money," Richard agreed. "But Cassidy is largely unaffected by her wealth and is a very sincere, honest, down-to-earth person." His eyes stared off into empty space for a moment.

"Richard," I said. After getting no response, I repeated, "Richard."

He seemed to awaken. "Yes?"

"Why are you so concerned about time? Is Cassidy's trial still ongoing? Is she about to be convicted and you want to absolve her of the murder?" I don't usually use words like "absolve," but Richard inspired a certain formality.

"No," Maxie said. "They suspended the trial when Richard here was found dead of blunt trauma to the head. Won't start up for another week."

"I'm concerned because Cassidy's life is in danger," Richard said.

I was starting to see why Paul and his brother had not been the closest of siblings in life. I closed my eyes briefly and let out a little air. "Richard," I said, "you have a habit of doling out information in short bursts whenever you feel like it. That's not helping. Can you give it to me all at once this time?"

"You seem upset," Richard said. "I don't understand."

"It's easy," Maxie, ever helpful, said. "First you tell us you're looking for Paul, but you don't say why. Then you tell us it's because you were working on this case and the girl is going to be convicted unless you can prove she didn't do it. Then you tell us you were murdered too, and that's got to have something to do with what we were talking about before, but you didn't bother to mention it. Now you're telling us the girl on trial is in danger, and you never said that before either. See how that's a problem?"

Richard's eyebrows twitched in various directions. "Not really," he said.

I closed my eyes again.

"I told you everything," Richard's voice said through my eyelids. "I honestly don't see what the order of the information has to do with the process."

Against my better judgment, I opened my eyes again and realized what a mistake that had been. Closed was so much more restful. But it was too late. "Forget it," I said to Richard. "Tell us why you believe Cassidy Van Doren's life is in danger, and then we can figure out what we want to do about it."

Richard, clearly glad to be on more solid ground (metaphorically speaking—he was still floating in midair in my library), nodded. "The night . . . this happened to me, I was doing research into Keith Johnson's business dealings to attempt to establish a motive for someone to have killed him other than Cassidy's simple dislike of her stepfather. In doing so, I came across some very serious malfeasance not in Keith's but in the handling of his household accounts, which held millions of dollars."

"You're a lawyer," I pointed out, in case Richard had blanked on the law school years and the bar exam he'd no doubt had to pass in Canada. "Why are you looking through Keith's books and not hiring an accountant to do that?"

"In addition to the legal degree, I hold a PhD in economics and accounting from McGill University," he said, puffing out just a bit.

I rushed back in before he could further fill us in on his curriculum vitae. "So you know what you're looking at. How does that lead to your concern for Cassidy's life?"

Richard held up his index finger like a person about to make a significant point calling for quiet. Nobody was trying to interrupt him, so the gesture felt a little pointless. "I saw that the moneys earmarked for a number of Richard's relatives, including his biological children Braden and Erika, were being diverted toward Cassidy's account."

I waited. Maxie waited. Anyone else living or dead on the planet would have waited for a further explanation if they had been in the room. But no more was forthcoming. Richard looked at me as if he had just proved his point beyond all question and was ready to rest his case. At the moment, his case was still resting in the cushion of my side chair, and the fact that he'd crossed his legs "casually" wasn't helping him convince anyone of anything.

"So Keith's kids weren't getting their money and Cassidy was?" I asked. I was pretty sure that was what he'd been saying, but it didn't add up at all, so maybe I was mistaken. You'll be shocked, but this wouldn't be the first time.

"That's right," Richard said. Okay, so I had not being mistaken on my side.

"She was getting money that was supposed to go to other people, and that's why you think her life is in trouble?" I've seen Maxie in many different moods under many different circumstances. But I didn't think I'd ever seen her this puzzled before. Usually even when she doesn't know what's going on, she's certain she really does.

"Not entirely," Richard answered, which gave me a little hope. "But think about it: if for some reason one of Keith's children were to discover what was going on with the finances, he or she would no doubt jump to the conclusion that Cassidy was manipulating her stepfather to cheat them out of their allowances and give the funds to her. They could very well decide Cassidy was an impediment to their fortunes and conspire to eliminate her from the picture."

That was flimsier than the wallboard Dad and I had installed over the gaping hole in my den ceiling. I really did have to get back to that repair soon. Maybe tomorrow. "That really doesn't add up, Richard," I said.

"How so?" He was asking in earnest. There are six jokes I could put in here, but you wouldn't like any of them.

"It assumes someone besides you found out about the scam with Keith's money, and instead of suing for it or confronting Keith, they decided to kill him. Why didn't they kill Cassidy if that was the case? Killing Keith doesn't move the money back; it just perpetuates the skimming, doesn't it?"

Richard shook his head. "When Keith died, his last will was immediately read and is in the process of going through probate. It's very complex, but the accounting of his estate will undoubtedly find the same malfeasance I discovered after doing a few hours of research. Certainly the funds taken from other accounts will be removed from Cassidy and given back to their rightful owners. It was Keith's death that made that process begin."

"How much money are we talking about?" Maxie asked.

"At least thirty-eight million dollars in the entire estate," Richard responded with no hesitation.

"That's not nothing," Maxie said. She has a talent for understatement—when she's not exhibiting her talent for overstatement.

"I think you might be overlooking one possibility," I told Richard. My job as an innkeeper, I'd discovered over the years, was more about diplomacy than it was about providing clean sheets and firm pillows. It was about delivering information in a way that made it palatable to the listener, as opposed to Phyllis's job, which was about delivering information intended to wake the audience up.

"I don't believe I've left anything out of my consideration," Richard said. It was almost like his words were starched; you got the impression they'd be a little stiff if they hit you in the face.

"What about the idea that Cassidy Van Doren really did talk her stepfather into siphoning off some money for her?" Okay, so I've been more diplomatic in my day. This wasn't my day.

Richard's neck stiffened. "You're saying you think Cassidy murdered Keith Johnson?" he asked.

I couldn't rule it out, but that wasn't what I was saying, so I moved forward. "I'm not saying anything about the murder right now," I told him. "I'm saying the impression that she was getting favorable treatment is clearly a correct one, and since she was the person to benefit from it, you can't simply say she's too nice a person to have done something like that."

"I will not allow you to insult Cassidy in my presence." Richard actually rose, in the sitting position, two feet out of the chair.

"I'm simply trying to get you to consider the possibility," I told him, "not to conclude that it's what happened. Paul would tell you not to reach a conclusion before you have enough facts to support it."

"Then get Paul and have him tell me that," Richard said in a huff. "I will not stay here and listen to more."

And then he was gone.

"Guy knows how to make an exit," Maxie said.

Chapter 6

It was the next morning that I heard the sound coming from the basement.

Melissa was upstairs getting ready for school. Maxie, as was her custom, had not appeared in the house yet, although Everett could be seen doing crunches in the sand beyond my driveway. I'm not sure why Everett feels it's important for him to work at staying in shape after death, but it makes him happy, and I am not going to get in his way.

I had not seen Richard since before he'd vanished the day before, when he told me to find his brother and stop denigrating the woman he loved, who was currently out on bail in the middle of her suspended murder trial. So I'd decided to do nothing on his behalf other than to attempt to contact Paul. Okay, so I'd called Phyllis to tell her about the murders in New Brunswick and Cranbury because she's a great source of information and a rabid snoop. I hadn't heard from Madame Lorraine, but I guessed she'd tell me there was no timetable in the afterlife. I could argue that the spook shows were at ten AM and one PM daily, but what would be the point?

Josh left promptly at six that morning, as one does when one owns a paint business that opens at seven, and promised to be home on time tonight, reminding me to catch him up by text if there were any developments in Richard's case. Josh doesn't see or hear the ghosts, but he definitely empathizes with them. He cares for his fellow humans whether they're alive or not.

Two of my guests, Eduardo DiSica and Penny Desmond, had not yet left their rooms and were presumed asleep. Vanessa, Eduardo's wife, had gotten herself a cup of tea and headed out to walk on the beach "to clear her head." She had reported no further "stretching noises" in the room above hers, but I would ask Maxie to do some research on what might have caused that kind of sound.

Abby Lesniak had passed through, made herself an iced decaf, and asked me if I'd had a chance to talk to Mr. Lewis yet. I confessed I had not, as Gregory had left very early in the morning to watch the sunrise, having informed me he would do so the night before. I didn't tell Abby about that because then she'd want to know why I hadn't Dolly Levi–ed my way into fixing her up, and that was a situation I could put off for a bit.

I was in the kitchen getting some orange juice and looking forward (sort of) to cleaning up the movie room, where some of the guests had been watching *Field of Dreams* the night before. Movies with ghosts go over big in the guesthouse.

And that is when I heard a definitely nonstretching noise coming from the basement.

It was more like an animal had gotten into the house somehow and was knocking over some of the detritus I (and everyone else in every part of the world) keep in the basement.

Melissa's ghost puppy, Lester, was presumably in her room, where he was supposed to stay. Even if Lester had gotten into the basement, he couldn't knock anything over. He would pass through it.

Now, I like animals as well as the next girl, as long as they're not in my house uninvited. Even Lester had taken some getting used to, given that his transparency had not seemed to make a difference to my allergies. So I was faced with the dilemma of letting some creature take my basement apart or waiting until my husband arrived home in eleven hours and making him deal with it.

The second seemed like the coward's way out, which was not at all the reason I decided to go downstairs anyway. I'm not some little scaredy-cat who needs a big strong man to save her—I told myself. So I was investigating another strange noise in my admittedly strange house. I was a fierce ghost seer or something. I could handle it.

I did pick up a four-battery flashlight, though. I'm not stupid.

The basement door leads to the requisite creaky staircase, which I was now descending as loudly as possible. If there was some creepy critter down there, I wanted it to scurry away in fear so I wouldn't see it and could pawn it off on my husband. There's being a coward, and then there's just being practical.

That strategy seemed to have worked, because after turning on the basement light (which is at the top of the stairs because nobody's that dumb) and stomping down the admittedly noisy staircase, there was absolutely no evidence of a loose raccoon, opossum, or other animal I didn't want to deal with right now or, to be fair, ever. There was one box of

Melissa's old books that she couldn't bear to part with that had been knocked off a shelf, spreading Dr. Seuss all over the basement floor. That was it.

Whatever had gotten in here, it could reach a shelf about three feet off the floor. That wasn't comforting.

Had a stray ghost passed through and accidentally disrupted the box? It was possible. Most ghosts steered clear of the place, I'd surmised. Maybe they had known Paul and Maxie—and now Everett—had taken up residence here and didn't want to intrude. Maybe the place just wasn't good enough for the ungrateful wretches. Huh! Imagine such a thing. I go out of my way to put up a sign that says, "Haunted Guesthouse," and ghosts won't even . . .

What was I talking about?

I picked up the books and replaced them in the box, which I now resolved to donate to the Harbor Haven Public Library on my next visit. What Melissa didn't know wouldn't hurt me. And since there had been no further unusual noises, I saw no reason to linger in what was a fairly well-organized basement, but still a basement. I'd toyed with the idea of finishing the basement some time ago, but there just wasn't much utility to the idea. I was having enough trouble filling guest rooms without adding another belowground.

A quick scan of the area with the flashlight—because lighting down there is always inadequate—revealed nothing out of the ordinary. I told myself I'd ask Everett or Maxie to come down and look around when I wasn't there because they are capable of actually making no noise at all, and they don't smell like anything, so animals don't always notice them.

So much for that. I could come down here the next time the pilot light in the boiler went out or I needed an extension cord or a power tool. Right now, there was cleaning to be done upstairs in society.

The stairs were just as creaky on the way up, but that didn't seem quite as significant on the return trip. I was intent on drinking that orange juice I'd promised myself back when I was young. Five minutes ago.

And that's why it was somewhat disturbing to hear someone opening and closing drawers in my kitchen before I got through the upstairs doorway.

It seemed unlikely that an opossum had been stealthy enough to elude me, climb up the stairs, and take up residence in my kitchen, but stranger things happen pretty much every day in the guesthouse. And when I considered I was about to enter a room full of sharp knives and heavy frying pans, the flashlight in my hand didn't seem like so dandy a weapon anymore. But it was all I had.

I suppose I could have used the cell phone in my pocket to call the police, but then I'd tell them . . . what?

The upstairs door was already open, and I didn't want to alert the intruder to my presence, assuming it wasn't just Maxie, Liss, or one of the guests getting more milk for their coffee. I was (pardon the expression) spooked now. Maybe I could get a signal to Everett, who was probably into the "running in place" part of his morning workout.

Instead I made a point of being light on the top step of the staircase and stuck my head—which was after all the part with the eyes—into the room.

Nothing, but my vantage point was not optimum. I could see only the refrigerator and the sink, with the window to the driveway, from here. Another very careful step into the room. For sure it was Liss or Maxie, I told myself. No reason to be—

Floating in the light from the back door, refracted enough to be difficult to see, was a ghost, fairly tall and with dark hair, as far as I could tell. Direct sunlight makes it awfully hard to make out details in a transparent spirit.

This one turned toward me and clasped his chest. "Alison," he said.

I knew that voice. "Richard?"

"Richard!" the ghost said. "Has it been that long?"

Now that I knew there was no danger, I walked into the room and got a better angle on the ghost. And my voice must have risen half an octave as I ran toward him.

"Paul!" I shouted.

Chapter 7

When you see someone you haven't spoken to in a long time, someone who means a good deal to you, naturally you want to give that person a hug. In this case, that was something of a problem. My arms just went through Paul's torso, which felt warm and calming. He chuckled and put a hand on each of my shoulders. When he does that, I can sort of feel it.

"It has been a long time," he said finally. "You called me Richard."

"It was the sunlight," I explained, pointing at the window. "I couldn't see you very well, and your voices are similar."

Paul looked at me for a long moment. "But Richard is alive," he said.

There was going to have to be a lot of explaining in the next few minutes. I decided to avoid that particular issue for the moment. "What brought you back?" I asked.

Paul looked at me with some puzzlement in his eyes. "You did put an ad in the *Harbor Haven Chronicle* trying to contact me, didn't you?"

Wow. The power of the press. "Yeah, but it never occurred to me you'd actually look there. I was trying to figure out a way to access the Ghosternet."

He nodded. "I've gotten some garbled messages from other spirits who claim to have heard from a Madame Fontaine," he said. "But the messages were never clear or complete, and everyone assumed it was simply another crank trying to pretend she could talk to the dearly departed."

"They weren't far off. Where have you been?"

"In Boston," Paul said. "I've been traveling the country the past few months trying to have experiences I didn't have when I was alive. I went to Fenway Park yesterday to see a baseball game between the Red Sox and the Toronto Blue Jays."

"You grew up in Toronto. You must be a fan," I said.

"Not really. I liked hockey when I was a boy. It just seemed like something to do." He focused on me. "But your advertisement said my brother, Richard, is here and needs me. Where is he?"

I'd also written that all was forgiven, but he probably knew that was just boilerplate. "Okay, you need to get filled in on a lot of stuff, Paul," I said.

And with perfect theatrical timing, Richard phased his way through the kitchen door and saw the two of us standing—okay, one standing, one hovering—there. "Paul," he said, slightly more animated than if he had just run into a business acquaintance at the country club, "you've come back."

Paul fell back a little, and his eyes widened. "Richard," he gasped, "you're . . ."

"Yes, dead like you," his brother informed him. "In fact, I was murdered much as you were, only with a blunt object to the head, it would seem."

Paul shook his head in spurts as if to clear it. He was trying to process the information, and it was taking time. "How could that have happened?" he finally said.

Richard looked at me. "You didn't tell him?"

Sure, blame it on me. "I just found him two minutes ago," I said.

Richard simulated a sigh and looked at his brother. "I suppose it's up to me, then." What a chore, to have to explain to your dead brother how you were murdered. Surely the servants should have handled it.

While he told Paul his story (in considerably fewer installments than it had taken him to tell me), the following things happened:

- I finally got myself that glass of orange juice;
- Melissa dragged herself down the stairs looking for coffee, saw Paul, and had a very touching reunion, which seemed to annoy Richard because it slowed down his recitation;
- Penny Desmond knocked on the kitchen door asking if there was more cream, which I provided;
- Everett came inside, wiping his brow as if it were wet, saluted Paul, and retreated to a corner of the kitchen opposite the brothers' somewhat-less-than-touching reunion, which he watched silently;
- I also got myself an English muffin because I remembered we had some in the fridge;

- Maxie drifted down from the ceiling, saw Paul, said, "Oh. Hey," rubbed her eyes a little to show me how cruel I was being by requiring her to be "awake" at this time of the morning just for a spook show, and rose back up into the ceiling again;
- Melissa asked if she could skip school because Paul was home, and I said no.

By that point, the somewhat-incomplete (in my opinion) story had been related, and Paul was in full investigator mode, pacing back and forth in thin air and stroking his goatee furiously. If it had any substance, it probably would have been completely worn away.

"There are many threads to these events that require investigation," he said. Then he turned directly to face me. "Get Maxie."

"Get Maxie? You need help in an investigation, I go to all this trouble to get you back here, and your first reaction is, 'Get Maxie'?"

I saw Everett rise up into the ceiling. No doubt he would let his wife know her presence was being requested.

Paul seemed mildly surprised. "You told me you were finished with investigations, and I agreed because I wanted to travel and not fulfill my obligations here," he reminded me. "I was simply assuming you would not be interested in assisting on Richard's case."

That made me stammer a bit, but I managed to squeak out, "Well, you're right about that. I don't want to be an investigator anymore. I mean, I got shot, sort of, the last time." I walked over to where Richard, arms folded impatiently, was floating. "But this is family."

Melissa's eyebrows met in the middle. "You *want* to help?" she asked. "Mom?"

She was reacting to my unexpected change of heart, which I'll admit was a surprise even to me. But Paul investigating Richard's murder, and perhaps that of Keith Johnson, presented a number of problems in logistics, not the least of which that Paul and Richard were both dead.

"You're going to need a living person to go and talk to people involved," I said to Paul. "You need someone with access to transportation even if you're going to do the snooping yourself. You need someone who can ask questions and come back here with the answers you need." And as my daughter started to raise her hand to indicate she was about to speak, I added, "I don't want it to be Melissa."

"Mom!" She was, after all, thirteen. I was lucky it hadn't been *Mother!*

Before she could protest any further, Paul nodded. "You're right. I am not comfortable with Melissa being involved in this kind of case, at least not on a face-to-face basis with any of the principals. And we will need access to a motor vehicle."

"You know I'm here in the room, right?" Melissa said.

"Can you drive?" I asked her. She remained silent.

"Very well, then," Paul said, the matter apparently being settled. "Alison, if you would, I think you and I should sit down and discuss the people and places you need to visit."

"I'd pay money just to see you sit down," I said.

Maxie descended from the ceiling in her trench coat, laptop tucked inside. Everett followed, having let his wife know there was an investigation brewing and her expertise might be needed.

"What's going on?" she asked.

Paul got her up to speed fairly rapidly. Richard, I noticed, was watching his brother with an expression approaching interest on his face. I guessed he'd never seen Paul work before.

After her briefing, Maxie looked determined. "So what do you need me to do?"

"Find out whatever you can about Keith Johnson's business dealings. How did he make his fortune? Were there changes in the structure of the business lately? Who besides his stepdaughter might have benefitted from his death?"

"Gotcha." Maxie started back up. She stopped midair, something I always find surprising even after seeing it for years. She looked at Paul. "Where ya been, anyway?" she asked.

"You name it," he said.

Maxie smiled and floated up through the ceiling. She likes to work in Melissa's attic bedroom, or sometimes on the roof where she can be left alone. Liss has given her and her alone permission to enter her room when Liss isn't there (I occasionally go in there under the authority of being her mother), and Maxie, who calls herself Melissa's roommate, takes advantage or goes up on the roof. This, I imagine, leads to people in low-flying planes wondering why a laptop is suspended in the air above a large Victorian on the shore, but I tend to doubt that happens very often.

"What can I do?" Melissa asked. She considers herself a vital part of the investigative team, and to be honest, she's right. Her insight and perspective is usually much more analytical and considered than, say, mine.

"Right now, you can go to school," Paul said. "You are still in school for the year, aren't you?"

"Yeah. There's another three days before we get out for the summer. But—"

"Don't worry," Paul told her. "I'll make sure you have things to do. I've only been back for fifteen minutes. Give me time to remember where everything is."

Liss smiled. "Okay, Paul." That was the moment, movie-style, when we heard a car honk in the driveway. "That's Wendy's mom," she said. "I've gotta go." And with that, my daughter was out the door and on her way to the other life she leads, which becomes a little more important to her every day. That's how it's supposed to go, and I hate it. Just for the record.

Everett, who had stayed behind after Maxie left for higher ground, did not ask for an assignment. He merely stood by while Paul paced some more, thinking. "Everett," Paul said finally, "are you trained in reconnaissance work?"

"I have been on some covert missions," Everett answered.

"Good. I have an idea for you, if you're interested."

"Anything I can do to help, sir."

Paul smiled his wry smile. "Don't call me 'sir,' Everett. That's something you should reserve for my brother, here." He pointed at Richard.

"Yes . . . okay, Paul."

Richard gave his younger brother a look that indicated he was less than pleased with that wise guy stuff. But he remained silent, watching with his hands clasped behind his back, not dissimilar from Everett's "at-ease" pose.

"It'll be something after Alison and I figure out what she's going to do," Paul told Everett. "You're welcome to sit in, but I can tell you later if you prefer."

"I'll skip the briefing and wait for your instructions, if that's all right." Everett correctly assumed it would be (all right) and left through the back wall onto the beach, no doubt to do even more exercises he would never need.

Paul turned toward his brother. "Richard," he said, "is there anything about this case that you have not told me? Anything that will be relevant?"

Richard made a show of thinking about it, then shook his head. "I don't believe so."

Paul's eyes narrowed, and I got the impression he didn't care for his brother's answer. But just when I thought he'd have pressed the point, he looked down at the floor and nodded. That was odd. "Very well, then."

"Wait," I said. Somebody had to. "You're leaving something out, Richard. You said you are in love with Cassidy Van Doren."

"That's correct, yes."

Paul made eye contact with Richard, which his brother had been subtly trying to avoid. "Was Miriam aware?" he asked.

"I am not certain," Richard said.

This was new. "Miriam?" I asked.

Richard had no qualms about making eye contact with me. "My wife," he said.

Chapter 8

"Well, I guess we can add another suspect to Richard's murder," I said.

Paul and I were in the bedroom Josh and I share, a larger one than what I'd been using before we were married. We'd decided on the location for this meeting because it was certain that none of the guests would come up here looking for me unless there was an emergency.

I sat on a chair next to the bed, and Paul was considerably higher in elevation than was his habit. He was excited about being on a case, but I imagine the involvement of his recently deceased brother wasn't making things easy for him.

"Miriam?" Paul said. He looked skeptical. "I'm not sure she cared enough about Richard to kill him. Their marriage had taken on the air of a formality, really. Even when I was alive."

"Even so, there's nothing like a little competition to bring out the worst in a woman," I said.

"She can't be ruled out, certainly, until we have physical evidence, but it seems more likely Richard's death had something to do with his vigorous defense of Cassidy Van Doren than with his marriage." Paul's head rocked back and forth. "We have a lot of work to do."

"It's good to see you too, Paul. Tell me about your travels."

He stopped his back-and-forth midair pacing and regarded me carefully, apparently remembering who I was and what our friendship had been like. "Of course. I apologize, Alison. It has been a very eventful day."

"And it's still only eight thirty in the morning," I pointed out. Hey, he left it hanging there for me; it would have been rude for me to ignore it.

"Indeed." Paul has a sense of humor so dry you could light a match on it. He stopped to think for a moment, closing his eyes briefly and slowly nodding his head. "Well, when I left here the last time, you had just been married." He looked at me.

"I'm still married, Paul. It's only been four months, and I expect this one will stick."

"I was setting the time. I was lucky in that the first car I entered on the road outside was headed for Philadelphia, and I managed to find my way to the airport. It is remarkably easy for me to get on a plane, Alison."

"Yeah," I said. "You can probably even bring all the shampoo you want."

Paul looked at me strangely and then shrugged his left shoulder, deciding not to follow up on that, which was wise. "I decided not to leave the country just yet, although a flight to Rome or Istanbul would have been interesting. Instead I headed to Seattle and figured I would work my way back by car."

"Seattle?"

"I'm from Canada, Alison," Paul said. "I like to start in the north. And I stayed there for a few days, then caught a car heading east. I did that for some weeks. Butte, Montana; Grinnell, Iowa; Chicago; Painesville, Ohio. I saw Mount Rushmore, which is quite impressive."

"Was the trip what you wanted it to be?" I asked. Paul had been very unhappy when he was bound to my house and its grounds. I hoped the freedom to move around had satisfied him.

"It was interesting for a while," he answered thoughtfully. "But it is odd not to have a base of operations."

I hadn't expected that from him. Paul had never seemed comfortable staying in the house with a family that wasn't his and guests who stayed for a week or less. "That's sweet," I said.

He blinked. "I meant for the investigation agency," he said. Paul truly believed that what we'd had was a working detective operation, and no amount of argument on my part could convince him otherwise. What we'd actually had was the occasional client—usually a ghost—who didn't pay us (Paul obviously didn't care about that) and got me involved in something dangerous I would seriously have preferred avoiding. "I didn't do any work the whole time I was away."

"But you weren't expecting your brother's murder to be something you'd find when you got back," I said.

Paul lowered himself a foot or so, an indication of his mood, I think. "No, that was something of a surprise."

I didn't want to say what I said next, but there was no avoiding it. I'd already committed myself to the current lunacy and was already mentally kicking myself for it. "So what do you want me to do first?"

Paul inexplicably perked up. Well, maybe not "inexplicably." He loved nothing more than a juicy case to solve, and if his brother was dead, well, that was unfortunate, but it provided him with the mental challenge he needed. He rubbed his hands together, which is a weird sight to see when the hands are mostly transparent.

"The first thing," he said, "is to go to Richard's house and his office. We need to find his laptop and his case files, especially those concerning Cassidy Van Doren and Keith Johnson's murder."

That was not what I'd been expecting. Usually Paul had me interview witnesses or suspects and record it so he could hear it later. Now he wanted me to go to Richard's *house*?

"If I heard correctly, Richard said his wife . . ."

"Miriam."

"Yes, Miriam," I said. "He said he wasn't sure whether Miriam knew he was love with Cassidy Van Doren."

"You did indeed hear correctly," Paul said.

"So you want me to go to his house, meet his wife, who you did not rule out as a suspect in bludgeoning him to death in a jealous rage, and ask her for Richard's laptop?"

"Unless you find it at his office," Paul said, nodding.

"Uh-huh." Actually, I'd been wrong. This might not have been what I was expecting, but it had a queasily familiar feel to it.

"Is that a problem?" Paul asked.

"Nah. I was just thinking how much like old times it all seemed."

He held up an index finger like a master debater about to make a devastating point. "Ah, yes," Paul said. "But this time, I'll be there with you the whole time."

"Imagine my relief."

He had the nerve to look surprised.

#

Paul volunteered to star in the morning's spook show "for old times," but I knew it was because I was helping on the case he was investigating and he felt obligated. Good. I made sure to include a number of the stunts he didn't especially care for, including playing ukulele badly and answering questions from guests he considered mundane, like, "What's it like to be dead?"

Worse, Richard was watching the whole time. My father had also appeared on cue, not knowing Paul was available, and insisted on doing his own patented ghost tricks, like tightening the screws in the switch plates for the overhead lights and measuring the hole in the den ceiling. Again.

"We're going to have to get a steel beam in here, baby girl," he said to me after his amazing tape measure trick ended.

Since I had no desire to consider the cost of that kind of construction or to discuss my renovation plans with the four guests (everyone but Penny, who was at Stud Muffin getting breakfast), I did not answer my father and waited for the morning show's grand finale.

That consisted of Maxie and Paul having a "swordfight" using two umbrellas that had long given up the whole rain-fighting part of their existences and now lived strictly to amuse tourists when being wielded by dead people. Such is the nature of my inn-keeping business.

"Someone's going to put an eye out," Vanessa DiSica murmured at one point. That would have been quite the feat, as neither of the umbrellas had a pointy end, and the ghosts, who had performed this little charade more than a couple of times (even if Paul was rusty), were actually much farther from each other than they would have appeared to the mortal eye. Not to mention, the umbrellas would have gone straight through them.

Finally, as planned, Maxie "defeated" Paul by knocking his umbrella out of his hand (he threw it into an unoccupied corner of the library as the guests gasped) and held her "weapon" up as Everett had taught her to do with his parade saber. Which Maxie had lobbied about using in the sword-fight game and had been roundly shouted down, especially by her husband. The guests applauded.

"That's it for this morning, everybody," I said, giving them a good excuse to exit the premises. "If anyone needs a recommendation for lunch or directions anywhere, you know where to find me." I have an agreement with some local businesses to steer some guests in their directions for a small cut of the profits the guests rack up. You call it a kickback; I call it mutual benefit.

Nobody asked for a place to go to lunch. They'd been here a few days already and probably had some local favorites identified; Harbor Haven isn't a very large town. But I did notice Abby Lesniak eyeing Greg Lewis as he shuffled out of the room, as usual saying nothing but smiling a little weakly at me as he went. Greg, I had been told in the paper work from Senior Plus Tours, had some problems with his feet.

Abby sidled up to me just as the room had cleared out to her eye. The ghosts, of course, had not left, so Dad was actually sticking his head, flashlight in his mouth, up into the gap in my ceiling, something he'd done almost daily since the bullet hole had been made. Maxie was, to be fair, heading for the ceiling, relieved her morning obligation had been fulfilled. Maxie won't admit to enjoying the performances and, for a rambunctious poltergeist, has an odd distaste for strangers. She prefers to be alone or with people she knows. Mostly Everett, whom she adores, and Melissa, whom she considers a younger sister.

Paul was conferring with Richard quietly near the window, making it difficult to see either of them clearly.

"Have you said anything yet?" Abby asked me in a stage whisper. She wasn't cognizant of the dead people within earshot and was being careful because of those who had just left the room the conventional way.

"To Mr. Lewis?" I said, not waiting for her exasperated nod in return. "I haven't had the chance yet. It's not the kind of thing you can just spring on a guy, Abby. The topic has to be broached."

"Broached!" She didn't exactly shout so much as she *emphasized.* "Am I such a terrible person that you have to soften the man up first?"

First, no, she wasn't. Second, you never want to get within driving distance of insulting a guest. "Of *course* not," I answered immediately. "It's not about you at all. I'd be this way no matter who had asked me to fix them up with Mr. Lewis." That hadn't come out the way I'd rehearsed it.

"I'm sorry." Abby seemed to shrink a little bit. "I realize I'm putting you in a difficult position. But I'm really the shy type, and it scares me to have to make myself vulnerable. If you don't want to say anything, I'll understand."

Wow. My mother and Abby could have been cocaptains of the Olympic Passive-Aggressive Team. They'd probably win the gold too. I found myself assuring Abby I'd speak to Greg Lewis as soon as I had the opportunity. She smiled a beatific smile and thanked me again, confident in the knowledge that her powers to make others bend to her will had not been diminished by age. She walked out of the library.

The conference between Paul and Richard seemed to break up as she did, as Richard simply evaporated into thin air, which seemed to be his signature way of leaving a room. Paul floated over to me. "Ready to go?" he asked.

I looked around the room and saw seven things that needed to be cleaned or straightened. "Go where?" I asked, putting a bookmark in a hardcover novel *Written Off* and closing it, as the reader had left it open on a side table. We frown on breaking the spine here at the guesthouse.

"To the offices of Filcher, Baker, and Klein," he answered, like I knew what that was. "The law firm Richard was working for on the Cassidy Van Doren case."

Ugh. "Oh, do we have to, Paul?"

He shrugged. "We can go see Richard's wife, Miriam, first," he offered.

"Law firm it is," I said. "Let me find my bag."

Chapter 9

Paul regaled me with tales of Evanston, Illinois; Mechanicsburg, Pennsylvania; Ann Arbor, Michigan; and Hyde Park, New York, as I drove from Harbor Haven, New Jersey, to Woodbridge, New Jersey. Woodbridge was home to the branch office for Richard's law firm and the one he'd been loaned when he needed to consult on Cassidy Van Doren's murder trial.

And he was making sure to catalog his travels during the forty-minute trip to Woodbridge, no doubt as he would on the forty-minute trip home. I was glad Paul had returned, but I had to keep reminding myself of that as I drove.

I wasn't bored. I want to make that clear. I was not bored listening to the stories of Paul's adventures, such as they were, because he couldn't actually do much besides look around as he explored America. But after a while I did want to change the subject to pretty much anything else, and luckily I knew a way to do so that wouldn't for a moment annoy the blatherer in question.

"Paul," I said when there was room for a breath, "how are we going to get Richard's laptop or his files out of his old office? I don't have any credibility there. I'm not even sure how to identify myself when I get to the front desk."

Paul switched modes beautifully, like a luxury car shifting gears. He cocked his head to the right side and considered. "That, you'll find, is the advantage of having me along from now on, Alison," he said. "You don't have to get *anything* out of Richard's office. You just have to identify where the items are being kept and then create a distraction while I conceal them in my clothing and meet you back at the car."

"A distraction? You want me to pull my skirt up like Claudette Colbert in *It Happened One Night* so the next car will give us a lift? For one thing, I'm wearing pants."

"That is unquestionably not what I had in mind," Paul said, and I wasn't sure how to take that. "I was thinking more in terms of your asking very specific questions, the type more likely to gain attention in that office, and being, let's say, conspicuous in your asking."

"You want me to shout," I said.

"I wouldn't object, but 'shout' might be overstating it. Just make sure you're audible beyond the one person in front of you."

We (that is, I) pulled the car into a parking lot my portable GPS insisted was my "destination." At least it wasn't my "final destination," the way the airlines like to put it. You have to take your signs of hope where you can get them.

It was as nondescript a building as you can imagine, glass and steel and only four stories high. Some of the parking spaces—those for employees and not visitors like me—were on the level where the ground floor should be, and the building itself was raised over the lot. It was like the offices were on stilts.

I walked into the lobby, taking off the sunglasses I'd been wearing to drive. It was a lovely sunny June day, which meant there was enough glare to blind a person on New Jersey's chrome-and-glass-infested highways. I put the sunglasses in my tote bag and walked toward the building's directory.

Filcher, Baker, and Klein, attorneys at law, was (were?) located on the second floor, which meant the third floor if you were counting the level with the cars. I'd decided I would because I had to walk up a flight of stairs to get to the lobby. I walked up another flight, Paul rising effortlessly and annoyingly beside me, and was immediately confronted with the law offices, which took up the whole floor.

It was one of those bright, busy, frantic (aren't you glad I didn't say *bustling*?) hubs of activity that might or might not actually justify itself but certainly wants you to know about it. Young people rushed from one cubicle to another with actual paper files, which was odd if you thought about it, but I didn't. Ringed around the bullpen area were the partners' offices, which had actual wooden doors and blinds in the windows to disassociate them from the riffraff in their outer offices.

Right inside the front glass doors was a very welcoming reception area, settled to the left but unmistakably the first stop in a visit to the office. Behind it sat a woman of Asian descent, maybe twenty-five on a bad day, dressed more expensively than I had been at either of my weddings.

"How may I help you?" she asked pleasantly. I thought the question was a hair presumptuous. How did she know she could help me at all?

Paul saw the look on my face and said, "You're not being confrontational, Alison. You're here for a very specific, completely legitimate purpose. Project that."

I didn't nod, but I did take his words to heart. Paul was right; this was his operation, and I was just the distraction. I remembered to raise my decibel level a bit. "I'm trying to find the office for Richard Harrison," I said. I was playing it a little brassier than I'd intended, but that note was right for the character I decided I was playing.

The young woman, whose nameplate identified her as Isabel Chang, didn't flinch as I might have expected. But she did take a beat to answer. "I'm sorry to be the bearer of unpleasant news," she began.

"I know he's dead," I told her and a few other people in the immediate area. "I'm here to pick up some of his things. Which one's the office he was using?" I looked around at the offices to choose one for Richard, but Paul watched Ms. Chang's eyes, no doubt to see which way she would look reflexively.

"And you are . . . ?" she said.

"I'm his assistant from New York," I said, hoping that Richard's real assistant hadn't come by already or wasn't known by the local staff. "I'm boxing up his things and taking them back where they belong."

"I'm afraid Mr. Harrison was working out of a hotel in New Brunswick during the trial," Ms. Chang said. "He didn't have an office on these premises."

"They surely put his things somewhere," Paul said. He had, in fact, asked Richard where to look, and Richard had replied that since he had been working out of the hotel, there was no telling where his personal effects and professional materials might have ended up.

I channeled my inner Joan Cusack in *Working Girl*. "He had a laptop. He had case files. They're not in the hotel, so they must be *someplace*." I was especially proud of the spin I put on that last word. Even I was a little uncomfortable with myself in the room.

But it got the response Paul had hoped for: just for a moment, Ms. Chang's eyes moved toward one of the vacant offices to her left, our right. He headed in that direction immediately.

"I'm afraid the police confiscated everything Mr. Harrison left in the hotel room," she said, once again holding eye contact with me. "The county prosecutor's office probably has it now."

I needed to buy a little time for Paul to look through the room Ms. Chang had unwittingly pointed him toward. "There were no copies of anything? No backup files in the server here? I find it hard to believe you guys in *New Jersey* don't have a protocol to save things like that in case of an emergency."

Ms. Chang looked, as she should, offended at the idea that New Jerseyans can't keep up with our evil overlords in the Big Apple. I had hoped that would irritate her enough to make her composure slip a little but was disappointed. "I'm sure in the *New York* office you have the same procedures that we do. A deceased attorney means every file is sealed. And no doubt your office has the proper forms to request access to any files you might need."

I was trying very hard not to look like I was watching the empty office into which Paul had vanished behind drawn blinds. He was not emerging, but then I wasn't able to keep a constant eye on the room.

"You want me to fill out a *form*?" I answered, hoping the increase in volume might alert Paul to the idea that I was running out of improv material and might need him to hurry his see-through butt out of the area. "A man is dead! I'm just trying to retrieve what he left behind so he can be remembered appropriately." Yeah, I was running on fumes, all right.

"You know the rules," Ms. Chang said. "Right?"

Uh-oh. What did that mean? "I know, but—"

"Do you have your ID on you?" she jumped in. "Your company key card?" As if to intimidate me (which she could do easily on her own), she indicated a lanyard around her neck with a very professional swipe card hanging on it.

"Um . . ." I was going to argue that the New York office didn't have those, but what were the odds? "I didn't bring it with me. Figured I wouldn't need it to get in here."

"Right." Ms. Chang looked toward a young man standing to my left, who wasn't wearing a uniform but whose stillness gave the impression he was working as a security guard of some sort. Of course, how many sorts of security guards are there, really? "Gary, would you check with the New York office? Ms. . . ." She looked at me. "I'm sorry. I didn't catch your name."

That was probably because I hadn't thrown it. My job here had been to create a distraction, not to actually obtain anything. "I'm Mr. Harrison's assistant," I said. It sounded stupid even to me.

"I imagine it doesn't say that on your driver's license," Ms. Chang said. Gary the security guy, who frankly wasn't all that scary in a polo shirt and blue khakis, moved a little closer in case I tried to bust my way into the law firm. I guess.

For a Jersey girl, there is only one option when backed into a corner, and that is to exhibit righteous indignation. "Look, if you think for one second that you can tell me I'm not *me* because you don't feel like going through your own computer files, I don't have to put up with that!" I huffed. "I don't get paid enough for this!"

With that I turned on my (flat) heel and headed for the office door. Paul, I decided, could fend for himself, largely because no one could see him anyway. Even if someone had stumbled into the office he was searching and saw files flying around, what was going to happen to Paul? Very hard to get *him* arrested, but I was still quite visible, and my hands were solid enough to hold cuffs.

"Just a moment," I heard Ms. Chang say, and against my better judgment, I stopped and looked at her.

"What?" I asked in my best confrontational tone, which wasn't very good.

"I need you to sign out," she said, pointing to a sheet on a clipboard in her hand.

I made a rude noise and left the office.

I walked down the two flights of stairs and went to my battered, weathered Volvo wagon in the parking lot among the Lexus SUVs and Mercedes sedans. Hovering just over my car was Paul, arms folded, in his usual jeans and dark shirt, looking as if he'd been there for hours.

"What took you so long?" he asked.

"I figured while I was up there I'd file a lawsuit against somebody, but I don't currently have an address for my ex-husband," I said. "What do you mean, what took me so long? Why didn't you come out and relieve me at the front desk?"

Paul looked stumped, the question clearly never having raised itself in his mind. "The window was so much more convenient," he said. "It never occurred to me you would stay out there. I just needed to find the right office and get inside."

"And here I thought I'd missed you. Did you find anything useful?" I got into the car and watched Paul drop through the roof and into a position approximating sitting in the front seat.

"Not very much," he admitted. "It's very possible much of what Richard was working on was confiscated by the police, and that could very well be a factor in the delay in Cassidy Van Doren's trial."

"The receptionist said that's what happened and that it's now with the Middlesex county prosecutor," I told him. "And I'm not doing this show in their offices, so don't ask me. It would take weeks to wade through all the files there, and I don't want to stand at a reception desk for weeks."

"I will not point out again that you need not have stayed at the reception desk," Paul said.

"You just did point it out again."

He plowed on through, which was probably the right decision. I pulled the car out of the parking lot to head back to the Garden State Parkway. "I believe you are right about the prosecutor's office. There's no quick and simple path through there."

"What about asking Richard to access his files through Maxie's laptop?" I suggested.

Paul didn't answer immediately, which meant my idea might have some semblance of merit. But then he shook his head. "I'll ask him, but I'd be surprised if his account is still active," he said. "And someone signing on to a dead man's account might seem odd and be detected by the site's Webmaster."

"So they'll trace it back to a dead woman's computer," I said. "That'll keep them up nights." My world is so much different than that of most people. I often envy most people. There was a silence of a few seconds in the car as we each retreated to our own thoughts. "You and Richard weren't very close, were you?" I asked Paul.

"Not especially, but we harbor no animosity toward each other. At least I don't toward him," Paul said. "How is that relevant to his murder?"

"It's not," I answered. "I don't think you killed him."

"Then why did you ask?" Paul said.

"I wanted to understand. I never had a sibling. Neither does Melissa, and she's not getting one. So it's always interesting to me to see the dynamics in families with more than one child."

Paul folded his hands in his lap, and the expression on his face told me he was trying to be tactful. "It would probably be best to keep your focus on the case, Alison."

"I can multitask."

He sighed a little. There's just no getting rid of a girl like me. "Richard was the older brother in a family with a single mother," he said, staring out through the windshield. "My father left when I was very young, and Richard is twelve years older than I, or was twelve years old than I was, anyway. He became a surrogate parent. We are less like brothers than most. It was as if Richard were my guardian for much of my life." He leaned back a little and melted into the passenger seat.

"That must have been rough," I said after a moment.

"I came through it all right," Paul said, eyes closed.

"I meant for Richard."

Paul seemed as if he were falling asleep, which was odd. Ghosts don't exactly sleep. They do recharge, more or less, mostly at night or in the early morning hours, but they don't have the need for sleep that we living folks do. I took it as a sign that Paul didn't want to discuss the subject any further, which at this point was fine with me.

But when I switched on the turn signal to move into the on-ramp for the Parkway, he sat bolt upright and said, "Where are you going?"

"Home. Why?"

"Don't get on the highway. Keep going straight." Paul pointed so I'd know which way straight was.

I turned off the signal and kept going, which did not stop the guy behind me from honking his horn in exasperation. It's New Jersey. That's literally how we roll. "You know a better way back to Harbor Haven now that you've been out in the world?" I asked Paul.

"What? No. You should be continuing on to the Garden State Parkway, I believe."

"That's what I was doing."

"But you were going south when we need to head north," Paul corrected me. He thought.

"Paul, I realize you're originally from Canada, but north isn't always the way home. I need to head south."

He shook his head. "We're not going home yet," he said. "We're going to Montclair."

That made no sense. "Montclair! That's like forty minutes out of the way! Why are we going there?"

"Because that's where Richard lived, and that is where his wife lives now."

I moaned. "Miriam?" I thought he'd promised that if I was good about going to the office, I wouldn't have to go to the house.

"Miriam," Paul agreed. I guessed I was wrong.

Chapter 10

I had seven very good reasons not to drive to Montclair today to talk with Richard Harrison's widow, Miriam. Four of them involved the inconvenience to my day, and the other three were about not wanting to confront a woman who might have known her husband was in love with someone else and was at least technically suspected of hitting him with a blunt object until he became transparent and showed up at a haunted guesthouse.

Paul, being afflicted with a very specific type of crime-related tunnel vision, refused to hear any of my very good reasons. Of course, it could be said that I was driving the car and therefore could have taken us back to Harbor Haven, where even if my life wasn't normal, it was at least familiar. But if you've ever had an argument with a single-minded ghost, you'll know the prospects of winning aren't great.

I drove to Montclair, given the address Paul managed to program into my GPS.

We pulled up, eventually, to a very sprawling colonial-style home that was desperate for everyone to see it. Clearly the paint job was fresh and probably redone every year. Every shrub was trimmed within an inch of its life, and the lawn was so mowed, the people who invented AstroTurf (who were from Rutgers, the State University of New Jersey, if you're asked) had probably used this grass as a model.

The windows were recently washed. The Infiniti Q50 parked in the immaculate driveway shone so bright, my sunglasses practically begged for relief. Honest to goodness, the front doorknob looked like it had been polished that day.

I considered calling the Ocean County Board of Health and recommending that my own house, which I keep up nicely, be condemned.

"This is Richard's house?" I asked Paul.

"Yes. Richard said it was easy to get to his job in Manhattan and that Miriam liked the layout of the property." Well, that explained it. Surely you spend millions (easily) on a well-laid-out property.

I put the car in park and looked at Paul. "What do I need to know about Miriam before I ring that doorbell?" I asked.

He did not, thankfully, pretend not to know what I meant. "She is a short-tempered woman who bristles whenever anyone suggests anything she believes or desires might not be correct."

"I imagine you and she had few disagreements in your day," I said.

He didn't move a facial muscle, assuming he still had any. "There were some . . . spirited discussions," he said.

"You ever think of haunting her? Just for kicks?"

"That's what we're going to do now," Paul said. "Are you ready?"

I didn't think I was, but that wasn't going to slow Paul down, so I didn't answer and got out of the car. We each got to the front door in our own way. Paul looked at me, then at the doorbell. That's Paul being subtle.

Well, I hadn't come all this way *not* to ring the doorbell, I supposed. That didn't make it any less ominous, but it did have logic behind it, which is a plus. I pushed the incredibly clean button and heard the chimes ring inside.

"I don't suppose just running away at this point would be enough retribution for you," I said to Paul.

"We are not here for retribution. We are here for information." I made a mental note to invite Paul to my next party; he's a fun guy.

There was no time to answer because that was the moment the door opened. A woman in her late forties, tall and imperial, looked down her considerable nose at me and asked, "May I help you?"

"Mrs. Harrison," I began. Paul shook his head.

The woman twitched an eyebrow and asked, "Who shall I say is calling?"

"That's her assistant, Joan," Paul told me. Miriam had an assistant? In her house?

"My name is Alison Kerby," I said, because it was. "I'm a licensed private investigator." Also technically true, as I had renewed my license online before leaving this morning. "I have a few questions to ask Mrs. Harrison." I was willing to bet there would be more than a few questions, especially since Paul was there to ask them through me.

"Regarding what?" Joan deigned to ask.

"*Mr.* Harrison," I said.

"Mr. Harrison is deceased."

"That's why I'm here. Can I talk to her?" This was getting tiresome, and I tend to react to people who look down on me by punching up.

"I will ask," Joan said, then closed the door in my face.

I looked toward Paul, who was pretending to notice something in the doorway above our heads. "I realized Richard was doing well at the law firm, but I didn't realize he was this rich," I said.

"Much of the money is from Miriam's family," he told me without looking me in the eye. "They own a very large soft drink company in Canada."

"This place comes from sodas?"

The door opened again, and this time the woman behind it was in her late forties, short and imperial. It wasn't much of a change.

"I am Miriam Harrison," she said with an affected accent that was for sure not from Saskatchewan. "And you are?"

"You know all that from your assistant," I reminded her. "You know who I am and you know why I'm here. May I come in?"

Miriam clearly wasn't used to having people talk to her like that, which I enjoyed. She pursed her lips as if to speak and then didn't. Instead she took a step back and to the side and gestured with her right arm for me to enter. So I did. Paul phased through the door as Miriam closed it and followed us into a room to the left.

The entrance foyer was impressive in itself, with a very high ceiling and a rail that ran around the room halfway up the walls. "This room was modeled after the entrance hall at

Monticello," Miriam said as I stared upward. I wasn't sure why, but she seemed to want to impress me.

But we were out of there before I could answer and into a room lined from floor to (again) high ceiling with bookshelves, crammed to the last inch with books. They looked like they had not been taken out to be read in years.

"What was this room modeled after?" I asked.

"It's a library," Miriam said with some superiority, which appeared to be the only way she knew how to talk. She gestured me into an overstuffed easy chair and did not offer her brother-in-law a seat because she knew he had died five years before and for some reason didn't imagine he was in the room now. "What is it you are investigating, Ms. Kerby?" she asked as she sat in a chair opposite mine.

"I'm looking into the case your husband was defending when he died," I said at Paul's prompting. "I have some questions that his records could help answer. Can you tell me where he might have left a computer file or hard copies?"

"I have no idea."

That seemed unlikely. "Didn't you receive his effects after his body was discovered?" I asked. If Miriam didn't want to be sentimental, I saw no reason to be.

"I got his personal things, but the work things were confiscated by the police." Miriam wasn't explaining; she was lecturing on the workings of the New Jersey criminal justice system. "They are considered evidence."

Paul prompted me to ask, "What about the trial he was working on? Wouldn't the notes and other records he had be needed for that?"

"I imagine so. I don't get involved—didn't get involved—in Richard's cases."

"But I would guess there would be backups, copies, things like that," I said. "Where did he keep those?"

Miriam stood up with an air of impatience. It was barely discernible from her air of superiority, which was her go-to air. "I *told* you, I have no idea," she said. "Now if you don't mind, I have things I need to do." She turned toward the door. Paul even started floating in that direction. If Miriam had decided I was leaving, clearly I was leaving.

Except I didn't care what Miriam had decided. "I don't believe you," I said quietly.

"Alison," Paul said.

Miriam, halfway to the doorway, turned back with an expression similar to that if I'd told her we were now living on Mercury. "I beg your pardon?" she said.

"I said I don't believe you. You don't strike me as the kind of woman who would so easily disconnect from so important an aspect of her husband's life. I think you would have been very interested and involved. So when you tell me that he was working on a case at the time he was murdered and you haven't so much as lifted a finger to find his remaining records, I think you're hiding something."

Paul, who is transparent, looked pale. I didn't think that was possible.

Miriam regarded me carefully, something she had not done before. Until I'd defied her authority, I was not worthy of her attention. Now she needed to size me up more completely. She took her time, which I thought was excessive. A person's appearance can't actually tell you who she is, and she needed to know who I was if she was going to prevail. For people like Miriam, everything is a competition.

"I underestimated you," she said. "I won't do that again."

"Now, about Richard's case files," I said, not acknowledging what I'm sure she saw as a compliment.

"Richard's laptop computer and his case files *are* with the county prosecutor's major crimes division," Miriam answered. "I told you the truth about that."

"But there are copies somewhere, aren't there?"

Paul was floating, eyes wide, watching the scene as if he couldn't believe such a thing was happening. His right hand actually covered his mouth like he was afraid he'd say something that would betray him. I'd be the only one to hear it.

"There are. His firm saves everything on the cloud, and there are more hard copies than you can imagine. The law is one of the last areas that actually still relies heavily on paper."

"Where can I find those?" I asked her.

"I'm not sure I want to tell you," Miriam said. "The fact that you wouldn't take no for an answer isn't enough to give you everything you want."

I stood and faced her. Since the idea of my leaving immediately was off the table, giving up the chair wasn't a retreat. I needed to look her in the eye to retain her respect. "What do you need in return?" I asked. "Because I'm telling you right off the top, a pound of flesh is not a possibility for me." Not that I couldn't afford to drop a pound or two, but I wouldn't much care for Miriam's method of removal, I was pretty sure.

"It's not a barter situation," Miriam said, taking a few steps toward me. "You don't have anything I could possibly want." That was a point.

I toyed with the idea of telling her I could easily get in touch with Richard and talk to him for her, but I doubted she'd much want that, and she certainly wouldn't have believed me anyway. "There's the idea of finding out who killed your husband," I said.

"After you tell me who bludgeoned Richard to death, will he be any less dead?" Miriam said. "I'm not much for revenge."

"You weren't angry when you discovered Richard was falling in love with his client?" I asked. Paul audibly gasped; Richard had told us he wasn't sure Miriam had known about that. I might have been letting the family cat out of the family bag.

"Alison," he repeated. It seemed to be the only thing he could bring himself to say in this room.

"I was irritated," Miriam said. "I think *angry* would be an overstatement. Richard and I hadn't been a typical married couple for quite some time, so his interest in a younger woman wasn't exactly unexpected. It happens to middle-aged men all the time. At least he didn't buy himself a red sports car."

"How did you find out?" I asked.

"Richard made a few offhand remarks," she said. "He didn't exactly *tell* me so much as he didn't try very hard to conceal his feelings. I wasn't as worried about the betrayal as I was about his rather atrocious taste. A woman on trial for murder, after all. We didn't even know her father when he was alive."

"Did you talk to him about it?"

Miriam waved a hand to declare the subject irrelevant. "What you're after are his work records," she reminded me. "And this line of questioning isn't making me feel more inclined to give them to you."

"I could ask a judge for a warrant," I noted.

"You're not a cop," Miriam reminded me. "I'm not even sure you're a real private investigator."

I resisted the impulse to flash my state license. Instead Paul leaned over to me (as if proximity would make a difference to Miriam) and said, "Find a way that it benefits her and she will do anything to help you."

I've never taken an improv class, but here I was on my feet trying to make up a scenario without even any help from the audience. It was about motivation. I had to understand Miriam as a character. What would she want that I could promise her? What would matter to her?

"You're right," I said. That's the first thing someone like Miriam wants to hear. "I'm not a cop. I'm not attached to any police department at all. And that's lucky for you."

"I don't see how," she sniffed. "The police are investigating Richard's murder. I don't even know who your client is or why you're at all interested in the incident." *The incident.* Her husband is beaten to death and she calls it *the incident.* That's a new level of cold.

"Yes, they are, but they aren't aware that Richard believed he was falling in love with his client," I told her. I completely ignored her mention of my "client," since that would bring in the whole communication-with-her-dead-husband thing, and who needed that? "I can keep that part of the story private and make sure that your name is not mentioned in the investigation at all."

Miriam's eyes narrowed like a hawk's. "There is no reason to mention me in connection with Richard's death other than to say that I am the grieving widow."

"Unless it comes out that he might have been infatuated with someone else," I said. "Even if you're not considered a suspect after that, you would be known as the woman whose husband fell in love with a younger woman he barely knew. Was he beginning divorce proceedings?"

Miriam's voice dropped in tone and volume. "No. He was not. And I don't appreciate—"

"See, that's the kind of thing people from the press will be asking if this comes out," I said. "The police have no way of knowing about it, so they're not going to mention it to anyone. But if I have to make a noisier inquiry than I'd like, you never know what might come out."

Miriam cocked an eyebrow in her last-ditch effort to demonstrate the superiority of her class over mine. What she didn't realize was that my class was always phys ed or shop. "You are trying to blackmail me, young lady," she said.

I tamped down the impulse to say that *blackmail* is an ugly word. It's not nearly as ugly as, say, *mucilage* or *sludge*. "I am attempting to show you the advantage in helping me along," I said. "I'm not threatening you with anything at all."

"You're treading on very dangerous ground," Paul warned. "But it might be working."

Indeed, Miriam pursed her lips, and for a moment I was afraid she was going to spit, but let's face it, this was a woman who probably hadn't spit in decades, even when her dentist told her to. After a long pause, she barely opened her mouth and said, "What do you need?"

"Access to any of Richard's case files on Cassidy Van Doren and his e-mail password," I said. I had asked Richard about his passwords before we left for the office and he'd made a vague reference to "gaps in my memory" that made getting them from Miriam necessary.

"You will have them in five minutes," Miriam told me. "On the single condition that I never have to talk to you again."

"Nothing would please me more," I told her.

"Let's get out of here," Paul said.

Chapter 11

The first person we showed Richard's computer files to when we got home was Richard. It seemed the logical step to take. He'd understand the legalese better than anyone there and was intimately familiar with the case.

"What is it I'm looking for that I haven't seen before?" he asked.

"Anything that might have prompted someone to see an advantage in eliminating you," Paul told him. "The last time you looked at these files and these e-mails, you had no idea someone was going to kill you. Now you have that advantage."

"Some advantage," Maxie said from her perch on the movie room's ceiling fan. I was considering turning the fan on, which wouldn't have bothered Maxie's insubstantial body at all, but it's a little weird to watch the blades go straight through someone even when she can't feel it. Maxie actually thinks that sort of thing is amusing.

"Is there a quiet space where I can work?" Richard asked, wisely not answering Maxie.

"You have the room I gave you," I reminded him. "Nobody else is going to go in there. In fact, the door is locked and I have the only keys."

"There is no desk in that room," Richard said. "I need a desk and a computer. May I use this one?" He pointed at the unit we'd used to show him the files Miriam had given me on a thumb drive, which just happened to be Maxie's laptop.

"Hey," Maxie said.

"Yes," I said. "But only for short periods because Maxie will need access as well."

Maxie, who believes I never stick up for her, smiled and nodded in my direction. "Thank you."

"You're going to have to do some online research," Paul said.

Maxie pouted. "Figures. The only time you'd put me first is when you want something from me." She zipped up into the ceiling and was gone.

I felt bad, but mostly because my first impulse was to remind her that the second spook show of the day was coming up soon.

"I will get to work immediately and let you know what I discover," Richard said, and he too phased his way through the movie room ceiling, leaving Paul and me alone.

"Your brother and his wife are not exactly kickback kind of individuals," I said, sinking into one of the reclining chairs I have in the room for movie nights.

"Not everyone is as footloose and fancy free as I am," Paul told me. His thin smile indicated he thought he was being amusing.

"Will Richard be able to get anything out of the computer files?" I asked.

He shrugged. "It's a place to start. It will probably take him some time, and the information he gives us will be technical and difficult to understand, if I know Richard. But it's possible he will uncover something with his new insight that he didn't see before. My best guess is that he will find information pertinent to Cassidy Van Doren's case and not to his own. Richard has processed being dead faster than anyone I have ever seen."

It was true; over the years we had witnessed a number of people for whom the transition to a ghostly existence had taken weeks or months to sink in. Everett had not realized exactly what had happened to him until he'd overheard a conversation in the men's room at a gas station, and even then he'd had to understand it and accept it.

"So what do we do in the meantime?"

Paul did his usual Sherlock Holmes thing: he "paced" back and forth in midair while stroking his goatee, although not as fervently as if a juicy clue had been discovered. "We need more basic information on the Van Doren case from another perspective. The murder took place in Cranbury, which is not very close to here, so Lieutenant McElone probably won't be an enormous help on this." Detective Lieutenant Anita McElone is the chief of detectives in the Harbor Haven Police Department. She and I have collaborated on cases before, meaning I have annoyed McElone to the point of distraction and she has very reluctantly given me information to make me go away.

"I don't know anybody in the Middlesex prosecutor's office," I said. "But Phyllis might."

"It would be worth asking," Paul told me. "But we can also find out quite a bit, I'd think, from the subject herself."

"Cassidy Van Doren?"

"Yes. I'm sure Richard, especially armed with his files and passwords, can provide some contact information."

This opened up a subject Paul and I have discussed at length, and one that never makes me feel good. "You're talking about me going to see an alleged murderer," I said. "I've had enough guns pointed at me, you'll recall."

"I believe Cassidy's modus operandi is drowning in a bathtub," Paul noted. "Allegedly. In any event, I doubt that will be possible if you arrange the meeting in a public place. Besides, I will be there with you."

"How about you get on the Ghosternet and ask Keith Johnson who killed him?" I proposed. "He's been dead a while. There's no reason to think you won't be able to find him."

Paul nodded. "That will be my first order of business. When we see Richard again, you can ask him about Cassidy's cell phone number. Maxie should be looking up any details we can find on Richard's murder, which took place in New Brunswick."

"Richard has her laptop," I reminded him.

Paul nodded again. "Can she use yours?" he asked.

I groaned a little bit. My laptop was probably one of the beta units Steve Jobs rejected in the California garage where Apple got started. "She's not going to be happy about it. And I assume you remember what it's like when Maxie's not happy."

He closed his eyes. "I remember."

Before I could answer, Gregory Lewis appeared in the archway entrance to the movie room. "Excuse me, Alison," he said. "Am I interrupting"—he looked around, then up, as your typical mortal will—"anything?"

I'd barely heard Mr. Lewis speak at all since he'd gotten off the Senior Plus Tours van on arrival, but he was a guest, and my favorite kind too—the ones who don't ask for much of anything. "Not at all, Mr. Lewis," I said. "What can I do for you?"

"I don't want to be a bother." He turned and started to shuffle away.

I walked around him and more or less blocked his path. "You are anything but a bother, Mr. Lewis. Please, tell me what you need. I'm happy to help." With guests like him, that's actually true.

Was this the right time to do my John Alden impression on behalf of Abby Lesniak? Was there such a thing as the right time to do that? I had promised Abby but had hoped the whole thing might be forgotten. I decided to see what Mr. Lewis's request was first because that gave me more time to think.

"Well, if it's not too much trouble . . ." Mr. Lewis was doing his best to back out of asking me a question, but I'd mentally vowed to see this through.

"No trouble at all," I said.

"I was wondering if you might be able to direct to a good gift shop in town," Mr. Lewis said quietly.

A gift shop? The town was lousy with them. It's a Jersey Shore town. You can walk down the street and be pelted with gifts if you move slowly enough. "What kind of gift are we talking about?" I asked. This might be a clue toward proceeding with Abby's request. If Mr. Lewis was buying perfume or jewelry, for example, it might be an indication that he was at least interested in someone at home.

Paul floated by looking impatient. Anything that is not about the case is a waste of time in Paul's eyes. If he wore a wristwatch, he'd have been checking it frequently.

"You know, T-shirts, postcards, balloons, that sort of thing," Mr. Lewis said.

Sounded pretty standard to me. "There are plenty of those on the boardwalk in Seaside Heights, but here in town, if you walk down Ocean Avenue, they're pretty hard to miss, Mr. Lewis."

He looked up at me; Mr. Lewis was a diminutive man. "Please call me Greg," he said.

"Thank you, Greg. There are lots of those gift shops in town. I'm sure you know."

"Yes," Greg allowed. "But I need something a little better. Higher quality. Something that will stand out. You know what I mean?"

Saying I did might have been an overstatement, but I nodded because there was a store I could recommend. "Go to Shanahan's on Surf Avenue," I said. I walked to a table near the windows and opened a drawer where I keep business cards of those local concerns I can confidently give to guests. "Their quality is a little higher than everyone else. No obscene T-shirts, no toys that'll break on the ride home." I handed Greg the card.

"Thank you, Alison," he said. "You've been a big help." Greg turned and left the movie room, prompting a melodramatic sigh from Paul.

"Finally," he said.

"This is a business," I reminded him. "And it's what's keeping a roof over your see-through head, so don't knock it. It's always going to be my priority, and that means you need to cope with it."

"Yes. Now. About Maxie using your laptop." Paul had given up pacing, his momentum completely interrupted by what he saw as an intrusion.

"She's not going to be happy."

"We can't ask Richard to use yours. His work would be slowed down immeasurably. But Maxie can use yours because she's accustomed to it and she has less data to analyze." Paul even looked like he wasn't just giving his brother preferential treatment.

"Fine. But you have to tell her." Never let it be said I can't be vindictive when the occasion arises.

Paul sputtered. "That's a dirty trick, Alison."

"Welcome home."

He smiled. "I probably deserved that. Okay. I'll talk to Maxie. If you hear the roof come off the house, you'll know why." He rose up and flew through the ceiling.

I was alone for the first time that day. It actually felt pretty good. So naturally my phone rang. I reached into my pocket and pulled it out.

My best friend, Jeannie Rogers, was calling, and I had to decide if I could summon enough energy to talk to her. Jeannie is one of the best people I've ever met, but she operates at a level of kinetics higher than I could achieve if I were a raging cocaine addict. I'm more into caffeine as a drug of choice (and even that in moderation), but I can imagine.

I love Jeannie. I'd let her go on and try to relax while she talked herself out. It was a plan. "Hey, Jeannie," I said when I pushed the *accept* button.

"Alison!" See what I mean? Right off the top, energy. "How's the old married lady?" This was a question she'd asked me four times a week since the day Josh and I made it official right before her very eyes. She finds some strange pleasure in reminding me I'm married, just in case I've forgotten or something.

"Tired," I said. "I'm working on an investigation, and I have five guests." After the speech I'd just given Paul about my priorities, I probably should have said that the other way around.

"An investigation!" Jeannie speaks quite often in exclamation points. "I thought you'd given that up."

"Well, I did, but then this came up and I sort of have to get it figured out so I can give it up again." That made sense, right? Because I figured once we solved Richard's case, Paul would be back on the road—or a couple feet above it.

I gave Jeannie a very brief rundown on the investigation and tap-danced a little about who my client might have been by saying it was "someone close to the lawyer who was killed." You really couldn't get any closer.

Jeannie is a fantastic listener, a skill she has cultivated through decades of being an excellent gossip. She said nothing while I was talking, not even asking a question. When it was clear I had finished my sordid tale, she waited a moment while digesting the information. "Wow," she said. "Somebody didn't want that girl to get off, did they?"

"What do you mean?"

"Well, everybody was telling this guy the case was open and shut, that she'd put her stepdad under the water and held him there, right? But he comes in and starts finding stuff that might get her declared innocent, and the next thing you know, he's got a pipe upside the head." Jeannie thinks she's street. She's more cul-de-sac.

"So you think this was about Richard finding something out that got too close?" I hadn't thought through the motives enough in this case. Which wasn't even slightly unusual, I'm sorry to say.

Jeannie made a rude noise with her lips. "Plain as the nose on your face," she said. "Not that I'm saying anything about your nose, you understand."

"No offense taken."

"It's just real clear that the dead guy found out something that was going to show somebody else killed that stepdad, and whoever it was didn't want him to say so. Otherwise, you could probably ask *him* what happened."

That was precisely what I intended to do.

Chapter 12

It turned out that Jeannie was calling just to pass on some fairly uncontroversial news about a high school classmate of ours who had married one of our high school teachers eighteen years after graduating. And to invite herself; her husband, Tony; and their two children over for dinner the following night once she found out my mother and Melissa (mostly Melissa) would be cooking. I sort of hustled her off the phone because I needed to go upstairs and talk with Richard and, if I could find him, Paul.

Paul actually came looking for me to say that I owed him because Maxie hit the roof—or would have if she hadn't already been sitting on it—when she heard she had to stoop to using my laptop even for a few hours while Richard toiled away on hers. He said the fury of her tantrum was similar to what Hurricane Sandy had unleashed on much of the Jersey Shore years earlier, which was actually a sort of tasteless hyperbole. There are still people trying to get their shore houses back together from Sandy.

Nonetheless, Paul agreed we should go talk to Richard about his progress and the idea that he might have been holding back part of his story for reasons unknown. We checked on the room I'd given Richard but didn't find him there. Which was weird.

"I can't understand why he'd go somewhere else," Paul said. "He knows we need him to look through those files."

"He said that he wanted a room that has a desk so he could put the laptop down on something," I remembered. "Is it that taxing on your arms?"

Paul made a noncommittal face. "Not really. You'll recall Maxie managed to carry you in the air for quite some distance a while back. But Richard is not used to his current state of existence and might still be operating on the same standards he had when he was alive. Which rooms have desks?" Paul has been living in my house with all my furniture for years and there are still rooms I don't think he's ever visited.

"My old bedroom has a little pulldown shelf on the dresser that I used as a desk," I said. "But Penny Desmond is in that room now. You don't think Richard would use a room that a guest has taken, do you?"

"If Penny is not there now, it's possible," he answered. "Richard wouldn't concern himself with someone's effects, but he wouldn't want to be there working when she was present."

But a check of Penny's room did not locate Richard. It's a small enough room (albeit with a private bath, which means I can charge more for it) that one glance told the story there. I stood on the outside landing with Paul and ran through the furniture inventory in my mind.

"The only actual *desk* desk is in Liss's room," I said to Paul.

He nodded and started rising toward the ceiling. "Hang on," I said. "That's my daughter's room. Only I get to go up there when she's not around. So I'll check. And if Richard is there, that's what I'm going to tell him." Paul offered no protest.

There's a dumbwaiter/elevator to Melissa's attic bedroom that Jeannie's husband, Tony, installed when I decided to convert the space for my daughter. But the ceiling in the hallway beneath that room still has the pulldown stairs I used when it was just an attic. I reached for the handle, pulled down the stairs, and unlocked the hinge on the panel to get inside.

Richard wasn't there either. I found that comforting and oddly irritating. Was this ghost playing hide-and-seek with us? I climbed back down the stairs, folded them back up, and reported my lack of progress to Paul.

He looked thoughtful, and then his eyes brightened as much as they can. "Richard is my brother," he said.

"No kidding. I have a cousin named Roberto. What's your point?"

"Some of the thought patterns are the same. It's genetic. We have personalities that aren't identical, but the basis is roughly similar." He continued this babble as he sunk into the floor.

"Where are you going?" I asked just before his mouth reached the carpet.

"The basement."

Of course Richard was there when I arrived a minute later, panting a little from running down two flights of stairs. The basement had always been Paul's place to do his best thinking and to get away from the chaos my house can become. I should have thought to look for his brother there first.

Richard was using a huge stereo speaker from the good old days as a rest for Maxie's laptop computer, and the two ghost brothers were already involved in conversation when I got there.

"I believe that is something I had said when I arrived," Richard was saying. "I was killed because I was getting too close to discovering who had actually murdered Keith Johnson."

"You didn't say that," I said when I'd caught my breath. "You said that you were working on the case and then somebody killed you. I'd remember if you'd mentioned being close to making a breakthrough that might have led to your own murder."

"Whether you said it before or not, you're saying it now," Paul pointed out. He's all about getting things back on topic as long as it's about the case. Ask him about anything else and he'll look slightly pained, like you're trying to divulge deeply buried emotional baggage. Is that a mixed metaphor? You can bury baggage, although the manufacturers don't recommend it. "What had you found, and who was the murderer you had discovered?"

Richard held up a finger like a professor about to reveal an especially interesting law of physics. Assuming there is such a thing. "Well, I hadn't discovered the actual murderer *yet*, but I was very close. Looking at these files just reminded me of the process."

"Show me," his brother said.

"Well, hang on. As a defense attorney, my job was not to solve the crime. My job was to prove that the accused, Cassidy Van Doren, had not committed it. So that had been the thrust of my research the whole time. But in researching the physical facts of the murder, it had become clear, as I'm certain I *did* tell you before"—he gave me a telling glance, but I chose not to respond—"that Cassidy could not have lifted her stepfather into the tub nor held him down long enough under the water to drown him."

"Surely not," Paul said. "But that does not lead to another possible killer."

"It does when you realize that if Cassidy didn't drown Keith, and he was still drowned, someone else might have done it," Richard said. Surely he had missed his calling in life when he'd turned his back on the lucrative line of telling people obvious things. "So I focused on discovering exactly who *could* have had the strength to perform these tasks, particularly among those who might have had access to his room in the bed-and-breakfast."

"Was it common knowledge that Keith was taking a long weekend in Cranbury?" Paul asked Richard.

"Well, he wasn't hiding it as far as I can tell," Richard said. "I'm not sure he went around telling everyone he knew, but it wasn't an illicit affair with anyone. He was just taking a break at a rustic inn called the Cranbury Bog."

That was so adorable, I wanted to adopt it. But Haunted Guesthouse had never really been my first choice for my own place. When I was planning it, I was calling it the Sea Breeze in my mind. That went out the window when I got hit with a bucket of wallboard compound.

"So who would have known he was there?" Paul asked. "Did his wife go there with him?"

"No. Adrian was at the house in Upper Saddle River. They were having new appliances installed in the kitchen, which was one of the reasons Keith wanted to be away, but his wife felt she needed to be there to supervise. Adrian is very good at supervising."

If she were half as good at supervising as Richard's wife, Miriam, was at being imperious, they could start a business where Miriam intimidated the contractors into dropping their rates and Adrian Johnson stood over them every step of the way through the job. Believe it or not, I think there might be a market for such a thing.

"Who was there, then?"

"Well, clearly Cassidy, since she was found with the body." Richard seemed to be teaching a class in which Paul and I were not the brightest students. Which was a pity, seeing as how no one else was here. "But I think Keith's business partner, Hunter Evans, had taken a room in the inn as well. The innkeeper, Robin Witherspoon, would know if he had any visitors while he was there. I was just looking into that when this happened to me."

Paul's eyes narrowed; that last part had sent off an alarm in his head. "Who in your firm, or anywhere else, knew your thinking on this case, Richard? Who knew what you were working on exactly?"

Richard's head seemed to back up on his neck a little as he straightened in his faux sitting position. "Paul, if you are suggesting that anyone in my firm might have been trying to send Cassidy to jail and murdered *me* to accomplish that, I will have to protest on their behalf. I have found no proof of that being true, and I have looked."

Before Paul could be cowed by his older brother, I jumped in. "Protest all you want," I told Richard. "Who knew what you were working on?" I think Paul gave me a glance of appreciation, but I didn't want to telegraph it to Richard by making eye contact.

Richard looked at Paul, who had asked the original question. "My assistant, Tracy Cheswick. The first chair on the case, Leonard Krantz. I imagine there are a few others in the Woodbridge office who saw some of my memos, although no one but those two were on my e-mail list."

I looked at Paul. "That's a lot of people."

He nodded. "And if Richard is right about Cassidy's life being in danger, we don't have a great deal of time. Perhaps the first thing to do is to contact her and ask to meet."

Again with meeting the potential murderess. Under the circumstances I supposed it was the thing to do. "It'll be outdoors, and you'll be there with me, Paul," I said. "And we're not doing it before tomorrow."

"Tomorrow?" Paul hates delays in a case.

"We have a spook show in twenty minutes, and then I have to pick up Melissa from school; it's my day. And I do intend to be here and not at Cassidy Van Doren's place when my husband gets home tonight."

Paul put up a hand as if to stop traffic. "Fine. But call today so we can set something up for tomorrow."

"Do you have Cassidy's cell phone number?" I asked Richard.

He pointed toward the screen on Maxie's laptop, which I decided was going to be returned to Maxie for the rest of the day right after the spook show. "Good." I looked at Paul. "You can text her and ask her for the meeting." When Paul couldn't leave the grounds and I had to go do detective stuff, I bought him a cheap cell phone so he could text me. He can't be heard on a phone, but he can push buttons.

"Me? Shouldn't it be you? You're the one she'll be able to see."

"I don't want her having my cell phone number," I said. "I don't care if she has yours, and neither do you." Then a thought struck me. "You don't have your phone on you, do you, Richard?"

"I'm afraid not. I imagine it was confiscated with the rest of my effects."

"Shame. That would have gotten a rise out of her."

But Paul was still protesting being pressed into service. "Alison, you can call on my phone. There is no reason to do this via text message."

I headed for the stairs out of the basement. "My house, my rules," I told Paul.

I didn't look back for his reaction.

Chapter 13

"I really didn't know what to expect when I got your text." Cassidy Van Doren, who looked to be about five years younger than I am, which put her in her early thirties, sat on a bench in front of Voorhees Hall on the Voorhees Mall (for rhyming purposes, no doubt) on the Rutgers University campus in New Brunswick. I was opposite her, close enough to keep our conversation private but not so close that Cassidy could pull a stiletto out of her purse and stab me if she felt like it. I felt it was a reasonable compromise. "I mean, I didn't recognize the number, and there you were talking about Richard Harrison."

"I wanted to be sure you understood that I'm not trying to ask you for money or anything untoward," I said. I immediately regretted the use of the word *untoward*, but it was out there and nothing could be done about it. "I'm looking into Mr. Harrison's murder, and naturally your case has been mentioned."

"I didn't kill my stepfather," Cassidy volunteered.

"For the purposes of our investigation, it doesn't matter whether or not she killed her stepfather," Paul said. Did I not mention that Paul was hovering between us, half in/half on the bench?

I felt it best not to convey his message of total indifference to the nightmare her life had undoubtedly become one way or the other. "I understand," I told her. "But because Mr. Harrison was working on your case at the time, it's possible that the two murders were somehow related. Do you have any idea what might have happened to Richard Harrison?"

Cassidy stared at me for a moment. "He was hit in the head with an iron," she said.

"An iron!" Paul shouted, then put his hand over his mouth, more I think because he was showing some amusement at the way his own brother had died and not because he was afraid the other ghosts in the area, who looked to date back to the 1600s, would take notice, laugh, and point at him.

"An iron?" I said somewhat less explosively. "Someone hit Richard with an iron? Like, the kind to smooth out your blouse and not to play golf, right?"

"Yeah, the iron from the hotel room. You didn't know that? Didn't the police tell you?"

I hadn't actually consulted the New Brunswick police or the Middlesex county prosecutor's investigators yet. "I just started investigating yesterday," I said. It was a poor excuse, and I knew it, but the battles over who was using which laptop had raged on well into the evening the night before, the final result being that not much of anything got investigated. Richard had literally not known what hit him, so it was something Maxie would have to research. Well, now I knew.

"Well, that's what happened. He was in the Heldrich Hotel, right over on Livingston Avenue, and somebody got into his room, took the iron they give you in the closet in case you have to all of a sudden press your pants, and clocked him with it in the back of the head." Cassidy was so matter of fact about it, I wondered whether Miriam Harrison really had any reason to be at all jealous of her. When Richard was alive.

"Ask her about Richard," Paul said, like I hadn't already been doing that. "What their relationship was like." I had to wonder whether his interest was professional or familial.

"Had you gotten to know Mr. Harrison well?" I asked.

"He was working on my case a lot," Cassidy said. She sat back on the bench but didn't seem at all relaxed. She watched the students walking by, even a month after the most recent class of seniors had graduated. Rutgers slows down in the summer, but it never stops. "So we spent some hours together. He asked me about my stepfather and how we got along, you know. Then about the night . . . it happened."

"How did you get along?" I said.

"We didn't," Cassidy answered. "Keith married my mom less than a year after my father died. I couldn't talk to her about it because she was so in love with him, or thought she was, but I felt like it was too soon, you know? She couldn't have processed all that about my dad and then just pushed it aside for this new guy so fast."

I was actually asking about how Cassidy had gotten along with Richard, but this was another interesting way to go. "So Keith knew you disapproved of the marriage. Was there a problem financially?" It had seemed like money was being funneled out of Keith's trust funds for his children and into Cassidy's, and I thought this was a tactful way to broach that subject.

Cassidy, apparently, disagreed. "I didn't know he was putting money in my trust accounts!" she snapped. "I never check those things; I didn't expect anything from him. I didn't find out about that until he was dead! And even if I did know, I had no reason to kill him, did I, if he kept giving me all this money?"

"I'm not trying to prove you killed him," I assured her. "I'm not investigating Keith Johnson's death at all."

"Yes, we are," Paul said. Ignoring him was getting to be my hobby.

"Then why did you ask about that?" Cassidy demanded.

"I was actually asking how you got along with Richard Harrison, not your stepfather." I thought Paul would be pleased we were getting back to dishing the dirt on his brother. This was a side of him I'd never seen before.

"Richard?" Cassidy said. "We got along fine. He was a good lawyer." She looked a little puzzled by the question. "You're not trying to say I was the one with the iron, are you?"

"No, not at all," I said, although I wasn't ruling out any possibilities out at this point. "I just wondered if your relationship had been anything more than professional."

Cassidy looked as if I'd suggested she might decide to sprout flippers and become a penguin. She didn't burst out in laughter, but the thought definitely crossed her mind. "Richard?" she said. "Richard *Harrison*? No! What made you think that?"

It was probably bad form to tell her that Richard had mentioned his feelings for her postmortem, so after glancing very briefly at Paul, I said, "It's sort of a standard question. People who are being defended often have some strong emotional ties to the person defending them." Yeah, it was a dodge, but it was at least an intelligent-sounding dodge.

"Look," Cassidy said, "I had no interest in my lawyer other than being a lawyer. Richard was a lot older than me, and besides, I'm pretty sure he was married. Didn't you look that up either?"

I hadn't had to because I'd spoken to Richard's wife the day before, but again, this wasn't the time for such explanations. "He was definitely married," I said, getting back a little of my own. "That's not always the roadblock we might want it to be." Ask my ex-husband. Accent on the *ex*.

"Well, it is for me," Cassidy said. "Anyway, there's not much I can tell you about Richard. I wasn't there when it happened, you know."

That was true. Probably. "Tell me about the night your stepfather died. How did you happen to find him there?"

Cassidy had told this story so many times by now that she didn't even hesitate to ask why that was any of my business. "I was going to talk to him without my mom there. I knew how irrational she could be about Keith, and I figured now that he was away from her, I could talk straight to him. Tell him I didn't like the way he treated her."

That rang a bell in my head. "Was Keith abusive to your mother?" I asked.

Cassidy didn't look at me. She seemed to be mesmerized by the sight of two Rutgers students walking arm over shoulder near Scott Hall, the incongruously bland structure in this grove of more historical-looking academic buildings. "He didn't hit her or anything, if that's what you mean. But nothing she ever did was good and nothing she ever said was smart.

He'd go out of his way to make fun of her when other people were around. He treated her like a stray cat he'd adopted—no, not even that nice. Like a cat someone had forced him into taking care of that he didn't even want. That's how he treated my mom."

"And your mother didn't see it that way?" Paul didn't need to prompt me to ask that one.

"No." Cassidy watched as the young couple walked into Scott Hall and out of sight. "She thought that man walked on water. You know, we didn't have much money when my father was alive. He worked for PSE&G on the line, and he did okay, but he didn't rake in money. When Mom met Keith and he could buy her all these nice things, I think she got seduced by the money, you know? She thought he absolutely adored her because he bought her bracelets."

"How is she handling Keith's death?" That one Paul *did* tell me to ask.

Cassidy shook her head. "She won't talk to me. She believes what the cops told her. She thinks I killed him because I didn't like him." She finally turned to face me, and there was a tear falling from her right eye. "I mean, seriously, Ms. Kerby. If you killed everybody you didn't like, how many people would already be dead?"

Some of my best friends were dead before I met them, but I saw Cassidy's point. "So you went to the Cranbury Bog to talk to Keith. How did you end up finding him in the bathtub?"

"I'd called him ahead of time and told him I was coming. I didn't want to just show up, you know? So I already knew his room number before I got to the inn. I didn't see anybody at the desk in front, so I went up to his room. I knocked, but the door was already a little open, so I figured Keith was letting me in. But he wasn't in the room. I looked around a little. The water wasn't running in the bathroom so I almost didn't go in. But I heard a drip in there, and I just sort of followed it. And there he was."

I felt it had to be clarified. "He was already dead?"

Cassidy nodded vigorously. "Way dead. But his eyes were open. He looked surprised."

Given Richard's warnings about her safety, I asked Cassidy if she was taking precautions for herself. "I had this bodyguard for a little while, but I got tired of having someone looking over my shoulder all the time," she said. "The cops said I probably didn't need anything like that. They figure Richard got killed over something that wasn't related to my case, and besides, they think I'll be in jail really soon and there's no need to worry. For them."

Paul urged me to press the point, no doubt so he could report back to his brother. "Well, I think you need to be careful," I said. I didn't want to scare her.

"I'm more worried about the trial," Cassidy said. "They say it'll start again next week."

There wasn't much more I could think of to ask. I looked at Paul. "I think we've done enough," he said. I thanked Cassidy for meeting me and gave her my investigator business card. I think in my years of investigating, I've given out maybe fifteen. I have plenty more in my desk at home.

Cassidy left, and I put on my earbuds, which were plugged into my phone. It makes me look somewhat less crazy when I talk to people who aren't universally visible.

"So what do you think?" I asked Paul.

"I think Cassidy made an excellent point. We really do need to talk to the New Brunswick police. Luckily, they're only a few blocks from here. You won't even have to move your car."

\#

It took the better part of an hour to get Detective Barnett Kobielski to talk to me. I hadn't called ahead for an appointment, wasn't known to the New Brunswick police at all, and at best was a pest of a private investigator who was going to ask him questions he didn't want to answer and waste his time. Aside from that, I'm sure he was pleased to meet with me.

"I have six minutes," he said as he sat down behind a crowded, messy desk. It was a refreshing sight in a police station. Lieutenant McElone's desk would look positively ravaged if there were so much as a paper clip askew. "Talk."

"I've been asked to look into the death of Richard Harrison, and I know you investigated the case," I said. "I'd appreciate it if you could get me up to speed because I was just hired yesterday and there's kind of a time factor."

"He'll still be dead." Cops love nothing better than to pretend that the crimes they see don't affect them at all. Kobielski wasn't selling it especially well.

"Maybe so, but I'm working under a deadline from my client." That sounded sort of official, if vague.

"Who is your client?" Kobielski asked.

"I'd prefer not to give out the name," I told him. "A family member of the deceased, okay?"

"You realize I'm not required to give out any information that isn't part of the public record, right?" Kobielski leaned back in his chair. Indifference to a private investigator was something he could sell quite effectively.

"Then tell me what's on the public record," I said. "Where's the report on Richard Harrison's murder?"

"Ask for it in records," he said with very little inflection. "Downstairs." He pushed his chair forward again and made a show of looking over something in the morass of paper on his desk.

"Come on, Detective. What does it hurt you to tell me what you know about this? Why make me read the basic facts on a sheet you filled out the next day? I'm not getting in your way. The county prosecutor took this case away from you anyway."

I knew that last part would irritate the detective, and I saw Paul, who was hovering over my right shoulder, wince a little when I said it. But I thought a guy like Kobielski might respond well to the perceived affront.

And for once I was right. "They came in here the next day and took everything we had," he groused. "I get Major Crimes after me all the time, and I understand that. But they didn't even give us a couple of days to find the most logical suspects. I could have closed this thing in less than a week. Somebody wanted the county on it."

When in doubt, commiserate with the aggrieved. "Who would want that?" I asked.

"That's a good question, lady." Kobielski scratched behind his left ear. I got the sense it was a sign he was thinking. "There was no reason for them to get involved so soon. I had a pretty good idea of what was going on in that room when the guy got himself clobbered."

Paul lowered down a foot and moved closer to Kobielski. Solving Richard's murder was going to be easy because Kobielski, it seemed, had already done it.

"What happened?" I asked. Seemed like Kobielski needed the setup.

"Harrison was staying in the Heldrich on Livingston Ave.," he said. "Room six-fifteen. The door showed no signs of forced entry, but he was completely turned away from the killer and kind of hunched over the desk in his room. So it looked like whoever it was had a key to the room and didn't make a noise coming in."

"Was he just so engrossed in his laptop that he might not have heard the door open?" I asked.

"There was no laptop in the room," Kobielski said. "I figured he was working on a tablet or something in his car, but I don't think the county cops found anything. They don't tell me inside stuff like that." The wound was obviously still fresh.

"Whoever killed him must have taken the laptop," Paul said.

"What's weird to me is that he was killed with the iron from the closet in the hotel," I said, mostly because Paul had pointed it out. "If someone was sneaking into the room with the intention of beating him to death, wouldn't he have brought something with him? This guy seems like he was improvising."

Kobielski looked at me with a little more respect than I deserved, but that was because he didn't know Paul was still about a foot and a half from him. He leaned forward, and his head actually went into Paul's a little. If only that was an effective form of mind reading, we'd be able to solve every case in no time flat.

"That's not even the weird part," he said in a stage whisper. "The iron was still in his hotel room. Whoever bopped him on the head brought in their own iron."

You know that scratch-the-record sound they use in commercials when something doesn't make sense? I swear I heard that. "Their own iron? They brought an iron specifically to kill Richard Harrison with?"

"That's what I'm saying, and that's why it's simple to figure out who killed him." Kobielski sat back in his chair, satisfied grin planted firmly on his face.

"Who?" Some guys just have to have the straight line.

"The hotel maid," he said.

Chapter 14

"The hotel maid?" My mother looked at me as if wondering whether I needed a nice bowl of chicken soup and some rest. "He thinks Richard was killed by the hotel maid? What possible motivation could she have to kill him with a steam iron?"

"It doesn't make sense," I said. We were in the den at the guesthouse, having been banished from the kitchen by Melissa, who was making a lasagna and could not be interrupted. My mother taught her to cook, but now the pupil had eclipsed the master. Mom didn't seem to think that was sad. "None of the staff in the hotel would have known Richard well enough to want to kill him. He'd been there a few weeks, but mostly he was in an office or the courthouse. He didn't stay in the hotel except at night."

"That's right." Richard was standing just a few inches off the floor, legs mostly encased in a sofa whose other end boasted my husband. Luckily Josh didn't know Richard was there and wouldn't much have minded if he'd known. He's so used to these one-sided conversations now that he's become really good at figuring out what the invisible (to him) people have said. I don't have to recap nearly as much as I used to. "I didn't know one name aside from the evening desk clerk, whose name was . . . Sam, maybe?"

Let's be charitable and assume that Richard's memory lapse was due to his still being recently departed and not because he was imperious and superior. He was Paul's brother, and Paul was neither of those things.

"Okay," Mom said. "We can assume it wasn't the maid unless Sam put her up to it. So where does that leave us? Why does the detective think that's what happened?"

"Because it fits his set of facts and it's the easiest solution that does so," Paul said. His quiet tone bore some authority, and he was avoiding eye contact, looking mostly at the floor. "It leaves us with two murders to consider and a very large pool of suspects we have not yet interviewed."

He was right about that. You could book a cruise ship with the number of people who could have killed Keith Johnson in the Cranbury Bog, and that was compounded by the fact that Paul had been unable so far to locate Keith on the Ghosternet. But luckily Kobielski had given us a few details we hadn't already known about Richard's murder, and that helped us eliminate some suspects from consideration.

"Keith Johnson's son, Braden, has a verifiable alibi for the night you were killed, Richard," Paul told his brother. "So do his business partner and his wife. His daughter, Erika, has an alibi, but it's just that she was home alone. And that doesn't take into account the possibility that the two murders were committed by at least two separate people."

I heard some clanging of pots in the kitchen but didn't react because Liss doesn't like it when you assume something has gone wrong. Because it almost always hasn't. She would no doubt be out shortly; she hates missing a conference on an investigation.

"I don't think we should be concentrating on my situation," Richard said. "Cassidy is still alive and needs our help. There's very little that can be done that would make the slightest difference in my circumstances."

I can't say why, but that struck me as incredibly odd. "Don't you care who killed you?" I asked him. "That's the worst thing one person can do to another. Doesn't it bother you to know somebody wanted you dead?"

Josh smiled a little. He loves it when I get assertive.

"I wonder about it, but it should not be the priority at the moment," Richard answered, back as straight as a two-by-four. Or if he had one stuck down his pants. "I have literally all the time in the world after Keith Johnson's killer is unmasked and Cassidy is out of danger."

"I am not convinced Cassidy is in any immediate peril," Paul said. "She has been under suspicion and out on bail for months now, and there has been no indication anyone is trying to do her harm. Investigating your murder might help us solve the other."

"Enough," Richard said. "I will not hear of it." He stared at Paul.

"Very well," my friend said.

I wasn't standing for that. We needed to investigate Richard's murder if we wanted to figure out the whole puzzle, and now that I was in for one investigation, both seemed only natural. Paul could curl up at Richard's supposedly wilting gaze, but I didn't have to. "It makes sense to do things Paul's way," I told Richard. "I've found that he really has a good plan most of the time if not all the time." Paul did not glance in my direction.

"Really?" Richard said.

"Really," I answered. Richard saw the look on my face and turned toward Paul.

Richard began to argue the point with his younger brother (who wasn't putting up that much of a fight, I thought) as my cell phone buzzed. I took it out to find a text message from Madame Lorraine: *No sign of Paul Harrison yet. Is it possible you meant George Harrison?* It was best to resist answering right away because having Madame Lorraine as an aggrieved party would probably end up with us in a witches' duel I would undoubtedly lose, not being a witch. I stuck the phone back into my pocket, then decided to take it out again and text back: *Have found Paul Harrison. Thank you for your help.*

Foolishly, I thought that would end it with Madame Lorraine.

I was distracted by my father floating in through the front room and announcing that Jeannie, Tony, and their two children had arrived. He needn't have bothered, since I immediately heard their minivan roll up the gravel driveway almost to my back door and the unpacking procedure begin.

It took a good five minutes of Paul and Richard hashing out their priorities and Paul finally acquiescing to Richard's wishes before Jeannie was, from the sound of it, herding her brood through my kitchen, where she had undoubtedly assumed I'd be (I spend a lot of time in there for someone who doesn't cook at all), and out the swinging door into the den.

Since it was June, there wasn't the shedding of many layers of clothing we'd been accustomed to a few months earlier. Oliver, Jeannie's elder child, was now a three-year-old and rushing from place to place in search of new things to discover and possibly destroy. Their daughter, Molly, who was determined not to be Oliver and so was already walking at a year old, was less steady on her feet and not as bent on causing havoc. She looked around the room; saw at least Mom, Josh, and me (I have a feeling very young children can see ghosts based on Oliver's occasional reactions); and stopped, maybe feeling a bit overwhelmed despite having seen all of us many times before.

"Who are these people?" Richard wanted to know. "Were you expecting them?" I wasn't sure if he was nervous about them being in the room with him or just upset about a brood of middle-class New Jerseyans descending upon him when he was trying to organize a murder investigation—or at least watch as his brother did so.

Naturally I didn't answer him directly. Tony gets the whole ghost thing and is fairly down with it, although he is nervous around Maxie, who luckily wasn't in the room at the moment. Maxie used to think (in the pre-Everett era) that Tony was cute, and Tony, married to my best friend and also still alive, did not respond as she might have hoped.

Jeannie, on the other hand, refuses to deal with the ghosts in any way, shape, or form. She is living under the delusion that I advertise a haunted guesthouse because I am a genius marketer (if only) and am running a brilliant scam on the people who come to my house to experience it. This despite her having seen things fly across the room, walls be destroyed, and other assorted unexplainable phenomenon. That's Jeannie, the Napoleon of denial.

"They are friends, Richard," Paul informed his brother. "There is no reason to be concerned."

There were plenty of reasons to be concerned, but Jeannie and her family were none of them. I just feel it's best to point that out.

Melissa walked out of the kitchen, from which a delicious aroma was already emanating. She surveyed the room, picked out Molly among the crowd of living and less-living entities, and walked over to pick her up. "Hi, Molly!" she cooed to the little girl. "What's new?"

Molly, who might be able to say "Ma" on a good day, just gurgled a little and smiled at her pal.

"In any event," Paul went on, "if we are concentrating our efforts on Keith Johnson's death, we are going to need a police report from the Cranbury officers who first entered the scene and whatever has been generated by the Middlesex County prosecutor's office. Are those in your files, Richard?"

Richard said they were, and Paul instructed him to wrest the laptop out of Maxie's hands or—less likely to cause an international incident—to ask Maxie to find those files and print them out on the printer I keep in a corner of the movie room for guests who can't completely disengage even when on vacation. Richard and Paul exited via the ceiling because Paul has had considerably more experience dealing with Maxie.

Jeannie unpacked her massive diaper bag, which had enough supplies for the baby population of Topeka, Kansas, and watched Melissa swing Molly in her arms. If it had been

Oliver at that age, Jeannie would no doubt have been instructing Liss on the proper baby-swinging method approved by the American Academy of Pediatrics. In fact, I'm fairly sure she did deliver that lecture on more than one occasion. But now with a second child her parenting style had become, let's say, more relaxed.

"She looks so cute with Molly," she said to me. "Melissa's going to be a great mom."

I inhaled sharply, then let it out, realizing Jeannie meant that to be a long-term compliment.

"Of course she will," my mother piled on. "That girl will be amazing at whatever she decides to do."

Not actually objecting to this meeting of the Melissa Kerby Admiration Society, I did try to steer the conversation back to something more present day. I looked at Tony. "Have you found me a steel beam guy for that hole in my ceiling yet?" I asked.

Tony, who hadn't examined the gaping hole in my den as often as my father (strictly because Dad has more frequent opportunities), reflexively looked up at the spot. "It's not that I can't find someone to do the work," he reminded me. "I could do it myself. The problem is that you don't want to pay for it."

"That's not true," I protested. "I don't mind paying for the work. I just mind paying *that much* for the work." The last estimate had been for four thousand dollars. I'd searched through every sofa cushion in the house and so far had $1.38.

"So we're at a stalemate," Tony said. "You know I'm not gouging you, Alison. I have to pay my crew. I'm not taking a dime on the job."

"Of course I know you're not gouging me. But *you* know I don't have that much lying around, and I'm not taking out an equity loan on the place."

Tony shrugged. We each knew the other's reasoning. There just wasn't anything either of us could do about it.

Paul came phasing through the den wall wearing a light windbreaker over his T-shirt. That indicated he had something small or flat hidden in his clothes. Sure enough, once in the den he looked for a spot out of Jeannie's line of sight—not that it would have mattered, since she would have just rationalized—and pulled out a fairly thin sheaf of papers.

That was the moment Jeannie scooped Oliver off the floor and ran at top speeds for the downstairs bathroom, a move every parent of a three-year-old knows all too well. It opened up the room for conversation because Tony just lets this stuff wash off his back and he was over at the exposed beam examining the bullet damage with my father. Tony didn't know Dad was there, but did that really matter?

Molly, I noticed, was watching the area in which Paul flew in with a delighted grin on her face.

"This is the Cranbury police report on Keith Johnson's murder," Paul said excitedly. "And I believe there is significant information here." He floated himself over quickly to a side table and spread the papers out on top for me to peruse. Melissa put Molly down, a tad reluctantly, and made her way to the table to have a look. She'd been denied this long and wasn't going to let it go one moment longer.

My cell phone buzzed. Madame Lorraine: *Paul Harrison is in great pain*. She says that about everybody. I didn't answer.

"See here," Paul said, pointing to the top form, which had been filled out by an Officer Hirway. "The cause of death was clearly drowning, but the officer notes that Cassidy Van Doren was absolutely bone dry when he and his partner arrived. For a larger man to have been held down by a woman Cassidy's size, there would have been a good deal of splashing, you'd think. Cassidy was not showing any signs of having interacted with water. There was a small towel nearby, which Cassidy said she'd used on her hands after checking Keith for a pulse."

"Richard said the physical evidence didn't seem to favor Cassidy as the killer," I reminded him. "This bears out that opinion, but it doesn't really add anything."

Paul was grinning broadly. He not only loved that I was engaged in the case, but he had a secret he was about to reveal that he could barely contain. The man is incorrigible.

"There was some denim fabric in the bathwater," Melissa said. She pointed at the form.

That took some of the wind out of Paul's sails. His grin faded to a tight smile. "Yes," he said. "That matches up with the idea that the person who killed Keith Johnson was in the tub with him, possibly to hold his head underwater while he drowned, because Johnson was not wearing denim."

"What about the water?" I asked just to remind them I had some part in these proceedings. When we had dealt with a drowning previously, the kind of water found in the victim's lungs had been a productive clue.

"What about what water?" Jeannie was walking back into the room with Oliver, who was looking quite pleased with himself.

"I was asking Melissa if she had water boiling," I said. While it's possible—and sometimes entertaining—to let Jeannie find her own rationalizations for the ghost experiences she has, it saves an endless amount of time if I just cover for myself right on the spot, I've decided.

"No, you don't have to boil the noodles for lasagna," Liss answered. Not only is she able to help me gloss over something for Jeannie, but she also likes to teach me things about cooking. It's adorable, as if I'll ever use the information she gives me.

Oliver toddled off to play with some toys Tony had laid out on the floor across the den. It's the largest room in the house and has the most playing space on the floor. Molly, not yet certain of her walking skills, sort of cruised after him, holding herself up on various pieces of furniture. I'd gotten a few of Melissa's old toys from the basement and left them—cleaned, of course—near where Jeannie had set up the kids' area. They headed for Liss's toys because they were not familiar.

"In any event, the denim fibers found in the water is interesting," Paul continued. He was on a roll and not to be denied. I pretended I wasn't listening to him as my mother sat in one of the closer armchairs claiming to be "tiring out." She wanted to listen to Paul without being blatant about it too. Josh even sat in a facing chair to make it look good. "Where did it come from, and whose property was it? If Cassidy Van Doren did just find the body of her stepfather, she was fully dressed when the police arrived, so it would appear someone else had clearly been in the room."

Jeannie started in on some story about her job at an insurance company, about how her boss was ridiculous, and

Josh, who at least could hear her, nodded dutifully. *I just love that man.*

Melissa smothered a small laugh.

Luckily my father was there and could talk to Paul. "So whose jeans were they? Were they a particular brand or something?"

"No, we weren't that lucky." Paul was pleased to have someone paying him attention even when he knew those of us still using oxygen couldn't do that. "We don't know anything about the denim except that it was there; the county lab isn't that well equipped. They could have been bought in any clothing store."

"Seems to me it's likely a woman," my father said. "The only male suspect you have is the business partner who was with him in the hotel, and I bet he wears a business suit to bed. Those business guys are like that."

"That's very good, Jack," Paul said.

My mother gave Dad a proud smile when Jeannie thought Mom was looking at a poster I have hanging on the wall of a pair of flip-flops left on the beach. It's a classy place, my guesthouse.

"I don't think we can find out anything else about the fibers, but the county investigator report should show if there was makeup or aftershave in the water," Paul, that master of mirth, answered. "That's something we'll have to get Maxie working on."

On cue, Maxie and Everett dropped down through the ceiling. She was in her usual outfit of skintight jeans and a black T-shirt, this one bearing the legend, "LEGEND."

"Where's my computer?" she demanded. "I was supposed to get it back."

I glanced at Paul, noted Jeannie was still bending Josh's ear, and moved over to the table where he'd spread out the printed documents. Paul knew I'd have to be very quiet so he moved down toward me to hear.

"I thought Richard was giving that back to Maxie when he was done printing out the police report," I whispered.

"That was my understanding." Paul was whispering too for no logical reason. "I'll find him." He moved through the wall and vanished.

"This is getting inconvenient," Maxie said. "I need that laptop or I can't keep up with *Grey's Anatomy*." Well, at least she had a good reason.

"We're working on it," I hissed, maybe too loudly because Jeannie looked up.

Paul phased back through the ceiling this time, Richard close behind him. "I understand there is some question about the whereabouts of the laptop computer," Richard said.

"Damn right," Maxie shot back. "You were supposed to give it back to me and you didn't."

"I did. I left it for you on the table in the room I was using, as we agreed."

Maxie had originally suggested Richard leave the laptop in Melissa's room when he was finished with it (which would be okay because Melissa had given permission), but he had been adamant about not going into "the little girl's bedroom" and said she could come get it at the appropriate time. I was guessing now that hadn't gone as expected.

"Well, it's not there," Maxie insisted.

"Yes, I've seen that. I went with you and looked. I know it isn't there. But it was when I left the room."

Maxie fixed me with a glare. "My laptop is missing," she said.

"That's not all," Mom said with a dry rasp in her voice. "Look." She pointed. We looked.

On the opposite wall, right next to my America's National Parks calendar, was a piece of paper with very bold print in a very large font reading, *DON'T LOOK FOR ME*.

And it was being held up on the wall by one of my thicker kitchen knives.

Chapter 15

A thorough search of the house—and I mean *thorough*, because Maxie wasn't kidding around—failed to turn up the missing computer. I'd excused myself from Jeannie's presence by saying I needed to change my clothes, which drew a few incredulous looks from my best friend, my husband, and my father, and checked the guest rooms myself. I don't like to let anyone into the rooms guests are occupying besides me and Melissa.

Paul had insisted on the search despite the warning on my wall, which I estimated I could repair with some wall compound and the paint I'd used on the kitchen walls, assuming I still had it marked properly. Go remember whether it was called "Mountain Peak White" or "Bavarian Cream."

After not finding the computer, I had to actually change clothes to make the story work and put on a pair of khakis and a blue scoop-neck top Josh especially liked. If I was going to perform a ruse, at least there should be an upside to it.

I went back downstairs after conferring with Maxie, Paul, Everett, and Richard on the upstairs landing. Maxie, furious with me of all people for "losing" her laptop, ended up zooming through the ceiling, no doubt on her way to Jupiter. Paul looked distressed and made a comment about Richard's files being lost with the laptop. Everett went after Maxie. Slowly. He knew when to hang back. Richard simply looked stupefied and didn't say much of anything.

The threat knifed to my wall was unspecific but effective; there was a knot in my stomach, and I wasn't even sure why. Maybe whoever put it there just couldn't find a thumbtack or some tape.

Halfway down the stairs, I ran into Abby Lesniak, who looked at me, opened her mouth as if to speak, waved her hand in futility, and kept on walking upstairs. I was a failure at so many things that day.

The center island in the kitchen was set for dinner, so those of us who weren't past the need for food sat down and started paying Melissa compliments on her work. The stools next to the island are kind of high for Oliver and Molly, but they're used to having their own little table near their mom and getting the same food as everybody else. Well, Ollie does. Molly is a little young for some of it, but she was getting a small piece of lasagna tonight.

"So what's the latest on this murder you're detecting?" Jeannie asked once we were settled in. I de-ghosted the story and told her everything "I" had found out so far, which added up to not very much. I left out the stuff about the knife holding up a threatening message (which I had quickly taken down), because Jeannie would try to help and end up scaring the living crap out of me.

"Sounds like you should hire out Yankee Stadium and gather your suspects together," Tony said. Then he looked at

Melissa and actually pointed at his fork. "Is this Worcester-shire sauce I'm tasting on the ground beef?"

Liss and Mom passed a conspiratorial look. "Yes," my daughter said. "It's Worcestershire sauce, but it's not ground beef. It's veggie ground meat."

"We call it fake meat," Mom said.

"Well, it's really good," Tony told her. Liss nodded her thanks.

"It's not about the number of suspects," Jeannie told me. "You have too many because you're not looking in the right direction."

Having played Ethel to her Lucy for years, I knew a cue when I heard one. "What's the right direction?" I asked.

"Motive. Right now you're paying attention to who *could* have killed these two people, but because the murders seem so different, the real question is who would have *wanted* to kill them, and you get that when you figure out why."

"Well, Mr. Johnson had a lot of money," Melissa told her. "That seems like the most likely motive to kill him, doesn't it? And you said yourself that Paul's—Mr. Harrison prob-ably died because he'd found out something that was going to expose the murderer. So don't we know the motives?" Liss is an excellent student and, I'm afraid, is taking to this investi-gation business a little too well.

Jeannie shook her head. "We're making an assumption," she said. "Just because this Keith Johnson had a lot of money doesn't mean that's the only reason somebody might want him dead. Maybe he was cheating on his wife. Maybe he cheated a business partner. Maybe he was mean to his kids when they were growing up. Maybe he complained when the staff in the bed-and-breakfast he was in short-sheeted him. We just don't know."

Paul, who had floated into the room just when Jeannie had started to speak, immediately began stroking his goatee, so I knew she was onto something.

"It's true," he said. "We have been following theories and not facts. I *am* rusty."

He'd gone more than four months without investigating a case before, so I didn't think lack of practice was the problem here.

"People tend to be more careful and distracted when family members are involved," I said.

"What's that got to do with it?" Jeannie asked. "You have something on some member of Johnson's family?"

"Families don't do that," my mother sniffed. Then she thought about it. "Except when they do." My father floated down toward her and put a hand on her shoulder. Mom has been sensitive to ghosts all her life and sensitive to my father for decades. I think she actually felt his hand because she smiled and had to stop herself from putting her own hand on his.

"So the first move we should make," I began, "would be to determine motive. We need Keith Johnson's financial records to rule out the idea that money is the only reason to kill him. And the laptop that has those records is missing."

Jeannie, who had been watching her children eat and not saying anything about the way they were doing so, looked up at me. "Your laptop is missing?" she asked.

Well, this was going to be tricky. Sort of. "Not mine," I said. "One of the guests'."

"Ooh," Jeannie said. "That can't be good, with you being the hostess and everything."

The guests actually do sign a waiver with Senior Plus Tours saying that any loss of personal property is not the fault of the tour service, and I have a form covering my own liability that they sign their first day at the guesthouse. I also offer them a safe in the movie room in which they can lock their valuables if they choose. But since the computer in question did not actually belong to a guest (because Maxie was kind of a resident, I guess), I wasn't sweating the issue very hard.

"It'll turn up," I said. "I'm not worried. But it's the files."

"Why would one of your guests have files from the case you're investigating?" Jeannie asked. Oh, yeah, that was why Melissa had been frantically waving at me over Jeannie's shoulder when I'd started this charade.

"I accidentally put a thumb drive into the wrong laptop," I said. "They look exactly the same." Kick save and a beauty, I thought.

Jeannie had other ideas. "Somebody else has a laptop as old as yours?" She laughed. "Who knew two of them had survived?"

"That's not the point. I need the information on those files."

"Why don't you plug the thumb drive into your own laptop?" Jeannie asked. Tony, mouth full of lasagna, knew something was up but didn't know what because he couldn't hear the conversation except on my end. He looked down at his children for a way out and found one.

"Ollie, you have marinara sauce all over your face," he said with a chuckle.

"It's actually a vodka sauce," Melissa noted.

But Jeannie had responded as Tony anticipated. She was off her stool and walking over to her son with a damp napkin. There was a time she wouldn't have approached Oliver with anything short of an antiseptic wipe and a Hazmat suit, but now a paper napkin would do. "You little monkey," she said. Ollie, sensing what was to come, tried to flee, but his mother was too quick for him. He complained a little, but in seconds his face was being sandblasted.

I nodded to Tony for the help.

Josh started clearing plates off the island and putting them in the dishwasher, which we use on the nights Melissa cooks and there are more than three of us creating havoc in the kitchen. Mom started to help, something I couldn't prevent. My father forgot himself and picked up a plate, then looked at Jeannie and put it back down again. Jeannie, in full disinfectant mode, did not notice.

The kitchen then went into a state of complete activity. Everyone who wasn't clearing dishes or cleaning a child's face was wiping the countertop or putting things back in the refrigerator. Paul asked a few questions about the financial records, but I couldn't answer him amid all the movement.

And that was just as well, because once the kitchen and Oliver (and for that matter Molly, who had actually tried to press lasagna into her forehead) had been declared both spic and span, I made a quick visual scan of the room.

Maxie's laptop was on the counter next to the cereal cabinet. And I knew for a fact it hadn't been there a short time before.

I walked over to it and put my hands on the case. Sure enough, the laptop was real. I picked it up and turned back toward the others.

I wasn't going to say anything, but Mom saw it first. "That's the laptop!" she said. "Where did you find it?"

Every head, living and not, turned toward me holding Maxie's old-but-not-as-old-as-mine laptop computer. And the only one that didn't understand what had happened (and, of course, none of us knew how it had been returned) was Jeannie. But that didn't bother me a bit.

"That doesn't look a thing like your laptop!" Jeannie said, laughing. "You really have no head at all for technology, Alison." See what I mean? She can rationalize anything. This was an easy one.

"I guess not." I chuckled, but I was looking at Paul. "I wonder how I missed it before."

"Well now you can give it back to your guest," Jeannie said.

My friend had, as she often does, given me exactly what I needed without meaning to do so. That's what besties are for.

"You're right," I said. "I'm going upstairs to do that right now."

"I'll come with you," Melissa said. Jeannie looked at her a little funny but did not comment. Melissa understood we were going to her room and has a certain sense of propriety about it. Nobody goes up there when Liss isn't around. That's fair.

My mother almost tried to join us, but I headed her off by suggesting she help Jeannie and Tony keep the kids entertained. Everyone agreed to that, and I noted that Paul was already out of the room, no doubt on his way to the attic.

Liss insisted on using her dumbwaiter to get us there, which meant taking turns (her first), and Paul had somehow found Maxie along the way so she was there when I arrived. Maxie, with Everett in tow, glommed onto the laptop like it was her missing puppy. It was not a puppy, and Lester, Melissa's ghost dog, wanted us to know that. He was happily wagging his tail and scooting (six inches off the floor) from person to person. I was already starting to get itchy around the eyes.

Maxie opened the top and started booting up before I could even grunt.

"See if you can find the files about Keith Johnson's financial dealings, particularly the personal ones," Paul suggested.

Maxie stopped midmotion. "No *Grey's Anatomy*?"

"Not just yet. Soon." Paul sounded like a patient father. "Right now, we need to see that the financial records are there so we can begin our analysis."

"What-ever." Maxie started pounding on the keyboard as Everett held the laptop up for her. Lester jumped up and tried to land on my lap but, not having gravity to gauge his jump, floated past my nose, making me sneeze, and kept going until he reached Melissa, who is always a more receptive audience anyway. "Okay, what do you want to see?"

Paul pursed his lips. It wasn't quite a goatee-stroking problem. "First, let's take a look at Keith's personal bank accounts. There was some money being exchanged that supposedly favored Cassidy. Pull those up and let's see the dates and amounts."

Maxie stared at the screen. Then she stared some more. Just a moment longer. "It's not here," she said.

Paul looked up with an expression of surprise, but his first reaction was to look at Everett. "Can you find Richard and bring him here, please?" he asked.

Everett nodded. He would have saluted, but his hands were holding the laptop, which he gently laid on Liss's homework desk. Maxie floated down to compensate. Lester, unconcerned with the state of Keith Johnson's bank statements, jumped off Melissa's shoulder, where he'd been perched, and floated around the room awhile taking everyone in. He loves company.

As soon as Everett was down through the floor in search of Richard, Paul asked Maxie to look for any business records Johnson might have left in the files we'd gotten from Miriam. These were still on the hard drive, and Paul asked her to open the first one she could find. Then he huddled over her shoulder to see what came up on the screen.

"There are gaps," he said after a moment. "These have been redacted."

"They've be re-what?" Maxie demanded.

"Edited," I told her. There was a time I had to give Melissa vocabulary words. That was then; this was Maxie.

Everett flew back in through the floor, and Richard was just to his left side. "What is going on?" Paul's brother asked. He had the air of a colonel in the British Army. In a Monty Python sketch. It was a wonder he didn't ask, "What's all this, then?"

"You were looking at these files before," Paul said. "Did you notice any gaps in the information?"

Richard's eyes narrowed. "Gaps?"

"Take a look."

Richard maneuvered himself through Paul to get a better look. He examined the screen closely and scrutinized the spreadsheet. "This is not the way it looked before," he said.

"Everything was there when you looked?" Paul said.

"Yes."

"Maxie, close this file, please," Paul said, and Maxie complied. She'd comply if I asked too, but she'd complain about it first. "Now show us the menu for Keith Barent Johnson's financial records."

Maxie opened the menu, and Richard gasped when he saw it. "It's been sabotaged," he said.

Paul leaned back from the posture he'd taken when he was staring at the laptop screen. Now his hand went to the goatee.

"Someone doesn't want us to see what's there," he said. "And it's what's *not* there that is interesting."

Chapter 16

I spent the rest of the evening with Jeannie and her family, letting the ghosts (minus Dad) search the house *again* for clues to our intruder's identity or to find an idea of how someone had slipped in, taken Maxie's laptop, performed surgery on Keith Johnson's files, and then put the laptop where I'd find it, all without being seen. It was easier to let them do it (with limited access to guest rooms as long as Melissa was present) than to keep making excuses to Jeannie.

The knot in my stomach had dissipated to the size of maybe a staple. There had been a threat and no follow-up even after we did exactly what the paper had said not to do.

Besides, I was pretty worn out on the whole Keith Johnson thing at this point. I'd never known the guy, but he didn't seem like he was an especially wonderful fellow, and besides, Paul couldn't even raise him on the Ghosternet. It didn't seem like finding his killer would make that much of a difference in the real world.

Mom and Dad cut out fairly early, with my mother making a pointed comment about calling me the next day. She'd want to know what the transparent contingency had discovered during the evening.

Jeannie gave me a look after Mom (to her eyes) had left and asked what was bothering me. I couldn't tell her because it would have violated our policy of my never actually mentioning the ghosts unless under duress, so I told her I was just tired, which was also true. She took that as a sign—unintended—that I wanted her and the family to leave, and no number of denials could convince her otherwise. She too promised to call tomorrow. I'd have to block off some time.

"The fact is, I'm worried about Paul," I told Josh when I emerged from the master bath that night. He was already in bed—because men have to just brush their teeth and they're ready to sleep—reading a book about the Marx Brothers. Josh is something of a comedy freak.

He closed the book and looked at me. "What's to worry about?" he asked. "Nothing bad can happen to him, can it?"

I climbed in next to him and leaned over to get an arm put around my shoulders. My husband complied because he is a wonderful husband, and with so little practice. "Not physically, no. Not as far as I know, anyway. But emotionally he's still capable of feeling pain, and I don't think having his older brother around is good for him."

Josh pulled me a little closer. "Why not?"

He's my husband, so I can tell him my crazy stuff. "Madame Lorraine told me he's in great pain," I said.

"Madame Lorraine says that about everybody. It's her catchphrase."

"I thought so too, but it's the way Paul acts around Richard. Sort of like Lester." Then I remembered Josh can't see

Lester, so he doesn't know how the puppy might act. "He's so desperate to please that he's not thinking about himself at all. He doesn't take charge when he should. He doesn't question Richard's opinions. It's not like he's just shrinking into the corner, but he's not being himself, and I wonder if Madame Lorraine might not have a point."

"Well, from what you've told me, Paul always looked up to Richard," Josh said. "It's almost as if he's a parent instead of a sibling. It's not easy to stand up to your parents."

"I never had any trouble."

Josh chuckled. "Nonetheless, for someone like Paul, who seems to respect authority more than most, telling Richard he disagrees with an opinion would be a big step. Just give him a little time. He's only been back here a couple of days. He'll remember he's a private investigator and start acting like himself again."

"I guess." I put my hands on his arm to get a little warmer even though it wasn't cold in the room at all. Not hot enough yet for air conditioning. This would be the week of perfect weather we get once a year. "So who do you think killed Keith Johnson?"

"You have an interesting concept of pillow talk, Alison."

"You ought to know that by now."

"I don't know as much as you about the case, but I always think the wife is the best suspect." He pulled me tighter toward him. "That's why I like to keep you close, where I can see you."

"Oh, is that why?" It felt so normal in his arms. That's why it was so jarring when a ghost's lips showed up in the bedroom wall.

I sat straight up and pulled the blanket to my chin. "What?" Josh asked.

"Someone's here."

The lips did not attempt to push their way any farther into the room, and when they moved, Paul's voice came through them. "I'm sorry," he said. "I did not intend to intrude on you."

"Nice compromise, Paul," I said so Josh would know who I was talking to. "Can you hear me?"

"Yes. I wanted you to know that we completed a thorough search of the house and found no evidence of anyone who might have taken Maxie's computer and deleted the financial files."

I knew that already. "Did you manage to recover any of the files?" I asked.

"Not yet, but Maxie thinks there might a way to dive deep into the hard drive and find some of them. She's going to get on that as soon as she catches up with *Grey's Anatomy.*"

There was no point in arguing. Maxie has her agenda, and it will always come before everyone else's. It's her world, and even she doesn't live in it.

"What else can we be doing?" I asked. I wanted to get those lips out of my wall as soon as possible, and this was a good way to wrap things up.

"Of course, right now we can do very little," most of Paul's mouth said. "But in the morning, I think we should discuss which of the suspects we should go to see first."

Again, offering any resistance would be counterproductive. And it would prolong this conversation, which was among the weirder ones I've had. It was like trying to talk to the opening to *The Rocky Horror Picture Show*. "In the morning," I said.

"Good night, Paul," Josh said. He can pick up that much.

"Good night, Josh." I had to relay the message, and then, thankfully, the lips receded back into the wall and joined the rest of Paul's face somewhere else in the house.

I looked at my husband, who had half a smile on his face. "What must it be like to be married to me?" I marveled.

He kissed me very well indeed. "I can think of worse things," he said.

And just when things were going to get interesting, my cell phone buzzed.

Normally I would have ignored this call entirely. The circumstances being what they were, it was remarkable I even glanced at the phone to see who might be calling me at this hour (which admittedly wasn't that late for regular people who didn't run a paint store or a guesthouse and didn't have to be up at the crack of dawn). But I do worry when my mother is driving home so I took a look.

I saw the number of Detective Lieutenant Anita McElone of the Harbor Haven Police Department.

That couldn't be good. McElone didn't call me . . . ever, pretty much, and I hadn't even gotten in touch with her about either of the murders I was investigating because neither of them took place in Harbor Haven. It's one thing to have a friend—of sorts—in the police department. It's another to abuse the privilege. I try not to do that.

Josh saw the look on my face and let go of me. "What?" he asked.

"It's McElone." I reached for the phone and took the call. "Lieutenant?"

"Do you know a Cassidy Van Doren?" she asked. She gets right to business when it's business.

My initial reaction was to wonder how many Cassidy Van Dorens there might be to know, but I suppressed that impulse and asked, "A little. How can you know about that?"

"Normally I'd say something pithy like, 'I know everything,' but I don't have time for that right now," McElone answered. "I looked up Ms. Van Doren's rap sheet, and what do you know, she's on trial for a murder in Cranbury. And she lives in Rumson. But she says I should call you, so I'm calling you."

"She says you should call me? She's there with you?"

Josh sat up a little and took in the phone call. This was a little different than watching me talk to ghosts because he could at least hear the sound of McElone's voice, but he still wasn't getting everything.

"Actually, she's in the hospital. Seems there's been an attempt on her life."

\#

Josh insisted on coming with me to the hospital. I'd reminded him that he had to get up before the sun rose even this time of year, and he'd given me a look that indicated further conversation would take place in the car on the way to the hospital.

We took Josh's delivery truck because it was fueled up, while my Volvo had been living on fumes for a full day and its negligent owner had not heeded the warning. Even my car can make me feel guilty.

"What was Cassidy Van Doren doing in Harbor Haven?" Josh asked. I think he was talking to keep himself awake, which was something of a concern because he was driving.

"McElone said she was coming to see me. She had my business card in her pocket and she was on her way to the guesthouse when someone tried to run her off the road and into a ravine."

"Are the police sure the driver was intentionally trying to harm Cassidy?" Paul asked. Paul was sort of on, sort of in the back seat. When he'd heard us getting ready to leave and asked what it was about, he'd insisted on coming along. The only reason I'd agreed was that I was afraid Richard would have decided to come along if Paul wasn't there to act as his agent.

"The lieutenant said it was pretty clear from the tire tracks and the way Cassidy's car had turned over that someone else had pushed her off the road," I said. I like to keep my answers general when there's a ghost present and Josh is there. Josh knew Paul was in the car, but I still didn't want him to feel left out. "No state troopers or local cops saw it happen. It was on one of the hillier areas of a back road off of Route 35. Nobody else on the road, Cassidy said."

"Odd," Paul said, but he didn't elaborate, and I was too tired to ask for the lecture.

Josh pulled the car into the visitors' parking lot at Jersey Shore University Medical Center in Neptune, and we got out to walk to the emergency room where Cassidy had last been reported. I'd tried calling the cell phone number she'd given me and gotten sent to voice mail.

We found her in one of the cubicles, dressed and waiting to be released by a resident who clearly found her charming and was asking for her phone number. There was a bruise over Cassidy's left eye, and her side had clearly been bandaged, judging from the bulge in her skintight top.

We waited until the young doctor had finished his "examination" and Cassidy was being wheeled out of the ER and toward the parking lot. Josh offered to push the wheelchair, but the orderly working the room said it was hospital policy to have a staff member escort every patient to the exit.

"Yeah, this black SUV just came out of nowhere and started bumping me," she explained during the trip down the hallway. "I couldn't figure it out. I mean, he could have passed me anytime he wanted. There wasn't anybody else on the road."

"What did you do?" Josh asked her. His face had an expression that I read and nobody else would indicating he found Cassidy's manner, let's say, artificial.

"I slowed up, hit the brakes," she answered. "I figured if he was in that big a hurry, he could go ahead. But he slowed up and kept bumping me from the left lane, toward the side of the road. No shoulder there or anything. Just a drop down the hill. I figured I'd stop flat out, you know? But when I did, he backed into my grill and pushed me back farther. I was lucky I could start the car again."

We reached the doors, and the orderly nodded. Cassidy reached into her purse and tried to give him a bill, but the young man said that wasn't necessary and walked back into the hospital wishing her good luck. He told her to have a good one. I thought that train had sort of left the station.

"You put the car back in gear?" I asked. "What was the plan?"

"Plan?" Cassidy laughed nastily. "I didn't have a plan. I was operating on survival instinct. It was all about getting away. When I realized I couldn't do that—the radiator on my car was already steaming—I figured my best bet was to find a safe spot to let him push me over. So I managed to get it past the big drop and over toward a little ravine on the side of the road, and the next time he came around I steered into it. But I didn't figure it that well. The car turned over, and I ended up upside down in the ravine. Then I heard sirens, and the guy in the SUV must have heard them too because he took off."

"You didn't recognize the driver of the SUV?" I said.

"I didn't *see* the driver of the SUV," Cassidy answered. "Tinted windshield, which you're not supposed to be able to do in Jersey, right? And he was way higher than me, because I have—had—a little Mazda Miata. I was looking up at him the whole time." She hesitated while we stood outside the hospital entrance and grimaced a little. "Can I ask you a favor? Can you drive me to my mom's house? My car's sort of . . . you know."

Josh nodded and went to get the truck without looking at me; he knew I'd agree. "Where is your mom's?" I asked.

"Rumson. Where she and Keith used to live."

We got into the truck, making sure Cassidy could manage into the back seat without hurting her cracked rib. Paul sat next to her, a few inches above the seat, watching her intently. If Paul had been visible, it might have seemed crowded. As it was, to me alone it appeared in the rearview mirror as if Paul and Cassidy were getting very, *very* friendly. Paul likes to get a very close look at a subject's face.

"Why were you coming to see me?" I asked Cassidy once the proper address had been programmed into the GPS. "Why did you give Lieutenant McElone my name to call?"

"I remembered you said that I should get in touch if anything occurred to me about Keith's murder that might be important to Richard's murder," she said, as if that didn't sound weird even to me. "I remembered something."

"You could have called," Josh said. "You wouldn't have been out on the road tonight."

"Yeah, I had something to show you," Cassidy said. "I didn't want to take a picture and text it. Didn't want you to think I'd just printed it out myself. Wanted you to see the actual paper." She reached into her red purse. It looked like she was reaching through Paul to get it. Let's leave it at that.

"What did you find?" I asked.

"Here." She extended her hand over the seat back. In it was a page of high-quality letterhead from KBJ and Associates.

"Is this Keith's company?" I asked Cassidy.

"Yeah."

I turned on the light on my side of the truck and saw Josh wince a little. He doesn't like driving with the light on and thinks he'll be pulled over by the police. I told him I'd be very quick.

The letter was formally written and precise, and in no uncertain terms it informed the recipient, Erica Baker of

Filcher, Baker, and Klein, the law firm handling Cassidy's defense, to seek out and retain one Richard J. Harrison on behalf of the writer and at the writer's expense. It was suggested that if any criminal cases were brought against a member of Keith Johnson's nuclear or extended family, Richard should be pressed into service.

It was signed by Keith Barent Johnson.

"Keith wrote to the law firm in Woodbridge and ordered them to get Richard on a retainer?" I said to no one in particular.

Paul's sputter would have been heard a mile away if it could have been heard. I shook a little on hearing it, and Josh looked at me, concerned. I turned off the overhead light on my side.

"Yeah," Cassidy said.

"Let me see," Paul said at the same time. I had an impulse to hand him the letter but then realized I couldn't possibly do that. I handed it back, open, to Cassidy and expected him to catch as much as he could.

"And it's dated the day that he died," Cassidy added.

I had to ask. "Keith or Richard?" And it occurred to me that together they could have played for the Rolling Stones.

"Keith of course. He was already drowned a long time when Mr. Harrison got bopped."

"So on the day he was murdered, Keith Johnson wrote a letter to his law firm in Woodbridge suggesting they retain a criminal defense attorney who normally worked in New York and didn't specify what he might be needed to do." That was Paul. He was processing. Otherwise, he'd never speak of his older brother as "a criminal defense attorney who normally worked in New York."

"Why would he do that?" I wondered out loud.

"I'm no professional," my husband said, "but it sounds to me like Keith Johnson knew he was going to be murdered."

Chapter 17

Adrian Van Doren Johnson was waiting in the doorway of her Rumson home (which Cassidy had referred to as "the beach house," pointing out it was not the primary residence of the family, which was in Upper Saddle River) when we drove up because Cassidy had texted her to let her know we'd be on our way. It made perfect sense for her to be there after midnight because she was concerned about her daughter, who was coming home from the emergency room after being run off the road by a mysterious black SUV.

What didn't make sense was that Adrian was wearing a business suit and three-inch stiletto heels and was in full makeup. Cassidy had told me in the truck that she thought she'd awoken her mother with the text.

"Cassidy." We had gotten out of the truck and helped Cassidy out of the back seat, which took a little doing. Cracked ribs are not fun. Adrian looked at her daughter and took a deep breath. "What *did* you do to yourself?"

"I didn't do anything to myself," her daughter protested. "Someone did this to me!" She slowly walked toward her mother, who stood on the bottom step of the stone stairs to the front entrance. "This is not my doing, Mom!"

"Of course not." Adrian wasn't going to have a "scene" in front of her home this late at night despite the fact that the nearest neighbor had to be a quarter mile away. In New Jersey, that's the Grand Canyon. "Why don't you introduce me to your friends?"

While I didn't dislike Cassidy for any particular reason, I thought her considering Josh and me friends might be something of a stretch. Cassidy didn't blink an eye and introduced us, leaving out Paul because as far as she and her mother were concerned, he didn't exist.

When she mentioned to her mother that I was a private investigator, I thought Adrian's eyes might have doubled in size. "Really!" she said. I chose to take that as a sign of respect and admiration.

"I have been looking into the death of Richard Harrison," I told her. "I met Cassidy a few days ago on the Rutgers campus to discuss it." I saw no reason to inflate how well I knew Cassidy.

Adrian's eyes were no longer so wide. Maybe respect and admiration had been going too far. "Really," she said again with no inflection this time. I guessed she hadn't known about the meeting with Cassidy in New Brunswick. And she did not seem to approve quite so much.

"Yeah," Cassidy said. "It really wasn't a big deal, Mom." Thanks for the ego boost, Cassidy.

"And what did you tell Ms. Kerby?" Adrian asked. Her tone was pure Rumson or even Upper West Side, but her accent was all Newark or Paterson.

"She told me—" I began.

Adrian held up an index finger to stop me. "I want to hear it from *Cassidy*."

"I told her I didn't know anything about what happened to Richard because I wasn't there," Cassidy said. *Her* tone was angry teenager tinged with just a little bit of fear. "And I told her I didn't kill Keith."

That was apparently what Adrian had been waiting for, as she cocked an eyebrow and this time addressed her question directly to me. "Are you investigating my husband's murder as well?"

"I don't have a client on whose behalf I am investigating that murder," I said. It was a lie, but technically I'd almost never had an actual client to do anything. I mean, go try to get a dead person to pay up on an invoice.

"That's very artful, but it doesn't answer my question," Adrian said.

"The two murders seem to be connected, certainly," I told her at Paul's suggestion. "There's bound to be some overlap."

"So you *are* investigating my husband's death."

"Where there is some connection, I suppose I am." I felt Josh pull a little bit closer to me in the dark. It wasn't that Adrian posed a real physical danger, but her attitude was definitely unfriendly, and Josh doesn't like that when it's pointed at me.

Adrian did her best to lighten her tone. She moved it from demanding matriarch to grieving widow with a hint of confidante just lingering around the edges. "I really wish you wouldn't," she said.

"It's not my primary focus," I told her. "But if I were to find something that might help clear your daughter, wouldn't you want me to bring it to light?"

Cassidy shook her head slightly. I didn't know what that meant, but she was looking at me and not at her mother.

"I do not believe you will," Adrian said.

"You don't believe I'll let people know if I find something?" I wasn't following her logic. How could she have made an erroneous judgment like that about me in the three minutes we'd known each other?

"Hardly," Adrian answered. "I believe you would publicize any discovery you might make. What I meant was I do not believe you will find anything that will help exonerate my daughter."

That took a second. "You don't?" It was the best I could do.

"No. I believe Cassidy did murder her stepfather," Adrian said. "I think she drowned him and should go to prison for the rest of her life."

Cassidy, clearly unable to run, put down her head and shuffled into the house. I think she might have been crying. Nobody, not even Paul, said a word as she left.

#

My guests had only two days left in the guesthouse, and we like to ramp up the spook shows a little bit toward the end of a tour, building to a crescendo at the final one the night before they leave (I give Paul and Maxie the morning off when the guests are packing). So we started with a little Flying Teenager as Maxie picked up Melissa at the top of the main stairs and "flew" her down into the library, where the show was taking place. Then Liss went straight to the front door, got in her BFF Wendy's mom's car, and left for school.

After that, there was invisible guitarist (Paul plays a tiny bit), the changeable hat (which flies from the head of one guest to another), and the interchangeable art (pictures on the wall fly across the room and hang themselves in different spots, something Maxie likes to do because she disagrees with my choices in decor).

The guests seemed quite pleased with the spectacle, although Abby Lesniak kept looking at me, then at Greg Lewis, then back at me with a significant amount of eye contact. I guessed there was no time left to procrastinate, although I would certainly have appreciated some. I told myself I'd say something to Mr. Lewis as he left the library.

We went out on a high note as Maxie wrapped a feather boa I'd found in a local consignment shop around the shoulders of Eduardo DiSica, who went with the joke and played it for all he was worth, strutting through the room and touching others with the end of the fashion accessory. He got quite the round of applause.

I moved toward Mr. Lewis as the crowd started to dissipate, but he was a spry one for a guy with walking problems and seemed to have a mission on his mind. He was out the door while I was still accepting praise for the quality of the experience. I walked out into the hallway and did not see Mr. Lewis anywhere nearby.

Abby Lesniak wasn't there to give me a disappointed frown, but I could picture it.

There was no time to consider that, however, because Paul had already turned the page and was back into investigatory mode. The truth is that Paul, once given a case, never leaves investigatory mode and simply waits through anything else he needs to do in the course of a day.

"I think it's time for a talk with Keith Johnson's children," he began as I made my way to the kitchen for some badly needed iced coffee. "Even though they have alibis that hold up for the night Richard died, there is no reason to think they had no involvement in their father's murder."

"Give me a minute, Paul," I pleaded. I'd already had some caffeine, but we'd done the show especially early because the guests wanted to be outdoors and Liss had to get to school. It was, in my opinion, cruel and unusual punishment to expect me to think this early after I'd been out investigating past midnight the evening before. "My brain isn't awake yet."

As I pushed the door open, Richard was already in the kitchen, looking at me disapprovingly, which I was starting to believe was his default expression. "Cassidy was attacked last night. I warned you that would happen, and it will happen again. What are you intending to do about it?"

The Harrison boys were starting to double-team me and that was more than I felt like handling at the moment. "Fellas," I said, "before you start to get on my case about everything you think I've done wrong or everything you think I should be doing that I'm not, let me remind you that I am your only liaison to the living population of the planet and I'm the only one in the house who can drive a car. So tread lightly."

I walked to the coffeemaker and saw it was empty. It was that kind of morning. I had put out the urn for the guests, though, so I grabbed a mug from the cabinet and walked back out of the kitchen into the den where the coffee cart was sitting.

Richard sputtered as I walked but kept his thoughts to himself for once. Paul, who has known me for years, could read my mood and understand I was serious. His voice took on a conciliatory tone.

"My apologies, Alison. You know how I am about a case."

"Yes, I do. But you know how *I* am about a case, and it's going to take me a couple of minutes and a decent amount of caffeine to get us on the same page, okay?"

"Certainly," Paul said. "Take all the time you need. How about now?" That is Paul's idea of a joke.

"That's good, Paul. I'm going to write that one down." And now I have. I am a woman of my word.

But the coffee urn was empty. The decaf one, which usually sells out in minutes, had all you wanted, but this crowd was a little more energetic than most I get, and the little lift hadn't bothered them a bit. I could put the urn back in the kitchen now that the guests were going outside. It bothered me that I had no coffee for me, though. I looked at Paul.

"I'm calling Keith Johnson's daughter, and she can get in touch with his son," I said. "But wherever we meet, there had better be a Dunkin' Donuts on the way."

Chapter 18

"Cassidy killed my father." Erika Johnson was a petite brunette in her early to midtwenties who had probably been born a cheerleader. No. She'd been born *head* cheerleader. And I was trying with all my might not to hold any of that against her. "There's no other explanation for it."

We were sitting outside on the sidewalk in front of a café called What Now? (question mark included) in Red Bank, a town that is nearly as cute as it thinks it is. The thing about sidewalk cafés is that they seem like a good idea, but you end up looking at cars driving by on a street that's way too close to where you're eating and drinking. Erika and her brother, Braden, who was wearing a T-shirt and jeans and looked like he'd be more comfortable in a business suit, had picked the venue after I'd called her and she'd called him.

Thank goodness there had been six Dunkin' Donuts outlets on the way here and I'd only stopped at two.

"Why do you say that?" I asked. "From what I can tell from the physical evidence that's been brought up at the trial, it would have been very difficult for Cassidy to drown your father in the bathtub. He was much larger and stronger than she is."

Braden's blue eyes were not as cold as one would expect. "What was also brought up at the trial was that my father's blood alcohol level was well above the legal limit, so it's possible he was very groggy or even unconscious when he was put under water."

Richard, perched over my left shoulder, snorted. "How'd she get him into the tub to begin with?" he said, seemingly to himself.

"Please." Paul, perched over my *right* shoulder so Richard could play the little devil to his little angel, held up a hand. "Let's help Alison conduct the interview. Alison, ask how they think Cassidy managed to get—" He stopped when he saw Richard's imperious glare.

"Wouldn't she have had to pick him up to get him into the tub?" I asked. *I* didn't care about Richard's imperious glare.

Erika shrugged. "I wasn't there. Maybe she threatened him with a gun."

Okay, so Cassidy brought a gun that no one had found and that there were no records of her owning and then, intending to kill her stepfather, had used it only to get him into a bathtub full of water to drown him. Then, instead of running out the back door to cover her tracks, she stayed in the room, called the police, and waited until they showed up to tell her story. Sure. That made sense.

"Do you wear denim a lot?" I asked Erika. Might as well start in on the denim fibers found in the bathwater.

She looked like I'd asked whether she once owned a wildebeest. "What?"

"There are some denim fibers that figure in the case," I said, saying more than we actually knew to be true. "Is that something you wear often?"

"I don't have to sit here and take this," Erika said, although she made no effort to stand up or not take it.

I decided to change topics. "Why would Cassidy want to kill your father?" I asked both the young people in front of me. "What would she gain from his death?"

"Satisfaction," Erika said without a hint of emotion. "She hated Dad."

Braden, appointing himself the family spokesperson and the voice of reason, held up both hands, palms out. "Cass and Dad had some disagreements. She thought he had swooped in on her mom after her actual dad died. I'm not sure what she thought he was using her for, but it wasn't to get her money. Dad had all the cash in that marriage."

So why not push the point and get to the heart of the matter? "There were large sums of money being moved out of your father's personal accounts and into Cassidy's," I said. "Both of you had to know about that at some point, didn't you?"

There was the pretense of a stunned silence between them. "You think we killed our father?" Braden asked.

I didn't even have to listen to Paul's feed; I had heard this enough times before. "I don't think anything yet," I said. "I don't have enough facts to form an opinion. What I'm asking is whether you were aware of what was going on with the money in your father's accounts."

"Very good, Alison," Paul said. He'd raised me so well.

"You *sound* like you think we killed him," Erika sniffed.

"I'm sorry if that's what you hear, but I really don't have any idea just yet."

Braden clearly decided to take the lead over his sister. "Well I for one didn't know anything about all that stuff until I heard it in the courtroom," he said. "It never occurred to me that my father's money was being funneled off to Cass. I've never touched a dime of his money; it sits in a trust somewhere accruing interest." He even managed not to look askance at his sister as he said, "I have an income."

"You have a job?" I asked. Richard was already nodding. He'd done his research for Cassidy's trial.

"I work for a financial firm on Wall Street," he said. Braden didn't realize that my ex-husband (the Swine) had worked for a financial firm on Wall Street, so that probably didn't have the same high-impact effect it might have on a recent college graduate after three cosmos. He paused a moment and added, "I don't need the money from my father."

"So what are you doing here on a weekday morning?" I asked.

"I'm still on call as a witness at Cass's trial," he said. "I have a leave of absence until that's over."

"If you didn't know anything about the bank accounts, what can you testify about?" I asked, noticing that Richard was shaking his head. I'd broken the attorney's first rule: Never ask a question you don't know the answer to. Because Richard knew the answer.

"I can say that Cass and Dad fought the day before he drowned," Braden answered. "I was there and I heard it. He told her never to come back to his house and never to speak to him again. And her mother agreed with him. She said she never wanted to see Cassidy as long as she lived. That pretty much devastated Cass. She's so devoted to Adrian."

I remembered suddenly that I wasn't an attorney in a courtroom and could ask any question I wanted because the point was to get an answer, not to convince a jury. Richard, hand cradling his chin (I bet he wished he had a goatee to stroke), was still shaking his head, but I went on.

"What was the argument about?" I asked.

Erika, apparently miffed that no attention was coming her way, waited until her brother was sipping from his iced cappuccino and answered ahead of him. "Adrian had gone out with Cassidy that day, and Cassidy had driven her to her dead husband's grave," she said.

"People visit the graves of loved ones all the time," I told her.

"Adrian didn't want to go. She thought she and Cassidy were going to go shopping or something and then she got taken to this cheap cemetery in Neptune." It seemed the social class of the cemetery was the especially appalling part to Erika. "She didn't want to get out of the car to visit the headstone, you know, but Cassidy shamed her into it, and when they got back, Adrian wouldn't even talk to Cassidy. So Dad threw her out of the house."

That confused me. "I thought Cassidy had her own apartment."

"She does." Braden had recovered from his sip and made sure he was once again the working spokesman for the Johnson family. "It was more a symbolic thing, like Dad was telling her not to come visit."

"How did Cassidy react?"

Richard turned away.

"She said she blamed Dad for everything. She said Dad was the one who had poisoned Adrian's memory of Cassidy's father. And she said she wished that Dad was the one who had died." Braden seemed to get special satisfaction out of that last part.

"And this was the day before he was murdered?" I said.

Braden nodded. "Less than twenty-four hours, actually. This was about seven in the evening, and the police called Adrian about Dad's murder the next afternoon."

"So your father hadn't left for the Cranbury Bog the night before." I was just trying to get my bearings and regain some sense of the conversation.

"No, he and Hunter drove up there together the next morning," Braden said.

"Hunter Evans, his business partner?" I thought that was the name Richard had told me, and floating next to me now, he acknowledged I had remembered it correctly.

Braden nodded. "They liked to take the occasional day or two and go away, remember why they'd started a firm to begin with. Hunter knew Dad at Princeton. They were friends before they went into business together. Going to Cranbury was just a way to refresh those batteries. Dad said neither one of them was allowed to mention anything about the business while they were there."

"So where was Hunter Evans when your father drowned?" I asked.

"I have no idea," Braden told me.

"Evans said he was in his room taking a nap," Richard said. "The innkeeper, Robin Witherspoon, said that as far as she knew, that's where he was; she had helped him with the key to his room just before it happened. Apparently she'd given him the wrong key when he checked in."

"Who do you think killed Richard Harrison?" I asked the two spoiled brats in front of me.

Richard made a sound with his mouth that probably would have been like a balloon deflating if he'd had the use of air. "We're not talking about me!" he insisted.

"We did agree, Alison," Paul reminded me. Had I been able to then, I'd have reminded him that *he* agreed and I hadn't even been consulted.

Luckily I didn't have to respond to either of them. Braden did his best to look thoughtful, staring off in a direction just over my right shoulder, where he would have seen Paul if that were possible. After the appropriate pause, he refixed his gaze on me and said, "If I had to guess, I'd say Cass killed him too."

"Yeah," Erika said, nodding. "That's what I was gonna say." She seemed peeved her brother had gotten to it first, but he'd given her plenty of time to jump in, and she hadn't done so. Opportunity missed is opportunity lost.

Richard was probably glad he didn't have a physical body at that point because I think he would have had a major health event. On the other hand, he was already dead, so the victory was somewhat Pyrrhic. "That's . . . that's . . . that's absurd!" he managed.

To be fair, I had to agree. "What possible reason would Cassidy have to murder her attorney?" I said. "It seemed like Richard was the only one who *didn't* think she killed your father."

"Cass never liked that guy," Braden answered. "She said he looked at her funny, and she thought he just wanted her money."

Richard vanished. Flat-out vanished. One second there and the next second gone. Paul looked stunned.

"He kept coming around to talk to her about the case," Erika added. "I think it was creeping her out a little."

"That's enough to kill him?" I asked. It seemed like a pretty big stretch.

Braden shrugged. "She'd already done it once."

I stood up and, against my every natural impulse, thanked Braden and Erika for their help with my case. Then I turned and headed toward my Volvo with Paul directly by my side, still shaking his head in wonder.

"What do we do now?" I said as I pulled out my phone to make it look like I was talking to a living person.

Paul pulled himself together. "About Richard? He'll be back at the house before we get there, I'm sure, or he'll be in your car when we get into it."

"About the case. Figuring out who killed everybody and saving Cassidy from whoever ran her off the road last night."

Paul's face moved back into deep-thought mode, but he didn't go so far as goatee stroking. "I think it's important we talk to Hunter Evans and Robin Witherspoon about what happened the day at the Cranbury Bog," he said. "That means—"

"I know what that means. You want me to drive to Cranbury and then up to Bergen County to talk to these people. And I'm saying no."

Paul actually stopped in what would normally have been his tracks. "No?"

"That's right. This is the twenty-first century, Paul. Nobody has to go anywhere to see anybody anymore."

He was right. Richard was in the car when we got there.

Chapter 19

"I helped Mr. Evans with a problem he had with his room key." Robin Witherspoon, who looked exactly like her name, was probably in her mid- to late sixties, had her mostly gray hair pulled back in a bun, and was, at least from the waist up, wearing a very modest and unassuming outfit.

We were sitting in my bedroom. That is, *I* was sitting on my bed in my bedroom. Maxie, who was apparently caught up on her TV dramas, and Paul, only a foot or two beneath the ceiling, were looking down at me. I had my own ancient laptop computer open on the bed and power cord securely in the wall outlet (this thing wouldn't run more than three minutes without a direct connection) and was looking at Robin, who had agreed to a FaceTime conference when I'd called her.

Richard had not even asked about joining the group. He had not said a word the whole way back to the guesthouse and had sunk into the basement immediately upon returning. Paul said it was not unusual behavior for his brother when things had gone badly for him. But he added that Richard always rallied.

It was amazing he had even shown up in my house after he died. How much worse can things go for a guy?

"Had you noticed you'd given him the wrong key when he checked in?" I asked Robin. That was the story Braden and Erika had told me.

"Oh, no," Robin answered. "To this day I believe I gave him the key to his room properly. How he had the key to another room still baffles me."

Paul lowered down a bit. "Interesting," he said. "Ask her which room the wrong key was for. If it was Keith Johnson's, that would be a clue I'd be amazed the police would ignore."

I asked and Robin said Evans had shown her a key for a room on the other side of the house. Not the one for Keith's room by a long shot. So the Cranbury police weren't complete idiots, anyway.

Robin said she had a four-bedroom house in Cranbury (that looked gorgeous on their website, the address of which I will not give you here because I want you to come to my far grungier place) and after her husband, Roger, had passed away had decided it was too quiet. She'd turned the place into a bed-and-breakfast catering to particularly upscale patrons and had been operating it that way for more than seven years now.

"You said you were sure you'd given Mr. Evans the right key. So was there a key to that room missing?" That was not a Paul question. That was a question an innkeeper would think of. Maxie told me to ask it.

"As a matter of fact, there was," Robin said. "My best guess now is that I accidentally handed Mr. Evans two keys and he dropped one somewhere along the way."

"I'm an innkeeper, Robin," I said. "You know perfectly well you didn't hand Hunter Evans two keys."

"I thought you were a detective," Robin said.

"I also own a guesthouse in Harbor Haven," I reminded her. I'd tried to establish this earlier, but Robin had been so excited about being called in the Keith Johnson investigation that I don't think she'd been listening. "But the keys. You'd never have done that."

"It's true," she admitted. "I don't really think that's what happened."

"So what *do* you think happened?"

"Between us?" Robin seemed to think that anything she told me would not be repeated anywhere else. That was largely because she couldn't see the two transparent people behind me and I had not mentioned any intention of going to the police or the prosecutor with any information she might give me. Oddly that hadn't come up.

"Sure." Whatever.

"I think Mr. Evans deliberately took the wrong key so he could come and ask me about it later," Robin said. "I think I was his alibi. I think Mr. Evans killed Mr. Johnson."

"There was no evidence of that," Paul said.

Meanwhile, I had the living person who could see and hear me to deal with. "What makes you think that, Robin?" I asked. "And why didn't you tell the police or the county investigators any of this?"

I could only see Robin from the shoulders up, so it surprised me when she stood up and seemed to look from side to side, making sure we were "alone." She sat back down and looked into her web cam. "Well I couldn't be sure, could I?

And I didn't want to get a regular guest like Mr. Evans in trouble if I wasn't certain. But it was very shortly before Mr. Johnson's daughter showed up that Mr. Evans came down to ask about his key, and that had been about an hour after he checked in. He said he'd been down in the garden relaxing, but his bags were already in his room when I opened his door. So he'd been able to get in earlier. He'd had a key *then*. I think he came and switched them when I was away from the front room."

I keep my keys locked up in a hanging box on the wall in my kitchen, but I wasn't about to question the inn-keeping practices of someone who was clearly attracting high-end guests when I was struggling to keep my magic show going. "You said Mr. Johnson's daughter came to see him. You meant his stepdaughter, Cassidy Van Doren?" I figured that's what she'd meant, but Paul was in my ear (almost literally) making me double-check.

"Oh, no, Alison. Cassidy came a little later. His daughter Erika was here first. But there wasn't any ruckus when she was in there. It wasn't until Cassidy showed up that she screamed and came out yelling for nine-one-one a couple of minutes later."

Instinctively I looked at Paul, whose eyes were widening a bit. "Erika was there," he said quietly. Richard said nothing, and I didn't look toward him. I didn't want Robin to understand I was with other people, even if they weren't actually there. If you know what I mean.

"How long did Erika stay?" I asked.

"Oh, not long at all. Ten minutes, maybe. But if you want to know the truth, I think she was involved in what happened." She didn't wait for me to ask the obvious question. "I found a pair of jeans just outside Mr. Johnson's room. Women's jeans. And they were soaking wet."

Aha.

"Whoa." That was Maxie. I was too busy processing that information.

"You found wet jeans outside Keith Johnson's room?" I know, I know. She'd just said that. So I went on. "How did Erika—or whoever—get out of the room with no pants on?"

"That's why I think Mr. Evans was involved," Robin said. Clearly she was an accomplished gossip and a snoop, like any good innkeeper. "The rooms were right next to each other. If Erika had gone out the glass doors in the back and left the jeans because she was afraid the police might search, she could have gone directly into Mr. Evans's room and changed clothes. Besides, I heard voices coming from Mr. Evans's room, and one of them was a woman." Her voice became very confidential. "He did not bring his wife with him."

"Did she give the jeans to the police?" Paul asked, and I passed the question along.

"I couldn't be sure it was evidence," Robin said coyly. "I can't infringe on a guest's privacy." Really. She said that unironically. "I hadn't actually seen Erika wearing them, after all."

"Who else could they belong to?" I said.

"Not for me to say." She wouldn't want to be indiscreet.

#

"Funny how Erika never mentioned she was at her father's hotel the day he died," I said.

Paul was floating in a somewhat tilted position. When he is thinking especially heavily, he loses some interest in staying completely vertical and tends to list a bit. It doesn't mean anything, but it sure does look strange. He rubbed his nose for a moment and said, "But she didn't have any water on her when she came out. Certainly ten minutes is enough to drown a man, but she wasn't wet. Maybe Robin . . ."

"Clearly Erika is lying," Richard said. He of course was absolutely upright. You could have put a level to his back and had all the bubbles come up in the middle, if he was capable of being touched. "She must be the one who really killed Keith Johnson. The wet jeans really make the point."

"We don't have enough data to reach a conclu—" Paul began.

"Oh, Paul, really!" his brother shouted. "It's as clear as the nose on Alison's face."

"Actually, Paul's nose is clearer," I pointed out. "So is yours. I can see right through it."

Richard looked at me with some impatience. "I think you have plenty of data," he went on as if I hadn't spoken. "I think you're trying to prolong this process because you enjoy it, and that's making you turn your back to what is obvious. Cassidy Van Doren did not kill her stepfather."

"That's not the point," Paul said. "Even if she didn't, we don't know for a fact who did, and that isn't going to help Cassidy until Alison can bring some proof to the prosecutor."

"I don't think you're grasping the situation clearly," Richard told his brother. "You are doing your best to keep this case active. Why don't you know who killed Keith Johnson yet?"

Paul looked positively wounded, and you don't do that to a friend of mine. "Because you just dumped this case on us a few days ago and there are enough suspects to fill Madison Square Garden," I told Richard. "Remember, you decided to come here specifically not because you missed your dead brother and wanted to see him but because you needed help and trusted him with this investigation."

"Now, Alison, that's not fair," Paul said. "Let's try to refocus—"

"Don't defend her, Paul." Richard looked like he was about to knight somebody he didn't care for much. "She made accusations that can't be recanted." He turned his body, what there was of it, toward me. "You think I'm being unfair to my brother? Where were you when I practically had to raise him myself?"

"In grammar school. But thanks for asking. Since you got here you've done nothing but order people around and tell Paul how he's doing everything wrong. So let's leave it at this, Richard: either solve this case on your own or shut up and let us do it."

"Alison!" That was Paul.

I didn't feel like I'd gone too far, but apparently everybody else did, because Paul looked aghast and Richard almost had color in his face, something I didn't think was possible in a ghost. Richard looked down at me—he'd risen about two feet—and pointed his right index finger at me. "You are insolent and rude," he hissed.

"Yeah, but I'm not wrong, am I? What have you done to help?"

Richard didn't vanish. He pretty much exploded, out through my bedroom wall and into the street, or the air above the street. And his velocity was impressive. You could practically see the vapor trail.

I looked at Paul, whose face was showing something on the fringe of despair. "I thought he'd never leave," I said. See, you try to lighten the mood with a little joke.

Paul's mouth opened and closed three times. "You . . . you . . . you insulted Richard."

"Paul, Richard came into this situation with a predetermined set of opinions, and he's been holding you back. You haven't really been able to investigate this case because Richard won't hear anything except that Cassidy didn't kill Keith Johnson. He needs to be removed from any work we're doing."

"So you deliberately encouraged him to leave like that?" At least Paul's power of speech was coming back.

"It wasn't my original plan, but things escalated. Paul, don't worry about it. Richard will be back. Right now we need to focus on the case. What do we have?" There's nothing Paul enjoys better than reciting the facts of an investigation.

Sure enough, that got him going. "We have two unsolved murders," he said. "Keith Johnson was discovered in a bathtub at a bed-and-breakfast in Cranbury. He'd been drowned, and not a long while before. As we've discovered, although his stepdaughter, Cassidy Van Doren, was present at the scene and actually called the police, his business partner, Hunter Evans, and his biological daughter, Erika, were in the hotel and possibly in his room not long before he was murdered. They must remain active suspects.

"But there is also, whether Richard cares to consider it or not, the matter of Richard being killed with what appears to have been a steam iron in his hotel room in New Brunswick. We have no idea how the killer got into the room or why an iron other than the one already in the hotel closet was used." Paul shook his head at the thought of it. "We have no particular suspects for Richard's murder. Miriam seems to have known about his infatuation with Cassidy but was, at least outwardly, relatively unconcerned about the matter. The more I think about it, the more it seems the two murders can't possibly be unrelated. If we investigate Richard's more deeply, we might very well find out who killed Keith Johnson."

"Now you're starting to sound like the Paul I knew before you went gallivanting about the country," I said.

"I did stop into Canada once or twice as well," he noted. "See some of my home country."

"There's also the question of who in the house swiped Maxie's laptop, took Richard's files off of it, and then returned it," I reminded him. "We haven't looked into that at all."

"Surely that's related to the murders as well," Paul said, nodding. "There is no motivation to vandalize Maxie's laptop other than to remove some information the person did not want us to see. In this case, the only advantage we have is that Richard had seen the files before they were removed and the person who stole them doesn't know we can use him as a resource, assuming he is willing to discuss the situation when he returns."

"And there's the stretching noise in the upstairs bedroom to the left of the stairs," I said, thinking aloud.

Paul's eyes indicated I might have actually had a mental breakdown before his eyes. "The . . . stretching noise?" he asked.

"That's right. You weren't here for that. The night Richard arrived, Vanessa DiSica told me she heard a stretching noise in a guest room upstairs, but it was one that wasn't being used and was locked. I thought maybe Richard had gone in there, but he wasn't anywhere to be found, and neither was anybody else when Maxie and I went in to look. Vanessa hasn't said anything about the stretching sound again, but we never did figure out what that was all about."

"Sounds like it's a good thing I came back when I did," Paul said. "There are many mysteries to be solved here."

"You came back because I took out an ad," I reminded him.

He looked at me a bit askance. "By the way . . . Casper?"

"Friendly ghost," I said.

Paul shook his head. "We have a great deal of work to do."

I had to agree. "What's first?"

"Nothing has changed. Our next stop is exactly what it was going to be before you spoke to Robin Witherspoon."

Chapter 20

Hunter Evans did not do FaceTime. He would not submit to Skype. Either he was a technophobe or a control freak, but at least I got him to agree to a telephone call. I supposed he was comfortable with any device that had been in use at the turn of the century. The twentieth century.

I put the call on speakerphone on my end so Paul wouldn't be thrusting his ear into mine and distracting me the whole time I was talking to Evans. If you've never had a ghost stick his head inside yours, do not judge me. Evans, who had been on countless conference calls in his life, never so much as asked why I needed to put him on speaker when I was, as far as he knew, the only person on my end of the phone.

"I can't tell you anything more than I told the police, the county prosecutor, and the court," he said with some air of irritation. I got the impression Hunter Evans was irritated a good percentage of the time. "Everything I know about Keith's murder is already a matter of public record. Who is your client, Ms. Kerby?"

"I think you'll understand that my client prefers to be kept confidential," I told him.

"I don't understand that at all. You are not bound by any privilege like an attorney or a doctor. You're a private detective working a case and you have a client. Why can't you tell me who that is? Do you have an agenda other than helping to convict the woman who drowned my friend and partner in his bathtub?"

"You believe Cassidy Van Doren is guilty of the charges against her," I said, although I had no doubt Evans already knew what he believed.

"Of course I do. I was there when it happened."

Paul stared. "Does he mean—"

"You saw Cassidy put Mr. Johnson's head under the water?" I asked Evans.

"No, of course not." Paul's eyes narrowed back to their usual size. "I didn't mean I was in the room when Keith was murdered. Of course I would have stopped her from killing him. I mean I was in my room, in the same hotel, at the time he died, and I heard her inside his room. They were right next door."

That required some clarification as well. "So you heard Cassidy call out for help and scream for nine-one-one," I said.

"A clever ruse to deflect suspicion," Evans said. "But I heard them before she did that. I heard Keith's voice speaking in anger and then I heard a struggle."

Now I could feel *my* eyes narrowing. "So you heard a struggle in the room next door, where your friend and business partner was meeting with his estranged stepdaughter, and you didn't do anything about it until you heard her scream for help?" Nice friend.

"I knew Keith and Cassidy didn't get along. I was accustomed to hearing them shout at each other. There was no reason for me to intervene; I had no idea there was violence going on in the room."

Except he would have heard a lot of sloshing, I was guessing. "The bathroom was off to the far end of the little master suite Mr. Johnson had," I said, based on information Robin Witherspoon had given me. "It was the farthest point from your adjoining wall." Paul was feeding me the question, but I had an idea of where he was going. "Did you hear the water running?"

"I don't remember hearing the water, but like you said, it would have been far away from where I was sitting, and I was trying not to listen to the heated conversation." There was some change in the tone of Evans's voice; he was going from irritated to annoyed, which was to be a quick stop on the route to downright resentful. "I don't see why you're asking . . . Do you consider *me* a suspect in Keith's murder? Is that how far that little harlot wants you to go?"

It wasn't easy to maintain my demeanor when I was being yelled at like that, but Paul was motioning with his hands, palms down, reminding me I had to keep calm. "The one thing I will tell you about my client, Mr. Evans, is that it is not Cassidy Van Doren."

"It's not? Who is it?"

"We've covered this ground. Now I want to ask you about your room key."

Evans had no doubt been prepped by the prosecutor and already had testified in Cassidy's trial, so he had a prepared answer ready and waiting. He sent it out without inflection like a fourth-grade student reciting *Trees* by Joyce Kilmer. "I had the wrong room key but I didn't know it. I tried opening the door to my room and was unable to do so. I took the key to Robin at the desk and asked her what the problem might be. She examined the key and saw it was the wrong one for my room, so she replaced it. The new key worked and there was no further problem." Very concise, to the point, and definitive. I came close to believing him.

"There's only one problem with that," I told him. "You had already been in your room before you asked about the key. How did you get in the first time?"

I waited. This was a question Evans had not readied himself to answer, and it had implications he was bound not to appreciate. It took him a good long moment before he could address it. And even then he fell back on the most time-honored dodge in history.

"I have no idea what you're talking about," Evans said.

"It's simple." I wasn't going to let him up off the mat that easily. "You say you had a key for the wrong room at the bed-and-breakfast."

"That's right," Evans said. Apparently he thought that ended the discussion.

He was wrong. "So you couldn't get into the room you'd rented until Robin gave you the right key and you could open your door. But the problem is, when Robin helped you with that key, your bags were already inside the room. That means you'd gotten in there earlier. So I'm asking, if you didn't have a key to that room, how did you drop off your bags?"

"That's a fallacy," Evans said. "You are operating on the assumption that my luggage was inside the room when Ms. Witherspoon let me in with the proper key, and it was not."

"So you had your bags with you out in the hallway when you asked her for help?" I asked. I knew I could confirm with Robin that was not the case. I just wanted to hear if Evans was going to try to change his story or flat-out lie.

But Evans was not a stupid man. He had clearly picked up on the fact that I'd already spoken to Robin, and he knew what he could say that would deflect suspicion without being immediately verifiable as wrong. "I don't remember," he said. "I did stop in with Keith when we first checked in. I might have left my one suitcase in his room. I was not made aware of whether the police found it there after he died."

"Robin Witherspoon says you were out walking in the garden before you came to her and asked for the key," I told him. I felt that didn't betray any secrets Robin might have divulged. I didn't want to hurt another innkeeper's business. "Could you have left your bag outside in the garden?"

Paul shook his head. He hates it when I give a witness a possible answer to hide behind. But in my view, this scenario was so ridiculous that if Evans decided to use it, he would be copping to more than simply lying; he'd be casting serious suspicion on his whereabouts when his business partner was drowned in a bathtub.

"No, I don't believe I had it with me in the garden," he said. Like I mentioned, he was not stupid. "I must have left it in Keith's room, although I was there only for a minute before I went down to the garden. He was tired and wanted to rest up for a while."

Now to start broaching the really touchy topics. "I'm told you weren't alone in your room," I said.

Beat, two, three, four . . .

"I beg your pardon?" A common delay tactic. I waited because I knew he'd heard me correctly. "I was alone. Whoever told you that was lying, or mistaken."

"So there was no woman in your room with you? One who might have . . ." And that's when it hit me how ridiculous the scenario I was going to bring up actually was.

"I was alone," Evans asserted. I was not going to challenge him.

"Mr. Evans, I have to ask you a question, and I want you to know it's meant with all the respect due to someone of your accomplishments and experience." I thought that was a nice way of saying, hey, I have a rude question to ask.

"Ask your question, young lady." Even my father has never called me *young lady*.

"Why weren't you a suspect in the murder of Keith Johnson?"

I couldn't see Hunter Evans, but I guarantee you he didn't even blink before he said, "That's something you would have to ask the police and the prosecutor, Ms. Kerby. Now if you don't mind, I have a meeting in five minutes." And before finding out if I minded or not, Evans disconnected the call.

For the record, I didn't mind all that much.

I had to ask Paul about my revelation. "Why would a woman who drowned a guy in the bathtub take off her wet jeans and then dump them out the window when she was staying with a man in a nice dry room next door?"

"Because she knew both rooms would be searched and didn't want the wet jeans found if they could incriminate her," Paul said. And that seemed logical. Sort of.

I looked over at Paul even before I put my phone back into my pocket. "Well, that's one thing I've gotten out of today," I said.

"What's that?" Paul followed me as I started out of the room. Melissa would be ambling through the door at any second, and I needed to check on my guests. Maybe I'd even play Cyrano for Abby Lesniak and Mr. Lewis.

"I'm pretty sure now that Cassidy Van Doren *didn't* kill her stepfather." I walked down the stairs, and Paul did his floating thing.

"What convinced you?" he asked.

"Everybody who's lied to me for the past few days has told me straight out that she did," I said. "That's got to count for something."

Paul smiled his oh-that-Alison smile. "It's not empirical, but it's a start," he said.

But that wasn't the odd part.

The odd part was that out of nowhere, Adrian Johnson called me at that very moment. And before I could express any surprise at that, she was already saying something that surprised me more.

"I want to hire you," she said.

Chapter 21

Now, you have to understand how my mind works. The whole private investigation racket, that's Paul's thing. In my head I am not at all a detective despite what my license and the state of New Jersey might think. I am an innkeeper. That's the license I really wanted and the one that I worked hardest to get. So when Adrian Johnson wanted to hire me, it took me a second to realize she didn't just want to take a room in the guesthouse.

"You want to hire me?" I said, largely for Paul's benefit. We were standing—in our own ways—at the bottom of the main staircase, and I looked around to see if any of the guests were nearby, but no one was.

"Yes," Adrian said with her best fake royal voice. She hadn't been rich for that many years and still wasn't all that comfortable making other people feel inferior, although I got the impression she was working on it. "What are your rates?"

Wow. A paying customer. That was a rarity in my investigation business. Paul looked at me strangely, probably because he didn't know my avaricious side very well. "That depends on what it is you want me to do," I answered. And I said that largely because I had no idea what to charge Adrian.

"I want you to stop investigating Keith's murder," she said.

Well, that took me by surprise. "I'm sorry?" Sure, I can think of snappier comebacks *now*, but I was under time pressure.

"I said, I want you stop investigating Keith's murder. I'm willing to pay you quite well to do so."

I looked at Paul, who I was sure had heard the exchange. He looked . . . interested. That didn't help.

"So you want to pay me *not* to do something," I said. Yes, I was reiterating what had already been covered in this conversation, but I was processing, and maybe it takes some of us a little longer than others. You ever think of that?

"Exactly. I think your investigation has been a distraction. It's been disrupting my family while we go through the difficulty of losing my husband and seeing my daughter go on trial for killing him. I think it's in the best interests of everyone involved for you to stop asking questions and upsetting people." Adrian sounded like that was the most reasonable argument anyone had ever put forth. Surely Socrates himself would have been proud of that one and asked Plato to write it up for posterity.

I fell back on the defense I'd been using since I'd started doing what Richard had asked me to do. "I'm not investigating your husband's murder," I told Adrian. "I'm investigating the murder of Richard Harrison, but there is some overlap between the two."

"That's crazy. Cassidy didn't kill the attorney."

Oh, well, there was a compelling argument. "Still, that is what I have been asked to find out, and the investigation leads in a number of directions." That sounded pretty true.

"If you are only trying to find out who killed the attorney, why are you talking to my son and both my daughters?" Adrian asked. It took me a moment to realize she was referring to Braden and Erika Johnson as her children. "Why are you asking Hunter Evans about the night Keith died?"

Wow. That meant Evans had pretty much gotten off the phone with me and called Adrian to complain. About me. You had to wonder who was really pulling the strings here, or at least I did.

"Like I said, there is some overlap, and some of the questions pertain to both cases," I said. I didn't even believe it myself, but it sounded like something. "It is quite possible that the same person killed both your husband and Mr. Harrison. It would be foolish of me not to try to discover who that person is, don't you think?"

Paul gave me a half nod of approval, but Adrian wasn't buying what I was selling. "What I *think*," she said, "is that you can have ten thousand dollars if you stop your investigation right now, but that offer will be withdrawn the moment we end this phone conversation. Now what do *you* think?"

Ten thousand dollars? I was seriously considering the idea until I realized exactly what she was asking. I swallowed heavily and said, "I'm afraid I have to turn down your generous offer," I said. "I have a client who has asked me to do a job, and I can't renege on that agreement."

"Twenty thousand dollars."

I know Paul was listening that time because he actually shuddered a bit. I must have given him something resembling a pleading look because he regarded me and then shook his head negatively. Sure. What did *he* need with money?

I closed my eyes. Believe me when I tell you I have more willpower than I would have thought possible because I took a breath and then told Adrian, "I'm sorry. I wish I could, honestly I do, but I can't."

She hung up.

I put down the phone and glared at Paul. "You just made me turn down twenty thousand dollars," I said.

"Twenty thousand dollars?" Melissa had just walked in and was approaching. She has great timing, that kid.

"You knew you weren't going to take that money," Paul said.

"I didn't *know*."

"What twenty thousand dollars?" Liss asked.

I explained what had just happened and got her up to speed on the other developments—such as they were—in the investigation(s). Melissa, usually eager to immerse herself in a case, seemed less engaged than usual, staring off at the walls and nodding as if she were just waiting for me to stop talking.

"What's going on?" I asked.

She blinked a couple of times and then looked at me. "Nothing."

"Nothing? I just told you about two murder cases and you looked like I was trying to explain the conjugation of Latin verbs." That was something I actually studied in high school, and although I think the ancient Romans were way cool, I remember not one word of their language. How often do you run into an ancient Roman and have to strike up a conversation?

"It's nothing, Mom." Liss walked toward the kitchen, so Paul and I naturally followed her. "It's just, I only have one day left of school for the year and I'm thinking about that."

"Is this Jared related?" I asked. Melissa had a crush on a guy in her class named Jared not long ago, but it had come to naught by mutual agreement. Spring, however, brings out the crush-ready impulses in many a girl.

"What? No! We're friends. You know that. So tell me again about this Adrian Johnson and how she wants to give you twenty thousand dollars to not do anything."

Her mood was clearly a subject we'd have to table for future discussion. "It's very simple," Paul said, grateful to have the discussion focusing again on his area of expertise and not human emotion, which he does not process like other people alive or dead. "We have clearly struck a nerve, and Ms. Johnson is afraid we're getting too close to some truth she'd prefer we not discover."

"You get a lot out of a simple bribe offer," I told Paul.

"There is no other scenario that fits the facts."

"What if she really just doesn't want her family to be upset?" Melissa asked. "I know it doesn't sound like that's the reason just because she said so, but it's possible." I could hear my mother in my mind's ear saying how smart my daughter is and how she'll no doubt be a Supreme Court justice one day. Who was I to argue with the mother in my mind's ear?

"I consider that possibility to be extremely unlikely," Paul told Liss. "Mrs. Johnson had not exhibited any special concern over her family members before this phone call."

"I'm not saying it's what happened," Melissa said, doing her best—which wasn't good enough—to hide a small smile. "I'm saying it's possible."

Paul, smiling only on the left side, nodded. "Possible."

"For the time being, let's assume Paul is right," I told Melissa as we walked into the kitchen. Liss went to the fridge to get some orange juice. I looked at Paul, who was floating in place near—partially inside—the stove. "What does Adrian's offer tell us, and what can we expect now that I've turned it down?"

"Ah." Paul loves this kind of thing. His eyebrows closed just over his nose, and his mouth turned downward in a cerebral frown. I'd never seen him look happier. "What we can determine is that there's likely something Adrian doesn't want us to find that she thinks we're close to finding. It's probably best, if we can, to bring Richard back in on that part of it." He looked around, as if just having thought of it. "Have you seen him?"

I was about to say, "Not recently," but my daughter beat me to it.

"Yeah," she said as she put the glass of orange juice down after a long gulp. "I saw him when I was coming in. Richard was flying in and out of the movie room like he couldn't decide if he wanted to be inside or out."

That was different. "Did he say anything?" Paul asked.

"I didn't want to get that close. He looked mad."

My cell phone buzzed, and there was a text message from Madame Lorraine: *Bring Paul Harrison here. I can help.* Madame Lorraine didn't know when to quit.

I looked at Paul. "Are you in great pain?" I asked.

He squinted at me because apparently I was blurry. Maybe I was an old VHS copy of me. "You know I don't really feel," he said.

"So you're *not* in great pain, right?"

Now even Melissa was looking at me as if trying to size me for a straitjacket. "No. I'm not," Paul said.

"Good enough." I put the phone back in my pocket.

"I should be the one to broach the subject of more research with Richard," Paul said, shaking off my weirdness. "He's more likely to listen to me."

Actually, in my experience, Richard was less likely to listen to Paul and more likely to listen to himself telling Paul what to do. "I don't think so," I said. "I think there's someone who could do it better."

Paul's eyebrows, which had returned to their traditional position, rose. "Really."

"Yes. Liss, would you see if Maxie is up in your room, and if she is, ask her to come down here?"

Melissa put her glass in the sink and walked toward the kitchen door. "I was going up to change anyway," she said. She smiled privately. "One more day." And she was gone.

Paul regarded me carefully. "Maxie?" he asked.

"Best possible solution. She's not related to Richard, she has no feelings about him in any direction, and he's seen that she's good with research, so she'll be asking him on a professional basis. The trick is going to be selling it to her."

Paul stayed very still for a moment, which I know is not easy for him to do; the ghosts are sort of ethereal, not really ever being solidly in one place or position. Then he held up a hand, palm out. "Very solid reasoning," he said.

Maxie, wearing the trench coat that indicated she had her laptop with her—nobody was getting that thing away from her now—dropped down through the ceiling and landed in the middle of the center island. I was just glad she hadn't ended up in the middle of food. "Melissa says you were looking for me," she said. The trench coat vanished, and sure enough the laptop was there with her jeans and black "I Know You Are, but What Am I?" T-shirt.

"Yes," Paul began, but I thought it was important to cut him off before he tried convincing Maxie of something on adult terms. As an experienced mother, I had some inkling of how to talk to a person of Maxie's emotional maturity level.

"We're glad to see the laptop is still with you," I said. "You should make sure it stays with you at all times until we find out what happened."

"I know." Maxie seemed a trifle suspicious because I don't often start by telling her something she was doing for selfish reasons was a good idea. "I haven't let it out of my sight since I got it back, and I'm not going to start now." I wondered what Melissa might have let on about the work we wanted Richard to do.

"Good," I said. "But since you have it with you—"

"I knew it!" Maxie had been primed to go off and needed only the slightest spark. "You're going to get this thing stolen again!"

"I am definitely not going to do that," I told her in my calmest tone. I'd been running this conversation mentally for the past few minutes and knew not to react emotionally. "But I do want to ask you to do some research since you have it with you. We need to know more about what happened with Keith Johnson's murder that might have gotten Richard killed."

Maxie, not entirely finished with her bout of suspicion, looked at me for a prolonged moment. "What do you need to know?" she asked.

"Our theory is that Richard was getting close to information that would prove Cassidy Van Doren was not the murderer," Paul said. I was grateful that once I had established the tone, he picked up on the conversation; it would have alerted Maxie if he'd stayed silent the whole time. "We think that the person who did kill Keith Johnson also murdered Richard to keep that information from surfacing."

"Aha." Maxie was taking some comfort in the fact that Paul was on board with the plan. She trusts him more than she trusts me, even after all we've been through together. I managed not to tear up. "So you want me to find out what Richard was working on."

It was so tempting to lead her in the direction we wanted her to go, but I believe both Paul and I exhibited remarkable restraint in not embellishing the story. Let Maxie get to the conclusion herself. "That's right," I said. I didn't even add a "very good," because she's not stupid and would know I was patronizing her.

"Isn't it just easier to ask Richard?" she said. Perfect.

"Well, yes, but he hasn't been like us for very long," Paul said. "He might not remember exactly what he was doing at the time."

"Well, that's what the laptop is for!" Maxie wanted Paul to know how much smarter she was than he. "He can look at the files we have left because the ones that were taken were about this Johnson guy's money. The rest of the stuff about him being killed is still on here, I think." She gestured toward her laptop. "Richard might be able to find whatever he was working on again."

"Good thinking!" I almost believed I was astounded by Maxie's amazing deductions. "Why not find Richard and ask him to help?" I didn't think that was overplaying the hand, but I did look at Maxie a little too long.

But she didn't flinch. She loves it when she gets credit for doing something well and is especially proud of her Internet research skills because she's developed them since becoming a ghost. "I'm on it!" she shouted. The trench coat reappeared, the laptop went inside it, and Maxie was through the roof, literally. Well, the ceiling, anyway. What happened after that was a matter of conjecture.

I would have high-fived Paul if I could have. Instead I grinned at him. "Nice work," I said.

"Yes, but only the first phase of our new plans." Paul is a lot of fun at parties. I'm guessing. He came to my wedding and was so exciting, I didn't even know he was there until afterward. "It's also necessary for us to concentrate more completely on Richard's murder. We have the idea of someone bringing a separate steam iron into the room and hitting him with it when there was one in the hotel room closet. What does that tell us?"

"That it was certainly premeditated," I said. "Nobody uses an iron in a crime of passion, and even if they did, they wouldn't bring one from home."

Paul snapped his fingers, which made a slightly squishy sound that didn't resonate throughout the whole room. "That's the key, I think," he said. "Nobody brings an iron from home. The odds are it was discovered in one of the housekeeping carts or a supply closet in the hotel. We need to know the make and model of the iron and whether it matches the ones that are supplied in the guest rooms."

"So you think it's possible Kobielski was right and it was one of the hotel maids who killed Richard?" That seemed awfully implausible. What motive would a maid have to kill a guest? He couldn't have been *that* rude. I've had plenty of unpleasant guests in my house, and the urge to brain one with a steam iron had never once leapt to mind.

"I doubt it," Paul answered. "But I think whoever came into the hotel with the idea of killing him might have decided somewhere along the way that a hotel iron would make a good weapon. We also need to know if there were any markings at all on the iron. I'm sure if there were fingerprints, they'd have long since been discovered and the culprit caught, but there might have been blood spatter or some other traces that would give us a direction."

Melissa walked through the swinging kitchen door having changed into her "civilian" clothes, in this case shorts and a plain purple T-shirt. Her feet were bare. "What are we talking about?" she asked.

"Fingerprints, blood spatter, and a stolen steam iron," I told her.

"Great. So I haven't missed anything." She sat on one of the barstools I keep next to the center island.

"I'd say you missed some," I said. "We got Maxie to find Richard and start working on his research again."

"Well, we got Maxie to try to find Richard," Paul pointed out. "The last we heard from you, Melissa, he was fairly upset

205

and possibly unwilling to cooperate with us on the investigation of his own murder or Keith Johnson's."

"She must have found him," Liss said. "I was going to tell you, I heard his voice when I was coming downstairs. I think they're in one of the unrented guest rooms on the second floor."

"Good. So that is beginning. Now we need to get a better understanding of the police findings and the medical examiner's report on Richard's murder." Paul was doing his "pace" floating back and forth in front of the refrigerator. It makes getting the orange juice really sort of creepy because he doesn't bother to get out of the way. I decided I didn't need a drink right away.

But that was just distracting me from what Paul had just said. "We have to get the police and the medical examiner . . ." I felt the trap spring around me as it had so many times before. "Where are we going to get that information, I wonder?"

"I think you know," Paul said.

"Paul," I was already moaning, "I don't wanna . . ."

Josh walked in through the back door. "So, what did I miss?" he asked.

But at that moment, Richard came bursting (for Richard) through the wall, gesticulating wildly (for Richard) with his hands. "It's not the files that are missing," he said. "It's the *reason* the files are missing."

I was about to suggest he switch to decaf, but I realized that would not be appropriate. "The reason?" I said.

"It's the pattern, really." Richard seemed to get a hold of his emotions. "The key has never been which files from the

Johnson case are missing; I was looking for the wrong things. What's important is how they've been redacted."

Paul was in full Sherlock mode, left hand holding the right elbow as he stroked his goatee. "Redacted? Not simply deleted?"

Richard gave him a superior grin, which was the only kind Richard could generate. "Precisely. The files might have been removed by whoever took the laptop, but the pattern of the removal is clear. Keith Johnson—or more specifically, his business—was being investigated by a government agency, in my view for some sort of misuse of funds or illegal compilation of funds, perhaps a Ponzi scheme."

That was finally something, but I didn't know what. "So where does that leave us?" I asked.

Paul was already pacing. "With a host of new motives for various suspects," he said.

Chapter 22

"So this guy gets hit in the head with an iron and you want to know who made the iron?" Detective Lieutenant McElone (think "macaroni") looked positively amused, sitting behind the desk in her relatively new office, which replaced her not-that-new cubicle.

Amused for McElone, of course, meant that she had the slightest hint of a smile and not the least bit of humor in her eyes, which were brown, large, and intimidating.

"That's among the things I need to know, yes." I sat across the desk from McElone and braced myself for the inevitable comments about having to work with an amateur detective when she had real crimes to investigate and my equally unavoidable comebacks about saving cats stuck up trees. "It's also important to find out if there was any, you know, debris on the iron when it was found and how much it weighs."

McElone and I have something of a history. I first met her during the Paul-and-Maxie investigation, when I was not a licensed investigator and therefore was more of an annoyance to the working police than I should be now. In theory, I am now a lay investigator with a license from the state who has had some training and some experience and will know how not to get in the way of the municipal officers.

In theory.

I had left Paul and Richard at the house working on various angles, including researching the investigation of Keith Barent Johnson's firm, which Richard assured us was governmental but would not show up on public records because it was not yet completed.

"How much it weighs." It wasn't a question. It was a judgment. McElone surely believed she had better things to do, and I would have been at a loss to change her mind. "And since the ME's report and the police report are both matters of public record that you could look up online in about six seconds, you're here to bother me because why?"

I was glad Paul had decided to sit this trip out. Normally he adores anything that involves police officers because he thinks he can pick up tips on how to operate by watching the sworn professionals at their jobs. But in this case he was more concerned with "staking out" the house for the person who must have "borrowed" Maxie's laptop with the hope that more information about the shady business dealings might ensue. It was Paul's belief that the thief had surely been in the employ of Keith Johnson's murderer or someone hired by the killer to cover up the crime. Either way, he said, it was worth laying a trap and seeing what happened at the guesthouse.

Toward that end, he had instructed Maxie—and by extension Richard—to be very obvious about moving the laptop around the house. And Melissa, home for the rest of the day, was to ask loud questions about the amazing discoveries they were in the course of making. Then Maxie would lay the laptop down on a flat surface like a table in the den, where the person (Paul didn't say he suspected my guests, but there were few other suspects) who had done the wipe job on the hard drive—his words, not mine—would think it was being left alone. Then they'd wait and see who came to steal the machinery again.

The upshot of all that was that, for the moment, I was on my own in McElone's office, and it was something of a relief. I liked having Paul in on the interviews of suspects because I always felt like he was more competent than me and therefore would keep me from missing the obvious questions I'd otherwise forget. But this felt more natural and easier than having the schoolmaster looking over my shoulder while I worked.

"You're right," I told the lieutenant. "I could have looked up some of this stuff on the Internet. But I know you and I trust you and I'm sure that if there's something in the report that's strange or wrong, you would be much more likely to catch it than me. I'm relying on you for your expertise." I actually meant a lot of that, but McElone did not look especially flattered. She curled her lip on the right side.

"Does that work with other cops?" she asked.

"I never go to other cops with my problems," I told her. "You're the only one I'm not afraid of."

Somehow that didn't make her appreciate me more. In another minute I'd have to remind McElone that I'd saved her life once. Then she'd remind me that she'd saved mine more than once and we'd be right back where we were now, so I skipped it. "What am I doing wrong?" she asked, but she was already working her keyboard to find the files on Richard Harrison's murder.

"Richard was the attorney working on a murder case in Cranbury," I explained. "I think he was killed because he was getting close to proving that the woman charged with the murder didn't do it."

"Lawyers don't investigate the crime," McElone said almost by rote. "They try the case based on the evidence they have. The police and the county investigators do the detective work."

"I understand that, but in this case, whatever evidence there was seemed to be showing that the wrong person was on trial, and I think whoever the right person was found out he was going to expose them and decided to do some quick ironing on his head." When you hang around with a cop, you start to talk like cops. There's a gallows humor that I'm told helps them cope with the misery they see on a regular basis.

"How do you know that?" McElone asked. "How do you know what the lawyer was working on when he died?"

That was a tricky question; it would be somewhat inconvenient to explain that the victim had told me what he'd been doing just before he died because he was the brother of one of my house ghosts come to visit. McElone knows about the ghosts and is, in fact, a little afraid to set foot inside my house. But above all she knows that anything I tell her based on my conversations with ghosts is not going to be admissible in court and is therefore not at all helpful to anything she might ever want to do. So I try to refer to the ghosts as little as possible in her presence.

"He left a very slight trail on his laptop computer," I said, which was at least true-adjacent.

McElone's eyebrow raised a bit. From her this was a sign of intense interest. "And how did you happen to get hold of his laptop?" she asked. "I'd think that would have been confiscated by the county prosecutor as evidence."

"Well, I wouldn't say his *laptop*, exactly," I said. "Files from his laptop. I have access to some of those."

McElone studied me a moment. "I'm probably better off not asking what I want to ask. You said this guy was defending a murder that took place in Cranbury?"

"That's right."

Her face took on what I would assume for McElone was an expression of amusement. "The guy who drowned in the bathtub?" she asked.

I nodded. "Keith Barent Johnson."

McElone bit her lower lip, I think to keep from busting out in a most uncharacteristic chuckle. "The guy who drowned in his bathtub in his clothes," she said.

"I think we've covered this ground."

The lieutenant, to her credit, managed to contain herself and recapture her sense of authority. Her face went back to being impassive. "So your theory is that Harrison was finding things he thought pointed to a suspect other than the one who the cops and the prosecutor charged with the crime."

"It does occasionally happen," I said. "You guys are good, but you're not infallible."

"Don't look at me," McElone warned. "Harbor Haven had nothing to do with that investigation."

"Of course you didn't. I'm just saying, it's not a given that every person ever brought to trial has to be guilty. That's why we have a court system."

"Go on. So Harrison finds evidence to acquit his client. Why doesn't it show up in court? As far as I know, that trial is ongoing."

I stretched my neck a little bit because I was feeling some stress and just let my head fall forward. McElone, apparently not concerned that I might be having some kind of medical seizure, did not comment. When I looked back up at her, she was punching keys and looking at her screen. "The trial is on recess because the second chair for the defense has been murdered," I told her. "And I'm guessing the reason the evidence never made it to court is that *the second chair for the defense has been murdered.*"

Of course, I knew the real reason was that Richard had not actually made the connection from the files he'd examined to an actual suspect he believed was the real killer, unless something really important was going on at my house right at this moment, but I'd guess that Josh, Liss, or Paul would have texted if there was that kind of breakthrough.

"Okay," McElone said, taking out a pair of readers from her top drawer (which was impeccably neat, naturally) and putting them on. She looked at her screen. "From what the ME is saying, the cause of death with Richard Harrison was seven blows to the head with a heavy object, in this case a hand steam iron that was found on the scene when one of the housekeeping personnel down the hall heard a scuffle and looked into the room. She called nine-one-one."

"She didn't see anyone leaving the room?" I asked.

"No, she didn't exactly come running because she didn't think it was that big a deal based on what she heard, according to the initial report from the New Brunswick PD. But the iron was there, and no, there were no fingerprints found on it, and I'm sure they searched very thoroughly." As often happens, McElone had started out acting completely uninterested in the case I brought to her attention, but now her cop curiosity had sprung into action, and she was intent on the document she was reading on her screen.

"So what physical evidence was found at the crime scene?" I asked. I had already activated the voice recorder I carry with me and put it on McElone's bare desk. She had noted it silently.

"Well, there was the body. The ME says the guy was an otherwise healthy specimen in his forties who probably hadn't even turned toward the killer when the first blow was struck." McElone's lips pursed and twitched back and forth. "That means the killer was unusually quiet. Angle of the blows indicates someone not especially tall, right-handed, and not unbelievably strong. It took a few shots to kill him even with the pointy end of the iron."

"How did the killer get into the room?" I asked.

"There was an extra key card found on the bed, no fingerprints on it, in addition to the one the victim had in his pocket. Maybe it was someone the victim knew who was staying in the room with him, a wife or a colleague, someone he gave a card. They talked to his wife, and she said she wasn't there, but then, what would she say? The first chair in the case lives in the area and didn't need a hotel room."

I was getting more questions to ask than I was getting answered. "Was there anything unusual on the iron or in the room?" I asked McElone.

"If by *unusual* you mean hair, bone, and blood, then yeah, those were on the iron. If you mean anything you wouldn't otherwise expect to be in a room where a guy got himself beaten to death with a laundry appliance, not really. His wallet was intact in his jacket pocket. The jacket was hung on the back of the desk chair where he'd apparently been working. Nothing appeared to have been stolen. The laptop was left there and, yes, was taken by the county prosecutor's major crimes division for analysis. It wasn't a pretty sight, as you'd expect. The maid hasn't been back to work since then, and no, she's not a suspect."

"Before she went on leave, did she report whether there was a spare iron missing from her cart?" I asked.

"The question was asked once they found the other iron in the closet," McElone answered. "But no, everything that was supposed to be on her cart and all the other carts was there. Which led to the question, where did the murder weapon come from? And the next day, with the housekeeping staff alerted to make an inventory, it got answered."

"So where did the iron come from?" I asked.

"It was a Sunbeam Classic 1,200-watt iron like all the others in the hotel, which they buy in bulk, as you might expect," McElone said. "And the only one in the facility that was not accounted for should have been in room 407, three floors away from where Richard Harrison's body was found."

This seemed like a simple equation. "And who was registered in that room?" I asked.

"Thomas P. Zink, a pharmaceutical representative from Ames, Iowa," McElone said, reading off her screen. "They couldn't find any reason he might have brained Harrison."

"So did the . . ."

McElone nodded vigorously. "The county investigators got in touch with Mr. Zink back in Ames because he was only here for the one night," she said. "He had no connection to the victim or anyone involved in the trial and had no idea how the iron from his hotel closet might have ended up in Richard Harrison's head. Said he never even realized there was an iron in the closet—or in this case, that there wasn't."

"So do we believe him?" I asked her.

She shrugged. "No reason not to. He's not a professional assassin. There aren't nearly as many of those as the movies would like you to think, and besides, an iron is a rough way to kill a guy. A pro doesn't do that. And he's left Iowa a grand total of three times in the past ten years. Seems like a bad way to make a living."

"So where does that leave us?" I felt like all this had left me with less than I had coming in.

"Leaves me with the same workload I had when you got here," McElone said. "I have no idea where it leaves you."

I thanked her and left. Hopefully Paul had gotten better results at home. In a hopeful mood, I picked up a pizza on the way back to the guesthouse.

Chapter 23

"We haven't found out anything," Paul said.

I hadn't even made it all the way through the door. One foot was still outside in the warmth of the June evening and already I was being hit with the news I didn't want. It was a lot like having CNN on whenever you came home.

Carrying the pizza I'd bought in town—a five-minute drive from here and it was already starting to cool— I assessed the situation in my kitchen: Paul and Richard were floating near the door, which didn't stop my progress but made it weirder. Josh and Melissa were nowhere to be seen, but Gregory Lewis was lurking just outside the swinging kitchen door, visible in his attempts to be inconspicuous. He was calling in from the den, "Alison? I'm sorry; is that Alison?"

It was in fact me, so I ignored Paul and his bleak report to put the pizza down on the island and went to the kitchen door. I opened it gingerly to avoid hitting Mr. Lewis in the face.

"Anything I can help you with, Greg?" I remembered he'd asked me to call him Greg.

"Just a quick question. I don't want to be a pest," Mr. Lewis said. He was trying out for the title of Most Timid Man in the World and wanted to start in my house. That was my best guess.

"You're not at all," I assured him. "Please, come in." It's best to show the guests they *can* come into the kitchen even if I do like to use it as a ghost-safe space. They chose to come to a vacation spot called the Haunted Guesthouse, after all. I felt it was important to own the idea. I gestured to Mr. Lewis to walk into the kitchen, and he followed my lead. "How can I help you?"

"Do you know how to make a mix tape?" Mr. Lewis asked.

"Oh, for the love of—" Richard felt that my business, the one that actually kept food and clothing coming for my daughter (although things had been easier since I'd married a man with a going business), was not as important as my listening to his story of how they hadn't found out anything of significance. I've never had a sibling, so I was starting to wonder what strange bond there was that made Paul tolerate his brother.

"A mix tape? What do you need done exactly, Greg?" Because although I was sure Melissa could no doubt create whatever it was he needed in a matter of minutes, I have some ethical questions about people taking music or other copyrighted material without paying for it—not that that was what he was asking, but I wanted to make sure.

"I wanted to take a recording I have and make a disc that would best showcase it," he said, telling me virtually nothing I needed to know. "Do you know how to do that?"

"I don't, but I'm sure Melissa does," I said. "But I have to make one caveat: I will not reproduce something that violates an artist's copyright. I think those people need to be paid for their work, and so does everyone who helps them create the music we love."

Mr. Lewis tightened his mouth a little and shook his head the smallest amount possible while still creating a visible motion. "Oh, I wouldn't ask you to do anything like that, Alison. I completely agree with you. I just need to copy some recordings I've made myself. Do you think that would be possible? I assure you, it's not infringing on anyone's rights but my own, and I don't really mind." I think that was Mr. Lewis attempting a joke.

"Well, then, I think we can help you, but it will be important to know what format you're using for your recording. I'll tell you what: I'm about to call Melissa in for dinner, and when she comes downstairs, you can give her an idea of what you need. How's that?"

Mr. Lewis seemed quite pleased and not a little relieved. He thanked me and left the kitchen, saying he'd be in his room but that I could text him after I'd spoken to Liss about his audio conversion, whatever that was going to turn out to be.

Once alone—at least technically—in the kitchen, I looked up at the two deceased brothers populating the upper reaches of the room. Paul was hovering in the area of the stove, his favorite for reasons I don't understand, and Richard was at the center of the room, arms folded with frustrated impatience.

"Have you completed your innkeeper duties for the time being?" he asked. Some haughtiness dropped off his lower lip and formed a pool on the floor.

"Unless something else comes up," I countered. "Keep in mind, Richard, that this is my business, and it's going to take priority at all times."

"There has already been one attempt on Cassidy's life, and there will probably be more," Richard said. "There is no time for mix tapes."

I saw no point in continuing this discussion since I was going to act as I saw fit and Richard had remarkably little he could do about it, but I did say, "I spoke to Cassidy briefly this morning, and she said she'd rehired the security firm that had been working with her. You don't have to worry."

"It's not worry," Richard sniffed. "It's concern." Of course it was.

"Let's try to keep our focus on what we can do," Paul interjected. I'd noticed him being just the least bit more assertive about his investigation skills since I'd spoken to him about his relationship with Richard.

"That's what I've been *trying* to do," Richard said, glaring at me.

"Of course," Paul said. Look back; you'll see I did say it was the least bit more assertive. Don't expect miracles.

"You said you didn't learn anything," I reminded him. I decided I would be petty and not talk to Richard until I had to.

"Not about the computer thief," Paul said. "We ran through that whole scenario and made sure we were audible all over the house, but after Maxie put the laptop down on the counter, right there, we stayed and watched. Nothing happened, and we gave it plenty of time."

We all looked at the laptop, which I noted was mine and not Maxie's—she wasn't taking any more chances—like it was going to tell us something. It didn't. But I only gave it a quick glance.

I was busy texting Melissa and Josh that dinner, such as it was, had arrived. In a house the size of mine, going to each person to deliver the news is time consuming and rough on the feet.

"We aren't distracting you, are we?" Richard was in an especially prickly mood. I stuck with my resolution and did not respond.

Instead I looked at Paul. "So you weren't any more successful than I was." I filled him in on my conversation with McElone and gave him the voice recorder so he could listen to it later and determine that what I had encapsulated for him in twenty seconds was indeed true by listening to it for fifteen minutes. Paul's philosophy of time, based on the fact that he's not going anywhere anytime in the next few millennia, is somewhat different from mine.

"It sounds like you did have some success," he said when I was done. "You found out about the iron and about Thomas Zink in Ames, Iowa. I think it might be worth getting in touch with him."

Thomas Zink? He was the person I'd decided was least interesting in this whole story. "You think this Zink guy killed Richard?" I asked.

"I never heard of the man in my life," Richard said. That was verifiably true. But I didn't answer him.

"Nonetheless," Paul said. "I don't believe he was the killer by any means, but the iron that was in his hotel room was the one that killed Richard."

"I'm right here in the room," Richard noted. Apparently he felt he wasn't getting enough attention.

That was going to compound itself because Josh walked through the swinging door and gave me a kiss. "Thanks for picking up dinner," he said and then set about putting out plates and utensils (we'd need the plates; the utensils were just because Josh can't stand not putting them out) for our meal.

Paul was plowing on despite the conspicuous display of domesticity going on directly in front of his eyes. "I don't think Thomas Zink killed Richard, but I doubt parts of his story and think they might be significant to our investigation."

Melissa came in and nodded hello to the two ghosts. She knows Josh is aware of their presence but doesn't like to be obvious about it and make him feel left out. My daughter is a just soul. She went to the cabinet and got cups for the three of us who would be having dinner.

"I'm going to talk to Paul for a bit, Josh," I said. "Sorry about that." I had specifically not said I'd be talking to Richard. Being petty and childish was feeling good.

"No big," said my husband. He just went about his business with the plates, got some paper napkins from the cabinet, and set about putting them out.

I kissed him on the cheek as he went by. "Okay, so that's your opinion, Paul. Why do you think that?"

There's nothing Paul enjoys more than being able to lecture. "There are things a man in town for one night might do in a hotel room that he wouldn't want to have to report to the police," he said. "I don't know for a fact that's what happened with Mr. Zink, but it is curious that his room was chosen for the theft of the iron. It would be helpful to know if he was with anyone the night in question."

"How will we find that out?" I asked as we sat down on the barstools next to the island. Yeah, I could have had an actual kitchen table, but the island is also good for cooking (Mom and Melissa tell me), and the barstools are actually kind of fun.

"We will ask Mr. Zink," Paul answered.

"I'm an attorney, Paul," Richard said, just in case anyone didn't remember. "I can tell you that if someone lied to the police, he is at least as liable to lie to an investigator calling from another state." Thanks for the incredibly obvious point, Richard.

"Perhaps so, but if the argument is offered in a way other than a simple question, we might be able to glean more information than the police. We are, after all, not an organization that can offer incarceration or other punishment for telling a lie."

The pizza was a little cold, but it was too warm tonight to put on the oven, and besides, I was hungry and didn't feel like waiting for my slice to heat up. "What have you got in mind?" I asked Paul.

"We can discuss that later. For now, I'd like to consider the day Keith Johnson was drowned. We have at least two people going into and coming out of his room before Cassidy Van Doren reported finding his body, and not one of them appeared to have been splashed with water, which is what we'd expect under such circumstances. That goes against the laws of physics, or it indicates that someone else was in that room at the Cranbury Bog. That also pertains to the wet blue jeans found outside the room."

I considered bringing up the possibility that the person who had killed Keith Johnson had brought a change of clothes, but even in my head that sounded too stupid to say out loud.

Then Melissa said, "Maybe the killer brought a change of clothes." It made perfect sense when she said it.

Paul stroked his goatee thoughtfully. "That is a very strong possibility, Melissa. I hadn't thought of that."

Go raise children.

Liss put down her slice of pizza and looked thoughtfully at Paul. "About Mr. Zink," she said.

"Yes?" Paul takes Melissa seriously, which I consider a sign of intelligence, and weighs her input in investigations very highly.

"If you think that he was with a prostitute that night, don't you think it would be worthwhile to check with the restaurants and bars around the hotel and see if he was noticed with anyone in particular?" She picked up her piece of pizza and took another bite.

Josh's amused smile was just a little tinged with discomfort. Just a little.

Richard made some noises that were not exactly words. He was an attorney, you know.

Paul, however, was not considering the source, just the suggestion being made. "It's a good thought, Melissa, but I was not assuming Thomas Zink was with a prostitute. A woman who didn't know Richard would have no motive to kill him with a hotel iron, and that part of the plan was clearly premeditated. I think we're more likely to find that one of the suspects we already know in this case—male or female—might have been Mr. Zink's companion for part of that evening."

"It still makes sense to check with the restaurants and bars, though," I chimed in. "Liss is right—and the hotel restaurant and bar are probably the places to start, don't you think, Paul?"

Paul nodded. "I would tend to agree."

"It still seems that the person who . . . did this to me should be less the focus of the investigation than Keith Johnson's killer," Richard insisted. "Cassidy's life is in danger."

Again with this. "I know, but we've explained," I told him before Paul could acquiesce. "The two murders are almost definitely linked. Finding one killer helps us find both, so investigating both murders doubles our chances of succeeding."

I think Paul looked grateful. It's possible I'm projecting.

"What about the research you and Maxie are doing?" Liss asked Richard. "Have you found out anything yet that might tell us who killed Keith Johnson?"

Richard's voice was subdued, which made it sound like a grumble. "We spent so much time with that ridiculous laptop charade that we barely had time to start," he said. "Silly playacting, if you ask me." Nobody had asked him, but that hardly seemed the point at the time.

All our eyes (except Josh's, which were sweetly trained on me, I noted) instinctively looked over at the counter where Maxie had laid the laptop waiting for someone to make an attempt on it.

And of course now it was gone.

Chapter 24

"Well, at least this time it wasn't my laptop," Maxie said.

We'd called for Maxie and Everett as soon as it was discovered my laptop—which might be old, but it's the only one I have—had pulled the same vanishing act hers had not all that long ago. Maxie had responded by immediately looking for her own notebook computer and clutching it to her bosom tightly. That is Maxie.

"That's a huge help, thanks," I said. "You didn't see anybody heading in this direction? And by the way, none of you geniuses thought maybe it would be better to choose a spot for the bait that *wasn't* right near the kitchen door where anybody could have slipped in and taken it?"

"We were watching then," Maxie said. "Location didn't seem to be that big a deal."

"So you saw no one," Paul said in hopes of clarification.

"No, sir." Everett was at full attention. "I had been pulled off guard duty before the incident."

Everett is a lovely man and a dedicated soldier—of sorts—so it's hard to get angry with him, and I didn't. But the thought of having someone I didn't know get access to everything that was on my laptop, complicated by the idea that I might have to lay out a good deal of money to buy a new one—money I was saving to repair my ceiling from a bullet's damage—wasn't making me good company just now. "Who pulled you, Everett?" I asked.

"I'm sorry, ghost lady?" he said.

"Who pulled you from guard duty? Who told you it was no longer necessary to watch the laptop in here?"

"Oh, that would be Maxie," Everett said. I would have been shocked with any other response.

I looked at Maxie. For a while. And she had the perfect Maxie reaction. She said, "What?"

"Nobody was guarding the laptop," I pointed out.

"You were right here in the room," she countered, and dammit, she had a point.

It was a point that seemed to land right between Paul's eyes. Melissa saw it first as his head twitched and his eyes grew wide. "What is it, Paul?" she asked.

"Maxie's right," he said.

"See?" Maxie said, pointing at me. Then she looked at Paul. "About what?"

"We *were* here the whole time. First Richard and I were here and the laptop was on that counter. Then you came home, Alison, and Melissa and Josh all came into the kitchen. There was no point at which that computer was left alone, and yet it is gone."

"It won't be for long," I predicted. "There's nothing on that laptop our thief is going to find interesting. I'll bet it's back before we finish dessert." I looked at Melissa. "Do we have dessert?"

"Ice cream in the freezer."

"You are losing the topic," Richard said. "The laptop was here the whole time and still it has gone missing." That only succeeded in reiterating Paul's last statement, but I guess the idea was to bring us back to discussing the stuff Richard cared about and not ice cream, which I cared about.

I decided to throw the ball back to Paul. "So what are you getting at?"

"Alison, ask Josh if he noticed when the laptop went missing. He is facing in that direction."

That seemed an odd request, but I've gotten pretty used to such things, and the word *odd* barely even registers in my house anymore. It's odd if something *isn't* odd. If you know what I mean. I looked over at Josh. "You didn't happen to be looking over there when someone took the laptop, did you?" I asked.

Josh was putting his plate into the sink because we only use the dishwasher when we have guests for dinner or Melissa cooks. Well, let's face it: we always have guests for dinner when Melissa cooks. My husband turned his head to look at me. "Yeah," he said. "I saw it vanish like that." He snapped his fingers.

Okay, I didn't see that coming. "You did?" It's not that I doubted Josh, you understand. It's that I really hadn't considered that he would see my laptop disappear and not even mention it. "Why didn't you say anything?"

Josh shrugged. "I'm sort of used to stuff like that," he said.

"Exactly," Paul added, nodding his head. "Josh is used to seeing strange occurrences in this house. He didn't know it wasn't one of us."

I looked back and forth between my ghost friend, who obviously had some point he was trying to make, and my husband, who was clearing dishes and getting ready to wash them. Always marry a man who's used to living by himself. He's broken in on having to do things. What Paul was saying just slowly dawned on me, but as usual Melissa was a couple of blocks ahead looking behind to see if I was going to catch up.

"I get it," she told Paul. "Nobody, none of the guests or anybody, could have come in here and taken the laptop. It was on a counter up against a wall, not near the door. They'd have been seen not just by Josh, but by anybody who was here, just like you guys planned."

"Exactly," Paul said. "And yet, even with both living people like you and people like Richard and me in the room, the computer managed to vanish right before our eyes."

"Is it possible?" I was catching on at the remedial rate. "Wouldn't Liss or I or any of you . . . let's face it, anybody but Josh . . . have seen someone come in?"

"Thanks, honey," my husband said, probably not even knowing why. He had his usual amused expression on.

"Melissa is right," Paul said. "The laptop was on a counter next to a wall. It's entirely possible someone could have reached through the wall, secreted it inside a coat or a sweat shirt, and gotten back out without being noticed."

"A ghost stole my laptop," I said.

Josh looked up from the sink. "Stole?" he said.

Chapter 25

We moved the discussion out of the kitchen because the barstools, although very enjoyable, aren't comfortable for long periods of sitting. I suggested we move to the den where there are plenty of soft chairs and sofas on which to sit. There were no guests around at the moment. It was a lovely June evening, the sun had not yet completely set, and we were on the Jersey Shore. There was no reason for them to hang around my house.

Except that Mr. Lewis did come in as soon as we adjourned to the larger room and asked if he could talk to Melissa. She, having been briefed, hustled him to a far corner of the room where our discussion about the stolen laptop would not be quite so audible.

"So since we can be sure the laptop wasn't stolen by you, Richard, Maxie, or Everett, there has to be another ghost somewhere around the house," I said to Paul. "How come we haven't seen him—or her—yet?"

Paul didn't look very thoughtful. He clearly thought the answer to that one was obvious. "I think we can assume this particular spirit has some interest in staying hidden," he said. "Whoever it is has gone to great pains in that area and has been very successful so far. What we have to determine is exactly what the ghost's motivation might be for taking data off first Maxie's laptop and now yours, presumably on Keith Johnson's business dealings."

"And why he doesn't want to be seen," Richard added.

Melissa walked back toward us as Mr. Lewis left the den nodding his head. "He doesn't want to be seen because he's stealing stuff from our house," she pointed out. She had the good taste and manners not to add, "Duh."

"Granted," I said. "But how is it possible we haven't seen this ghost? Most of us here have no problem seeing people like you, Paul. Why is this one different?"

"He's taking steps to conceal himself, as Melissa said," Paul suggested. "But if he's staying close to the house, and I believe that to be the case, we should search the property again. I think it will not take long to find this person." Paul very rarely uses the word *ghost* to describe people like Maxie and him. I don't know if he considers it demeaning or if he simply doesn't think of himself in those terms.

"Another search?" I, well, whined. "I don't see the point. We searched the house from top to bottom the last time and came up with nothing. If this ghost really is taking pains to avoid us seeing him—or her—there's no reason to think we'll have better luck this time." I, you have no doubt noticed, have no problem using the word *ghost* at all. If something's a table, you call it a table, don't you? Should Paul ever ask me not to say it, I'll be happy to accede to his wishes. But until he does, he and Maxie are ghosts. Period.

"I would be forced to agree," Richard added. Once he said that, I had to wonder if I'd been wrong to put forth my idea. If Richard agreed with it, I suddenly wasn't so sure that I did. "What's the differing factor this time?"

"This time we will be searching the property around the house as well," Paul said, as if that actually made some difference. "I can't imagine this person would go far before checking to see the information we said was installed on the laptop. When it is found not to be there, I would predict your computer will be brought back, Alison."

Well, that was sort of good news, I supposed. "But, Paul . . ." I started to say.

He cut me off. "I know what I'm doing, Alison. We'll split up. Melissa will take the upper floors, starting with the attic. Maxie, Everett, and I will go outside because we can move more quickly than you can and therefore cover more ground. You take the lower floors, starting with the basement." He pointed to the front closet door.

"Paul, that's not—"

"Please don't argue. The person we are seeking has your laptop and will quickly discover it is not the one he sought despite our having made bogus claims about its contents. We can't assume he will be as easily misled this time. So we are going to leave Maxie's laptop right here on the coffee table as bait."

This plan was getting crazier by the second. Predictably, Maxie was fighting mad—even more than usual—as soon as Paul said that. She zipped back down and stared at Paul. "Are you *nuts*?" she demanded. "He got my laptop once, and we were lucky to get it back! Now you want to leave it here with nobody watching?" No doubt whole seasons of *Grey's Anatomy* were flashing before her eyes.

"Don't worry," Paul assured her. "We'll see to it that Josh is here to guard over the computer."

Maxie's eyes widened to the size of baseballs. "The *husband*?" she yelled. "He can't see anybody! How's he going to keep my laptop safe?"

"He can see movement. We just want to be sure that your computer, the one with the real information on it, remains in our possession. I assure you we are taking every possible precaution. And our search will no doubt turn up this person before there is any attempt made on your computer. Trust me, Maxie." Paul was already herding Richard toward the back door. "Go ahead into the basement, Alison." He pointed again at the front closet door.

"Paul," I began.

"You have to trust me too. I believe the basement is an excellent starting point." Another gesture toward the front closet door, and this time I understood.

"Got it," Melissa said. She had no doubt picked up this subtle little subterfuge long before I had. The girl's a genius. Ask my mother. Liss started toward the stairs to the upper floors. She was walking slowly.

I relayed Paul's instructions to Josh, and although he looked puzzled at being selected for this particular duty, my husband asked no questions and offered no arguments. Where had he been before I married the first time? (Actually, I know where and it's a long story.) He promised to stay on guard and watch for any strange movements in the room, especially toward the coffee table.

Paul and Richard exited through the back wall. Maxie, grumbling loudly about the injustice of it all, nonetheless followed instructions and left her laptop—which I noticed she stroked affectionately one last time—on the coffee table in front of my husband. "Make sure he's watching," she said to me and then exited out toward the front room.

I saw Everett, who had not been involved in the conference, through the gap between the kitchen door and the jamb. He was still at full attention, no doubt distraught that he'd given up his guard post and let the laptop be taken. He would not move until dismissed. I walked over to the door and pushed it open. I saluted Everett. He nodded gratefully, relaxed, and silently followed Maxie toward the front room, from which they would probably scout the front yard up to the property line.

Then after kissing my husband for being himself, I walked directly into my front closet and stood there with the door slightly ajar. Because that's what one does.

It didn't take long. Josh was clearly intent on his task. I could see him from behind, leaning forward on the sofa, his head barely moving as he concentrated on the laptop in front of him. I understood that he was confused about his role, seemingly the least qualified person for the task at hand. But he was determined to do it well.

He leaned his elbows on the table, no doubt horrifying my mother long distance, and placed his hands on either side of the laptop in a clear attempt to be ready should there be any movement.

I could see from my closeted vantage point that there would be no immediate need for Josh to grab at the computer. There wasn't any ghost in the area that I could—

Wait a second! Coming straight up through the basement—which I noted was where I was supposed to be—was a spirit I had not seen before. It was a man, but he was difficult to make out because he was being so stealthy in his move upward. At first I saw only the top of his head, which was very close to being totally bald. He rose millimeter by millimeter, and it took almost a full minute before his eyes were visible. He stopped moving at that point certainly because he was scoping out the room. He looked in every possible direction except directly at the front closet, which was lucky for me.

I held my breath. The last thing I wanted right now was to alert Josh to the presence of the ghost (or, as far as I could see, the top third of the ghost's head), and I was too far away to do anything myself. To be honest, I wouldn't have been able to grab this guy or stop him in any way even if I were a foot from his head, which was about six feet from the coffee table where Josh was wiggling his fingers in anticipation.

The ghost's eyes did a last quick survey of the room, and then his entire demeanor changed. Instead of moving at an excruciatingly slow pace, he sprang up from the floor and launched himself directly at Maxie's precious laptop, right between my husband's considerably more precious hands.

The only thing I had going for me, largely because Paul had left me without any instructions at all, was the element of surprise. I shoved the closet door open and jumped out into the room, yelling, "Hold it, buddy!"

Josh, excellent man that he is, dived onto Maxie's laptop without hesitation and clutched it to his chest.

My problem was that I had no way to hold this intruder at bay. If he decided to evaporate, he could do so, and there was a grand total of nothing I could possibly do about it. I yelled, "Paul!"

He was there before the echo died away, and there wasn't much echo in the den. Luckily the new ghost, whoever he was, seemed stunned by the sudden turn of events and did not make a move to escape. By the time he probably thought of it, he was surrounded.

Paul, Maxie, Everett, and Richard had formed a circle around the new ghost even as Josh turned to look at me and say, "Did we get him?" I didn't know so I didn't answer.

Melissa appeared at the entrance to the den and watched. She knew she couldn't affect the action in the room either.

I actually found myself wishing my mother was there. Mom has a way of talking people into thinking things are their own idea, and it occurred to me that might be a useful skill in the next few minutes.

But Mom and Dad weren't coming over until tomorrow.

"Don't try to run," Paul said to the intruder. "We can hold you if we all try, but we don't want to do that. We only want to talk."

The new ghost turned out to be a man in his sixties or early seventies, dressed casually but well. I would bet that if he had fingernails, they were polished. He wore eyeglasses. I'd seen ghosts wear glasses before, but I wondered whether they were actually serving a purpose or were just for fashion reasons. That wasn't the first question I needed answered now, so I let Paul do the work.

"I have nothing to tell you," the ghost said.

"How about telling me where my laptop is?" I said. A person gets to set her own priorities.

"Who are you?" Paul asked.

"I have nothing to tell you," he repeated.

But Richard stepped forward and took a closer look at the intruder. "I know you," he said.

The ghost looked like he would be sweating if he could. "No, you don't," he said.

"Yes. From the photographs in the case file. I know you. You're Keith Barent Johnson."

The ghost looked at the floor, and if Paul's hands hadn't been on his arms, I think that's the escape route he would have used. "Yes," he said. "I am."

"Have you been stretching something in one of the upstairs bedrooms?" Melissa asked.

"Did you stick a note to my wall with a knife?" I asked.

They were both good questions.

Chapter 26

There was a lot of talking over each other for the next few minutes. The snatches I was able to decipher and recall included the following:

Paul: Keith Johnson!

Richard: Yes, I'm quite sure.

Johnson: I said that's who I was.

Maxie: My laptop! (She snatched it from Josh, who looked at me. I nodded that it was okay.)

Melissa: Okay, everybody quiet down. (Nobody did.)

Paul: Why are you trying to steal files that can help us discover who murdered you?

Everett (to Maxie): You owe Josh some thanks.

Maxie: He can't hear me.

Josh (to me): I think someone just passed through me. Sort of a cool breeze.

Me: That's Maxie.

Maxie: Oh.

Melissa: Everybody quiet down! (I was listening but doubted anyone else heard her. Except Josh.)

Penny Desmond (who had wandered in during the brouhaha she couldn't see or hear): Alison, dear, is there a good ice cream place in town you can recommend?

Me: Stud Muffin actually has good ice cream, Penny, but there's a soft custard stand about five miles away if you have a car.

Penny: Oh, that won't be necessary. Thank you, dear. (Penny left.)

Johnson: You can't make me say anything.

Paul: Why wouldn't you want—?

Melissa: *Quiet!* (This time everyone heard, stopped talking, and looked at her.)

She accepted the respect as her due (which she should) and lowered her voice to a more socially acceptable level. I appreciated that in case there were any other guests wandering about the house who might have heard the screaming and assumed someone was being attacked. No one showed up at the entrance to the den, which led me to wonder if I should be relieved or insulted.

"Now," Melissa said, "let's all figure out what we want to do right now. Richard is only thinking about clearing Cassidy Van Doren's name. Paul, you're trying to find out from Mr. Johnson why he might have been trying to erase some files from Maxie's computer that have to do with his murder. Maxie is just concerned about keeping her laptop safe, which is understandable. Josh is trying to keep Mom safe but doesn't know who's here or where anybody is except me and Mom. Everett is worried about Maxie but also wants to make sure he stands guard over the laptop and any other evidence. And Mom is most worried about me because that's what she always worries about."

She turned toward the new ghost in the room. "So that leaves you, Mr. Johnson. What's your concern here? Why did you come and take Maxie's laptop and then my mom's? Are you embarrassed about something we might find in your files?"

Johnson, caught up in the scene, had been watching like a spectator and seemed a bit startled when Melissa addressed him directly. He blinked twice, thinking about her question. "Embarrassed?" he said. "No. I'm not embarrassed by anything I left behind. I don't know why all you people are making such a fuss. You've been upsetting my family, so I came here to tell you to stop. It's clear what happened. I've gotten over it. Why haven't you?"

"Why haven't—?" Richard sputtered. Richard was an expert sputterer. It was almost an art form in his . . . mouth. It was a shame I couldn't draw attention to his art because I'm sure Josh would have found Richard's sputtering quite amusing. There are some things that we can't share even with our dearest ones.

Paul spoke over his brother. "It is not in the least bit clear what happened, Mr. Johnson," he said. "But since you are now here with us, we have the opportunity to get answers for every question we've had, so we're very glad to see you indeed."

It was an effective shift in Paul's tone, and at least in the short term, Johnson seemed to accept it and ignore the antagonism he'd been showing just a minute earlier. He looked at Paul, and his eyes didn't exactly show empathy, but perhaps a touch of understanding.

"I can tell you exactly what happened that afternoon," he said in a quieter tone. "I checked into the Cranbury Bog and went directly to my room. Hunter came in to talk but only for a minute. We had a rule about not discussing business, so he was asking about a place to go to dinner that night. We usually went to a restaurant nearby, but it had closed since our previous visit. I said I'd look up some possibilities and ask Robin about it later. So Hunter left.

"After that I unpacked my things. I don't like to live out of a suitcase, and I hadn't brought much because we were going to stay for only two days. I put pretty much everything I had either in the bathroom or in one drawer in my room's dresser. Then I got a call on my cell phone that Cassidy was coming up. I didn't want to see her and told her so."

I noticed that the visit by Erika Johnson was not included in her father's narrative. Paul's eyebrow twitched, which indicated he'd caught that as well. But he didn't want to contradict Johnson now that he was talking, so he let the ghost speak.

"Cassidy hung up on me and then appeared in my door-way only ten minutes later," Johnson continued. "We immediately began arguing. She had upset Adrian, my wife and her mother, only the day before, forcing her to visit her father's grave. I knew Adrian did not want to go; she considered her first husband a piece of her past she'd just as soon forget. But Cassidy had insisted, and Adrian had been agitated the rest of the day."

"Why didn't you bring your wife with you if she was so upset?" Melissa asked. "Why not just take her along on your vacation so she could feel better?"

"Hunter and I had agreed never to take our wives along on these trips," Johnson told her, his tone slightly colder than

I would have preferred. You watch the way you talk to my daughter. "Some rules just can't be broken." He didn't add "little girl," or I would have called my father to come and beat him up.

"What happened when you and Cassidy started to argue?" Paul said, bringing the conversation back to where I was sure he wanted it to be.

"She became violent," he said, looking away from Paul and not making eye contact with anyone else in the room. That was quite a feat because there was a living person or a ghost in pretty much any other sight line. "She slapped me and said I had been poisoning her mother's mind against her. I didn't raise a finger to that girl, and she slapped me." He sounded like he was asking for sympathy but did not attempt to elicit a reaction directly from anyone. He kept his eyes on a point on the wall where no being of any kind was in view. "And she tried to blackmail me."

Well, that set off an explosion in the room. "Blackmail?" Paul said. He thought for a moment. "Did she know something about the pyramid scheme you were trying to perpetrate?" It was a calculated risk.

Johnson didn't go for it; he was a practiced liar, but not an artful one. "I don't know what you're talking about," he said.

"Yes you do," Richard told him. "I saw the files that were missing from your hard drive, and I saw them before they were deleted. Some law enforcement agency is investigating your business and probably finding out things you didn't want them to know when you were alive."

"I don't know anything about that." Johnson stared at the floor. "All I know is that little ingrate was trying to get me to transfer money into her trust account."

"What did you do?" Paul asked in an attempt to go with Johnson's narrative and move the conversation forward. He tried to move into Johnson's sight, but the new ghost continued to look down at the floor. It would have looked remarkably weird for Paul to have dropped down that low just to make eye contact.

"I asked her to leave, naturally," Johnson said. "And I do not remember anything after that."

Paul didn't stroke his goatee, but he held his hand over it. "I think you do," he said softly.

Now Johnson raised his head and looked at Paul in disbelief. "I beg your pardon?"

Paul leaned into the stare. "I don't think you've forgotten at all," he said. "I think you've been like this for long enough now that you remember everything that happened that night, but you don't want to explain it. I think your animosity toward your stepdaughter is so acute that you'd rather have her convicted of killing you than name the person who actually ended your life. That is what I think. Would you like to know why?"

Johnson continued to stare, his mouth slightly open. He did not answer.

But Paul was on a roll. "Because Cassidy Van Doren was seen by numerous rescue and police personnel at the scene of your death, and she was wet only up to her elbows. She had tried to pull you out of that bathtub, not hold you down in it. I think you're lying because you didn't mention that your daughter Erika had come to visit you in the Cranbury Bog and left before Cassidy arrived. And surely Erika knew at that point that you had already been siphoning money into Cassidy's account, money that Erika and her brother, Braden, no doubt believed was rightfully theirs. Your will is still in probate, Mr. Johnson. I'm wondering how that situation will resolve itself. So, yes, I think you're lying. Would you care to explain why?"

"Don't be ridiculous," Johnson said, but his voice was less than persuasive. "Erika didn't drown me in that bathtub."

"Then who did?"

Johnson's eyes got cold as he assessed Paul. "Do you remember the exact moment you died?" he asked. "That split second when you went from being a breathing human being and became what you are now? I remember fear. I remember being held down, the arms from above the water that wouldn't let me up. The exact moment? I have no recollection at all."

Richard stepped forward like the attorney he would constantly remind us he was and put his hands in the pockets of his dress pants. The man had eternity to hang around, and he was wearing a suit. It's telling, don't you think?

"I've only been in this state for a little over a week," he said, his voice a low murmur that would no doubt build to a crescendo. "But I remember the moments before I was killed. If I had turned my head just a little, I would be able to tell you who was standing behind me with a deadly instrument. So please, don't try to intimidate my brother with your questions about his death. He has processed the event. And that means he knows that even if you don't remember the exact moment you moved into this state of existence, you certainly do recall the minutes leading up to that, when you were confronted by your killer and held under water. So please, just tell us who it was that murdered you, because that might lead to some information about who murdered me."

"I still want to know about the knife in my wall. Spackle doesn't grow on trees," I said. They ignored that. And I was *pretty* sure Spackle didn't grow on trees.

Keith Barent Johnson looked Richard straight in the eye with a resentment I had rarely seen in my life. "Cassidy killed me," he growled.

"No, she didn't." Richard countered.

Johnson regarded him for a long moment, and then he just simply wasn't there anymore. There is no defense for that; the ghosts do it rarely, but it's extremely effective. They vanish and there is no trace of them afterward.

We all just stood there for a long time. Nobody moved much, nobody spoke. There was a considerable amount of looking around and making very small noises that indicated frustration. Maxie didn't even leave the room, and I was expecting that first.

Josh looked up from the sofa and caught my eye. "So how is the interrogation going?" he asked.

Chapter 27

"I spent that whole night in the room alone." Thomas Zink was a very standard-issue-looking man, and he was sitting in a café of some sort, from the look of the place on Maxie's laptop screen.

We were video conferencing with Tom, as he insisted I call him, because he was back in Iowa and driving out to him was completely out of the question. Sitting in my backyard at a picnic table I leave out during the warm weather, I was enjoying the last school day of the year and the last full day I would have these five guests in my house—if by *enjoying* you mean sitting around watching a man on a computer screen explain how he hadn't decided to take a strange woman back to his hotel room while on a sales trip to New Brunswick, New Jersey.

"I went to this microbrewery a couple of blocks from the hotel, and I had a burger and a beer sampler," he said. "I sat at the bar because a guy by himself at a table is pathetic. I didn't talk to anyone but the bartender the whole night. I watched a Mets game on TV, and I don't even like the Mets."

"How was the burger?" I asked.

"Actually, very good. But I don't think I can tell you anything else that can help you, Ms. Kerby. I'm sorry."

"He's trying too hard to get you off the phone," Paul warned me. With this much sunlight outdoors, he was even harder than usual to see, but I could hear him just fine. "He's hiding something, all right."

After the confrontation the night before with Keith Johnson, which you'd have thought would clarify matters, we were even more in the dark than ever about Johnson's murder and by extension Richard's. *Everybody* seemed to be hiding something. The trick was going to be figuring out what and why. That had led us to our only current lead: Tom Zink. Although Richard was back upstairs analyzing the data to trace Johnson's pyramid scheme.

"Well, maybe you can, Tom," I said to the screen. Talking to a screen is weird, but it's better than hopping on a flight to Des Moines and driving for another hour to get to Ames. I was adjusting to life in the current century, although Melissa would certainly have told me I was at least seven years behind the curve. "Sometimes it's the things you don't know you remember that make the most difference." I like to make general investigator-y pronouncements to make the other person believe I actually know what I'm doing.

"The things I don't know I remember?" Tom didn't believe I was as effective as I did.

"Sure." I glanced over at Paul, who at least didn't have the same totally perplexed expression on his face that Tom Zink did. He wasn't going to be much help now that I'd started this silly gambit. "I'm not talking about hypnotism or anything. I just want you to walk me through that evening and tell me as much as you can remember about what you did."

Tom opened and closed his mouth, apparently censoring himself from what he really wanted to say. "I told you. I went to this microbrewery, had a burger and a sampler of their beers. Then I walked back to the hotel, went up to my room, watched some TV and went to sleep. That's all there was to it. It wasn't until the next day when the detective came in to ask me about the iron that I even knew anything had happened. I didn't even know there was an iron in the closet at all."

"Okay, the microbrewery. Do you remember the name?" I knew perfectly well there was such a business called Harvest Moon on George Street, a short walk from the hotel in which Richard Harrison had been murdered.

"I honestly don't. It had a big yellow sign out front." That meshed with the pictures I'd seen of the George Street place online.

"Was it called Harvest Moon?" I asked. You can jog someone's memory, whether he's lying or not, with a few unimportant details sometimes. Paul taught me that.

"Yeah, that sounds right." Tom wasn't terribly forceful about the statement, but it wasn't something he especially cared to dispute.

"And you didn't talk to anybody there except the bartender?" I asked. I would have put this month's mortgage payment down that he had, but I needed to get Tom to that revelation.

"No. He gave me the beers and the food. I didn't even talk to a waitress."

"Perhaps it's time to be a little more direct," Paul said.

I had been planning to do just that. Tom was feeling too comfortable about my questioning. No doubt Richard would say there was no chance I'd get my client off with wimpy questions like the one's I'd been asking. So I moved a little closer to the screen.

"If I told you that Harvest Moon has security cameras pointed at its bar and its tables, would you still insist you didn't talk to anyone the whole time you were there?" I had no idea at all whether such cameras existed, but then I wasn't really telling Tom they did so much as mentioning them as hypothetical devices. I sleep just fine at night, thanks.

The question did seem to make an impact on Tom Zink. He looked from side to side as if trying to determine if anyone could hear what was being said. Since he was wearing head-phones, it was a pretty safe bet no one besides Tom could hear what *I* was saying. His own reply would be a different story. I was hoping it would be the true one.

"Look, I was at the bar alone and had no intention of talk-ing to anybody," he said. I thought there would be more, but he stopped at that point and looked at me.

"We don't always do what we intend," I said at Paul's prompting. Paul is so much more polite than I am. It's the Canadian upbringing, I think.

Tom looked around again. The café he was sitting in, from my limited vantage point, did not seem particularly crowded. I think this was just a gesture Tom had seen guilty people do in the movies. It worked brilliantly; he looked quite guilty.

"I'm just saying, it wasn't my idea," he insisted. I didn't care what was his idea; I cared what had happened, but I suppressed the urge to tell him that specifically. I took a sip of the lemonade I'd brought outside with me and tried very hard to determine whether the figure a little to my right was Paul, Richard, or an especially large sea gull. I decided it was Paul. Richard had gone back to work with Maxie, and the sea gull idea just didn't help me at all so I discarded it. "I wasn't looking for anything to happen."

"But something did," I suggested. Maybe I could speed this process along. A nice lemonade on a lovely June afternoon was fine, but my daughter would be home in six hours and would stay for two months. I had stuff to do.

Tom's voice dropped to a whisper, and I had to lean in to hear it because I had not been intelligent enough to bring headphones like he had. I asked him to repeat himself.

"Yes," he now emphasized a little too hard. "I don't care if you're recording this. I had to come clean. Keeping a secret even for just a couple of weeks has been killing me."

Wow. Paul was always talking about the power of the right question, and I seemed to have hit on one without half trying. Maybe I really *should* try being an investigator for money sometime.

"What happened?" I asked in as respectful a tone as I could muster.

"I was sitting at the bar waiting for my dinner to show up and trying the dark amber beer, the third one from the left in the sampler," he began. That he remembered, yet the name of the restaurant had escaped him. "I wasn't even looking around the room. Some guys do that, you know, but I don't."

What some guys did or didn't do was not something I wanted to discuss just now. "Okay, so you're a good guy. What happened?"

"Well, this woman walks over to where I was sitting and takes the barstool next to me," he said. "The first thing that sprung to mind was, did I leave my wallet in my jacket pocket? Easiest place to be stolen from."

I thought it was an interesting way to go through life, thinking like that, and I'm from New Jersey. But I said, "She didn't steal your wallet, did she?"

Tom shook his head. "She didn't steal anything, as far as I knew. Except I guess she ended up stealing that iron." Bingo. Now we could place the mysterious woman in Tom's hotel room.

Paul advised me not to leap directly on that information but to build toward it. "Did she tell you her name?" I asked. If it was Erika Johnson, this would be easy.

It wasn't easy. "She said her name was Ashley. I didn't get a last name."

I knew better than to ask if Tom had taken any photographs of his one-night "friend" from the microbrewery. "What did she look like?" I said.

He looked down. At first I thought it was out of embarrassment, but then I realized he was just trying to remember. "She had blonde hair, but I'm pretty sure it was a wig," he answered after a moment. "She had big brown eyes. She was pretty, but she didn't hit you over the head with it. If she hadn't come over to me in the bar, I might not have noticed her at all." Tom seemed to realize what he was saying and looked around the café again. As far as I could tell, nobody was looking at him in shock.

The description he gave us hadn't really rung any particular bells. "None of the women involved in this case are blonde," Paul said. "But any one of them could have been wearing a blonde hairpiece of some kind to better disguise herself."

I thought but did not say that I didn't remember any blue-eyed women we'd spoken to, so anyone could be a suspect. It was possible Robin Witherspoon's eyes were blue. Somehow I found it difficult to believe she'd killed Keith Johnson in the bathtub in her own bed-and-breakfast. But stranger things have happened, and I've been there for most of them.

We had to move the narrative along. "How did the meeting at the restaurant turn into a . . . meeting in your hotel room?" I asked Tom.

He sat up a little straighter, not enough to move the top of his head off my computer screen, but enough that I could see he was wearing a dress shirt with no tie and an American flag pin on the lapel of his blazer. I wondered if Tom was running for office in Ames. "I want to be clear about this," he said forcefully. "*Nothing* happened when we got to my hotel room."

I had as much interest in Tom's marriage as my ex-husband had in ours, but it was a source of leverage over him, and I needed that right at the moment. "We'll get to that in a minute," I said. "What I'm asking now is how you ended up there."

The skin around Tom's lips tightened a little. He didn't want to talk about this. I couldn't say as I blamed him. But it's very difficult not to answer a question when it's been posed to you. "We stayed at the bar and had a couple more drinks," he said. "We didn't stay nearly long enough for the bar to close, but it was getting expensive, and I don't like drinking that much. So I said I was going back to the hotel. And Ashley said she would come with me. It just seemed natural to continue the conversation. I guess I'd had more to drink than I thought, because it never occurred to me that was unusual, but it had never happened to me before."

I could believe that. "So once you got back to the hotel, what happened?" I asked.

"*Nothing.*"

"Yeah, I get that, but what actually happened?"

"Oh. Well, I thought we'd just part at the entrance to the hotel, but Ashley came right in with me. Then I figured she'd take off when we got to the elevators, because I told her I was going up to my room and didn't want another drink. She just nodded like that was the most natural thing in the world and followed me into the elevator."

Paul was suddenly behind me, paying more attention to the screen than he had before. He clearly wanted to see if there were any signs that Tom Zink was lying, and he'd know better than I would.

"What did you think when she followed you to your room?" I said.

"I was thinking I'd better figure out a way to get rid of her or I'd get in trouble with my wife," Tom answered. "I mean, this was exactly the last way I would have expected the evening to end up. We got back to the room, and I said it had been nice meeting her but I was going to go to bed now. And Ashley said great and asked if she come in for a minute. I just didn't know how to tell her no without being rude."

"So rather than be seen as impolite, you let this woman you'd just met into your hotel room," I said.

"Pretty much." He looked embarrassed. I understood that.

"Once she was inside?" It was like pulling teeth with this guy to find out what happened when an attractive woman insisted on being let into his hotel room. I've known men who would tell you this story if you passed them in the street.

"She asked to use the bathroom, and that's when I was worried, you know? You always see those things in the movies where the woman says she wants to freshen up and comes out looking like she wants something else, if you know what I mean." For the record, I knew what he meant. "I walked over to the desk and turned on my computer so she'd think I was going to be working before I went to sleep. I checked a couple of e-mails, but I wasn't paying much attention to them, and then Ashley came out, thanked me, and left. She didn't even shake my hand. Just like that, a different woman once she opened that bathroom door."

"And that must have been when she stole the iron," I said.

Tom shrugged. "I guess. It was in the closet in the hallway outside the bathroom, they said, but maybe I wasn't looking when she took it. All I know is the next morning at six, the police were banging on my door asking about the iron." I knew he was going to tell me again that he hadn't even known there was an iron in the closet, but there was just no way to stop him. "I didn't even know there was an iron in the closet."

Paul suggested I send Tom photographs of Cassidy, Erika, Miriam Harrison (you never know, but she didn't strike me as the bombshell type), Adrian Johnson, and just for good measure, Robin Witherspoon to see if he recognized any of them as "Ashley." He said he would take a look but asked that I send

them quickly because he didn't want his wife to see him looking at pictures of women, one of whom might have come up to
his hotel room and . . . stolen an iron.

We disconnected the call, and I asked Paul to find Maxie
because I am a computer idiot and Maxie could put together
the pictures we needed quickly. He flew off in his search, and
for a glorious moment, I was left alone in my backyard on a
wonderful spring day.

It didn't last. I couldn't even complain because it was Abby
Lesniak who came by, and I actually ask for guests to come
to my house. You can't argue with the customers. I breathed
in deeply when I saw Abby walking from the direction of the
beach because she had asked me for a favor and I had failed
her out of my own sense of social awkwardness. I didn't want
to be Betty asking Jughead if Archie really liked Veronica. Or
something like that.

Abby didn't look especially displeased, but she trudged
up the dune a little and stopped at my table, which had a nice
umbrella in it to block the sun when you wanted that. At the
moment, I was perfectly fine with the sun. But I wasn't sure how
Abby felt about me.

Before she could speak, I held up a hand. "I know, Abby. I
know. I haven't spoken to Mr. Lewis yet, and that's my fault.
I'm sorry if I haven't done everything I could to make your
vacation all it could be. It was just a very difficult thing for me
to do, and frankly, I kept putting it off because I wasn't sure
how to go about doing it. I can't apologize enough."

Abby's eyebrows knit a little. She pointed at the chair next
to me. "May I?" she asked.

I nodded and Abby sat down.

"Alison," she said, "I was being unfair when I asked you to talk to Mr. Lewis for me. That's not something you should have to do as a host. I was just as uncomfortable as you—more—to think about it, and I figured I could just get someone else to do it. I thought you wouldn't have a stake in it so it would be easy for you. But if there was ever going to be anything between Mr. Lewis and me, it was either going to happen or it wasn't, and as it turned out, it didn't happen. That's because I didn't say anything myself. I'm sorry I put you in that position."

"No, no." I was going to prove to Abby that I was the jerk here no matter what. "You asked me as the host of your vacation to do something to make it more enjoyable, and I didn't do that. I failed you and I'm sorry."

Abby laughed. "Do you realize we're just trying to convince each other that it was our own fault?" she said. "It doesn't matter. I'll tell you what: I'll forgive you if you forgive me. How's that?"

We agreed on that plan and shook hands, and Abby went back into the house to shower off the sand. The beach is lovely in June, but the ocean is still really cold. A warm shower was probably going to feel good.

I didn't even get the moment of solitude this time because Paul and Maxie were floating down to the table before Abby made it all the way to the French doors. Maxie was carrying her own laptop, which had not left her possession since the night before.

She didn't even take a breath because, let's face it, she didn't need one. "I sent that guy the pictures of everybody we think might have killed Richard," she said. Maxie isn't one for niceties. "I even sent him separate pictures of them with blonde wigs put on their heads so he could have a better look."

"What did Tom say?" I asked.

"He e-mailed you," Paul said. "Take a look."

It takes a while for my Stone Age laptop to do pretty much anything, so we waited around while I checked for new e-mails. Sure enough, there was one from Tom Zink.

I can't be sure. I only saw her for a little while and I was drinking. But none of these women look like the one I saw that night. The closest is the one in the middle, but even she probably isn't the one I'm thinking of.

"Which picture did you put in the middle?" I asked Maxie.

"I did it in a star pattern, with two on top and two on the bottom, one in the center between the two rows," she answered. "Did that with the wig pictures too, in the same order."

"I'm not asking for your process," I said. "Which picture was in the middle?"

Maxie looked to Paul. She doesn't remember names when she actually cares who people are.

"Erika Johnson," Paul said.

Chapter 28

"Tom wasn't sure," I argued.

My mother and father had shown up for dinner just about an hour after Melissa, literally dancing with glee, had arrived home from her last day of school for the year. Paul and I (with some kibitzing from Maxie) had gotten everyone up to speed. Paul was uncharacteristically eager to conclude that Erika Johnson had murdered Richard, who was as straight and unmoving as usual in the kitchen, arms folded across his chest, looking like a statue of a ghost rather than the ghost himself. Richard last approved of something around the time I was in middle school. I thought Paul was trying to impress his brother with his skills and was therefore abandoning his usual method, which was to come to no conclusions until he could prove his theory.

Melissa had actually abdicated cooking tonight's dinner because she was "on vacation," so Mom had shown up with the fixings for a beef brisket, which she had seasoned and prepared and which my father was now grilling outside on the deck overlooking the beach. I relished the idea of passersby who weren't supposed to be on my property watching the massive brisket turn itself over. My days of apologizing for the ghosts were over.

"He chose that photograph out of the six he was given," Paul argued. "It was the only one he could say might have been the woman he knew as Ashley, who stole the iron from his hotel room."

"That's right. He said it *might* have been Ashley, and he said he wasn't sure. In fact, he said it probably wasn't. You're not acting like yourself, Paul. Where's the data you need to reach a conclusion?" I thought confronting him would make him revert to his usual process.

Maxie, lying on her side and floating aimlessly around the room like she was on a lazy river in a water park, stretched her arms out to show off how relaxed she was. "I don't see why we're not tracking down that Johnson guy and telling him we know his daughter killed him and Richard," she said.

That was the Maxie I knew—virtually no help at all. I shook my head. "Even if we were sure Erika was the woman in Tom Zink's hotel room, we don't know anything more than that," I said, talking directly to Paul. "We don't know that 'Ashley' killed Richard, just that she stole the iron. She might have given it to somebody else. We don't know that the person who killed Richard necessarily killed Keith Johnson either. And we don't know where Keith hides around here so we can't just scrounge him up whenever we feel like it. Besides, there's no reason to think he'll want to talk now any more than he did when we caught him last time trying to get the laptop."

Maxie looked worried at the mention of her notebook computer, tapped it on her horizontal midriff, and relaxed again.

I saw Josh walk in and stand directly underneath my father without knowing it. He looked over at me and smiled but saw I was working and didn't come over. He didn't want to be a distraction.

"On that note, Alison is right," Paul said. At least that. "The only thing we can tie to Erika Johnson is stealing the hotel iron. We don't know that she did anything else involved in these cases."

"We don't know it was Erika either," I insisted, mostly because I was right and he was wrong. "Tom wasn't sure."

Melissa couldn't really disengage from cooking, which had become a passion of hers, so she walked out to the deck and joined Josh and Dad there. She was carefully watching the meat on the grill and picked up a brush to put more barbecue sauce onto it. My mother, who had been uncharacteristically quiet during this discussion, excused herself and followed her granddaughter out. I could see where this party was going.

"Maybe I should set up on the picnic table," I said, thinking aloud.

"Young lady, this discussion takes precedence over your dinner plans." Richard's voice wasn't much different from Paul's, perhaps a little deeper, and I wasn't looking at him, but the message and the grumpy tone were enough. But at least he thought I was young. I made a mental note to annoy him whenever possible. "We are trying to prevent a woman from harm."

"We're trying to determine who killed Keith Barent Johnson and then who murdered you," Paul corrected his brother, but gently. "Aside from the alleged attack on the road the other night, there is no indication that anyone is trying to harm Cassidy Van Doren."

"*Alleged* attack?" Richard probably wished he had a bushy mustache at that moment so he could make it move around to show his frustration and annoyance. "Are you suggesting that Cassidy was lying?"

"I . . . I don't know." Paul was almost completely transparent, and he wasn't even in the path of a sunbeam. "I would like to hear more from Lieutenant McElone."

"This is absurd," Richard said. I'm sure he thought most things were absurd. He liked thinking things were absurd. This was weird, I'll grant you, but it wasn't absurd.

"I'll give her a call in the morning," I promised Paul, ignoring his brother just to get under his skin, despite his not having any. "But right now I'm setting up for a dinner alfresco and then our spooktacular last show for the guests before they take off tomorrow." I gave Paul and Maxie a glance at the reminder. Paul looked dutiful, and Maxie rolled her eyes. They'd done this a few times before.

I started collecting the outdoor dinner supplies I keep in a basket for easy transportation to the deck. This would be our first dinner out there this year, so I had to remember where I kept everything. But pretty soon I had plates, napkins, utensils, cups, and various condiments ready to go. I got a vinyl tablecloth from a side drawer and examined it. Wrinkles and folds never hurt anybody. On a tablecloth.

But Richard went on throughout, complaining about our focusing on the wrong things and the general lack of progress he saw in our investigation. When I'd heard enough, I turned toward him, picnic basket in hand. "If you're so concerned about our coming to a conclusion, why aren't you and Maxie working on those files so you can remember who you were closing in on when someone took an iron to the back of your head?"

I heard a sharp intake of . . . something . . . from Paul to my right. But Richard did not react angrily and did not simply vanish into thin air as I'd sort of expected he would. He did the last thing I would have anticipated, in fact.

He apologized. To me.

"You're right," he said. "I have been neglecting the one area in which I can legitimately contribute to this investigation." He looked over at Maxie. "Would you mind?"

Maxie, who had been floating on her back, looked down at him. "Now?" she asked.

"If it's not too much trouble."

Maxie tilted her head a little in a *whatever* kind of gesture. "I don't have to be anyplace," she said. She tapped her laptop again and gestured toward Richard, and the two of them floated upward and out of the room.

I turned toward Paul. "I'm going outside," I said. "Want to come?"

It wasn't like he had a choice; I was already making my way to the deck. If Paul wanted to continue our discussion and what I'm sure he thought was a conference of strategy, he'd just have to follow me. Of course, I don't think the location mattered at all to him, so he just maneuvered his way outside and made it there before I did, not having to worry about things like doors or carrying a large, overstuffed picnic basket. Luckily Mom saw me coming and opened the French door for me. I put everything out on the table and went over to kiss my husband hello.

"That was what I was waiting for," Josh said. "I'm going to clean up. Be right back." He walked to the French doors.

"You didn't want to clean up *before* I kissed you?" But he was gone already.

"We're eating outside?" Mom asked. She already had figured out that's what was happening. This was more in the area of *you didn't tell me we were eating outside*, but I let it go.

"It's a nice night," I said.

"You should spray for mosquitoes."

"The dry clothing on Erika Johnson is important," Paul said. "If she did drown her father, she should have been splashed repeatedly with water, assuming he resisted."

"Way to bring down the deck, Paul," I said.

"Assuming he resisted?" Melissa asked. "You think he just got down in the water and let her drown him?"

Paul considered. "I don't believe Mr. Johnson committed suicide by drowning himself in the bathtub," he admitted. "The autopsy report Maxie found suggested there were signs of pressure on his shoulders and his chest."

"And Richard thinks that lets out Cassidy because she's such a sweet girl, she wouldn't have the strength to hold Keith down," I reminded him. "His judgment is a little skewed."

"Perhaps, but Tom Zink chose Erika's photograph, not Cassidy's," Paul said.

"I've seen Cassidy and I've seen Erika," I said. "Frankly, I don't think either one of them could have held Johnson down without a well-stuffed bowling bag. Is it possible he was drunk or drugged?"

"Autopsy report says no," Melissa said, checking the temperature on a meat thermometer my mother bought her last Grandparents Day. My mother believes the point of being honored as a grandmother is to give the grandchild a gift. Who are we to argue? "I know one of his children said he was drinking, but the report says the blood alcohol level was only slightly above normal. So who's stronger than those two, or do you think they acted together?"

Paul and I exchanged a glance; we hadn't thought of that before. "I did not get the impression those two women were close enough to plan and execute such a crime," he said. "I kind of thought they weren't as close as some stepsisters might be."

"What Paul's trying to say is that Erika and Cassidy hate each other," I translated from the Polite.

"And what about the wet jeans?" Melissa said. "They could be the reason Erika was in dry clothing when she was seen. She could have changed in Mr. Evans's room if she was in there with him." Paul and I avoided looking at Melissa or each other for a moment.

"I'm still looking for a motive," I said. "If Johnson was moving his money out of personal accounts, away from his own children and toward Cassidy, why would Cassidy want him dead? Why would he do that, anyway, given that he and Cassidy didn't get along at all?"

From under the deck, the ghost of Keith Johnson rose suddenly, and everyone jumped back a little. Out of the corner of my eye, I saw a tourist woman about fifty look at us, her glance drawn by the sudden movement. She must have seen us leaping away from nothing. She walked by a little bit faster.

"Keith," I said when I regained my breath.

"Who are you?" my father demanded. He and Mom hadn't seen Keith before, and Dad is, well, a little protective of his daughter and granddaughter. Just a tad. Like a mother grizzly defending her cubs.

I found myself making strange, awkward introductions. "Dad, this is Mr. Johnson. You've heard us talking about him. Mr. Johnson, these are my parents, Jack and Loretta Kerby."

"You the guy who drowned in the bathtub?" Dad asked Keith. Dad cuts right to the chase.

"I've told you what I know." Johnson was looking straight at me and didn't acknowledge my parents. You don't do that in my house. "Cassidy murdered me. There is no reason for you to continue investigating my death because that is what happened. Now please stop doing whatever you're doing and move on."

Paul floated forward. The ghosts can affect each other physically, and he might have been thinking of trying to restrain Johnson. Judging from the way his T-shirt fit, Paul, for his college professor demeanor, clearly spent a decent amount of time in the gym when he was alive. Not as much as Everett, but Everett is an extreme case.

But Johnson saw the movement. "Stay back," he said. "I went away the last time and I'll go away again. You can't stop me."

"Mr. Johnson, why do you insist Cassidy was the one who drowned you?" Melissa is a very logical girl, which gets her

into all sorts of trouble when dealing with humans, alive or
not so much. People are rarely as sensible as my daughter. "All
the physical evidence that's been found indicates she couldn't
have done it."

"You're dealing with things you don't understand, little
girl," Keith said. Condescending to Melissa is a capital offense
in the guesthouse.

"Watch who you call 'little girl,' buddy," my mother said.
"And never assume she doesn't understand."

You see what I mean.

"On top of everything else, Melissa is right," Paul told
the offending ghost. "Every fact we know about your murder
indicates Cassidy did not hold you down and drown you.
What is your motivation for lying?" The word *lying* was
significant. Paul very rarely confronts someone with such a
bald-faced insult. In Paul's world that was the equivalent of
spitting in Johnson's face. Paul is unerringly polite to the
point of error.

But Johnson was not taking the bait; he remained on
his talking points. "I want you to stop trying to prove it was
someone else. Cassidy killed me, and she has been charged
with it. Let her be convicted and face her punishment. That
would do me justice." Then rather than dramatically evaporate before our eyes, he simply lowered himself through the
floor and was gone. Paul might have been able to grab him
before he was completely away, but he didn't even move
toward Johnson. Clearly we weren't going to get any new
information from the victim in this crime, and that was frus-
trating. All I could think was that finally we had contacted a

ghost who knew exactly what happened to him, and he lied to us about it.

It was enough to make me want to give up investigating entirely, but then, so is just waking up in the morning. But what he'd said had a strangely familiar ring to it.

"Could he be right?" Dad asked. "Could Cassidy be the one who killed him?"

Paul considered it. He trusts my father and will accept advice from anyone he believes is intelligent, even if he likes to pretend afterward that it was his idea in the first place. Paul is not without ego and prides himself mostly on being a detective.

"Until we have conclusive evidence, we have to assume anything is possible," he said after a moment. "But given everything we know about the crime, it seems extremely unlikely."

"Maybe we're approaching this the wrong way," Liss said, taking the brisket off the grill and placing it on a platter to "rest." I didn't see why my dinner should be peppier than I am, but I don't question my daughter's culinary knowledge.

"Approaching what?" Josh, in clean clothes and clearly showered, walked through the French doors and onto the deck. "Did I miss something important?"

Mom told him what had happened, and my husband listened carefully. They say men don't listen. They clearly don't know the right men.

"So this guy's saying he was drowned by his stepdaughter." Josh had clearly already known this part, but he was summarizing. "But Paul says that's probably not true."

"That's it in a nutshell," Mom told him.

Josh turned toward Melissa. "When I came out, you were saying this was the wrong way to approach the problem," he said. "I didn't mean to interrupt. What did you mean?"

Liss was removing potatoes I hadn't seen before from the grill. She put them on the side counter and started to slice them. "Something Paul said before just sort of hit me," she said. "He asked Mr. Johnson what his motivation for lying was."

"It was an attempt to anger him into making a rash statement," Paul said. "I don't usually speak like that."

Melissa, who has in her life heard most of the choice rude words, looked at him with a small smile, but she shook her head. "That's not what I meant. I don't understand it. Why would he lie about that? This is about his murder. What reason would he have to not want us to find out who did that?"

Josh looked at me, then at Liss, and he seemed surprised. "There's only one explanation," he said. "He's covering up for the real killer."

Everybody Josh could see and the ones he couldn't all stared at him for a moment. "But that's the person who killed *him*," I said. "Wouldn't he want that person to be found and punished?"

Josh raised an eyebrow. "Apparently not," he said. "For some reason—maybe he thinks he deserved it—he's trying to draw attention away from whoever killed him and shift it onto his stepdaughter, who he wants to see get blamed for it. I don't know why, but that's the only way this whole story makes any sense at all."

He sat down in the deck chair next to me and looked over at Melissa, who was tossing the grilled potatoes into a salad she was making. "Something smells good," he said.

Everyone else was still digesting, but not the food. We were considering everything Josh had said.

"It is the only reasonable explanation," Paul said finally.

"Keith really did resent Cassidy, from what Richard told us," Mom added. "I guess he's so mad at her, he's willing to let his real killer just go free."

"That's the part that doesn't add up for me," I said, holding up a hand with the palm out. "Cassidy most likely didn't kill Keith Johnson. But the person who did is getting a free pass with his blessing. Why does a man do that?"

Josh, who probably didn't realize the roll he was on here, did a little shrug that indicated that was obvious. "He must really have loved the person who killed him," he said.

Melissa was in the process of slicing the brisket. This makes Mom nervous because she still thinks Liss is eight years old and should stay away from sharp knives. I know for a fact that my daughter is thirteen and considerably more adept with such implements than I am, so I actually ask her to cut things up when she's cooking to save me making a hacking mess of it. Josh defers to Melissa because he believes her to be a cooking savant.

But her activity only seemed to make her mind work sharper. Like the knife, I guess. "So if Josh is right, there's someone who was able to kill Mr. Johnson, and Mr. Johnson must have loved that person so much, he would let them get away with it. Who would that be?"

Every face in the room lit up, but no one said anything immediately because Maxie and Richard phased through the kitchen wall at a higher velocity than usual. Maxie shed her trench coat, and her laptop predictably appeared, clutched tightly to her midsection. Neither she nor Richard so much landed as stopped short of the deck and hovered.

And I realized who, like Johnson, had insisted that I should stop investigating his death.

"We've got it!" Maxie shouted as they approached. "Richard figured out who killed Keith Johnson!"

"Adrian!" Everyone on the deck yelled it. All at the same time. If we'd all said "Yo!" first, it would have sounded like a sing-along screening of *Rocky*.

Richard's face stiffened in surprise. Maxie just looked completely disappointed.

"How'd you know?" she asked.

Chapter 29

Paul looked dissatisfied. "Where is our evidence?" he asked.

I was busy setting up the movie room in my house for the last spook show of my guests' week and was not in a mood for rehashing what had already been, you know, hashed. I was hanging black bunting (I used to use Halloween decorations, but this was more reusable than crepe paper) over the windows. I would have hung some over the top of the large flat-screen TV I have over the mantelpiece, but I'm queasy about touching that thing for fear it'll fall off. The fact that it's attached to the wall with bolts directly into the studs and that I did that myself has no bearing on my emotions.

"You heard what Richard said," I reminded Paul. "The money from Keith Johnson's private accounts was being funneled to Cassidy, but based on his reading of the legal documents, Richard thinks that money was meant only to see to Adrian's needs as she aged or for any purchases Adrian wanted to make. It must have been part of the same deal where Keith wrote that letter about having Richard consult on any case if there were criminal charges against anyone in his family. We thought he meant Cassidy. Turns out it was probably Adrian. Keith was concerned that he wouldn't always be around to keep his wife in the lifestyle to which she'd worked so hard to become accustomed, and a trust fund is more tax exempt than an inheritance. Cassidy had a trust fund. Adrian just had what was in his will." The hooks for the bunting were now permanent, making the decoration process easier and faster. Give me a few years and I'll figure out whatever you want figured out, as long as it's not difficult. "He'd made that provision clear in legal papers connected to his will that Richard found when he was working on Cassidy's defense. He knew Adrian was mad enough to kill him, and he still didn't want her caught. The provision wasn't for Cassidy; it was for his wife."

"That's very subjective, and it doesn't make Adrian the murderer," Paul responded. "It's not clear she knew that provision was in place, and even if she did, it wouldn't give her motivation to kill her husband. She was already being given every material comfort she could possibly have desired."

Obviously that was true. But as I got down off my stepladder, I was less concerned with Paul's misgivings than I was with the cobwebs I'd seen in the corner of the ceiling. In my guesthouse, this poses a peculiar question: do cobwebs add or detract from the atmosphere? I decided on "add" for this particular evening for reasons aside from my general laziness.

"Paul," I said, "you were one of the people shouting Adrian's name when Maxie suggested they knew who killed Johnson. How come you're backing off now?"

We'd had a lovely barbecue brisket dinner with grilled potato salad (something I'd never thought about before) and discussed the virtues of this case for more than an hour, and here was Paul questioning everything that had been said, including things that were his ideas. I began to wonder why I'd gone searching for him again and then remembered it was because Richard had shown up and insisted on it. Had I missed Paul? I couldn't remember at this moment and didn't want to consider it.

Because as soon as the case(s) was/were solved, he might very well decide to be off on his travels again, maybe this time to Europe or Africa. Best not get myself too attached to the globetrotting ghost now that he had the ability to trot.

"I'm not backing off anything," he said with a hint of defensiveness. "I'm making sure our reasoning is based on facts and not simply our desire to see this case solved. I get the impression that you didn't care for Adrian much when you met her. That can color your judgment."

"You were there," I pointed out.

"I am impartial."

"Sure you are." I pulled the drapes shut on one of the windows. It wasn't quite dark yet as the days were among the longest of the year, but I did like to have a little gloom in the room when we were doing our last show of the week. The shows aren't exactly supposed to be scary for the guests, of course, because the ghosts in the house aren't the least bit frightening—unless you are scared of having your life disrupted. But a little traditionally spooky atmosphere adds something to the proceedings, I've found. "You want to show off to Richard about how brilliant a detective you are, and I get that. And you don't want him to be able to say that his research was what finally cracked the case. It's a very adorable brotherly competition—if you don't think about the fact that you're both, you know, no longer alive."

"I think you are misreading the situation," Paul attempted.

"And *I* think you respect your older brother, which is understandable, but you don't trust your own talents enough to overrule his judgment. That whole thing I just said about how the money in Cassidy's account was to keep Adrian solvent after Keith was dead? That's so sketchy even *I* don't believe it. Richard has a way of sounding authoritative, but you're the guy who actually solves the cases."

"I assure you that any imagined rivalry with Richard is not driving my skepticism," Paul attempted.

"Uh-huh, and I'm not the least bit intimidated when my mother is around," I said. And I did so while looking around to be certain my mother was not in the room, but she and Melissa had gone out to the 7-Eleven to get some large bottles of soft drinks. I have a little reception afterward, and while I can serve beer and wine as long as I don't charge for it, the guests are usually more prone to try the soft stuff. They have to get up in the morning. "But the fact is, it makes sense that Adrian killed Johnson, and it makes sense that she knew Richard was closing in on her and killed him too."

Mom and Melissa walked in from the hallway, the most direct route to the movie room from the kitchen, where Josh was still cleaning up what little there was from dinner (the great thing about cooking outside is you just need to clean the grill the next day). They were carrying the flash powder and sparklers I had asked for (Mom) and the cooler of sodas for later (Melissa). But they were clearly in the midst of a conversation when they arrived.

"There's nothing that ties Adrian to Richard or to his hotel room," Liss was telling my mother. "The closest we have is Mr. Zink saying maybe Erika was the girl he knew as Ashley who came up and probably stole the iron. That's not much."

I didn't even have to say a word. I just got Paul's attention and gestured with both hands toward my daughter: *See?*

"That is a valid point," Paul said to himself. That's what it's come to: my thirteen-year-old daughter's judgment is more valuable than my own. I was expecting this, just not quite so soon.

There was no point in bringing that up to Paul; there were more important things on the agenda. Besides, my mother had yet to weigh in.

"I suppose so," she told Melissa. "You're so smart."

That didn't help much, but it was sweet. Mom handed me the spook show supplies while Liss headed over to the little fridge I keep in the movie room for just such occasions and unloaded the sodas into it. Paul was pacing, such as he can, back and forth in the air almost above our heads so that we could go about our business and come close to not noticing him at all.

I moved the stepladder to the next window, which would be the last to be decorated. The spook show was set for eight PM, just as the sun would be setting, and that was in roughly an hour. "Let's assume for the moment that Adrian did kill Johnson, because that seems the most likely explanation," I said.

"Well . . ." Paul began.

"Just for the sake of argument." I cut him off. I was going to get at least one point in before everyone else explained to me how I was wrong. Paul nodded and "stood" still for a moment, letting me continue. "If that's the case, and Richard was just starting to close in on her while he was working on the research for Cassidy's trial—something Keith had apparently asked for before he died—how did Adrian find out about it?"

"Find out about what?" Liss asked, walking over from the fridge to steady the ladder as I climbed. I taught that girl well, as my father taught me. And as he still taught her despite being dead for years.

"How did Adrian know that Richard had discovered something to tie her to Keith's murder?" I said as I reached over to hang the last piece of black bunting. "Richard wasn't in contact with her, and even if he had been, he didn't make a formal announcement that he suspected she was the killer. Why would she come to his hotel room and iron his head?"

"A very good question," Paul said. "One that I think might hold the key to Richard's murder."

I was startled because I rarely bring up a point that important and Paul even less frequently tells me I did a good investigator thing. So I turned my head abruptly to look at him.

And that might have saved my life.

I heard the whizzing right by my left ear but luckily didn't turn toward it until it had passed. That wasn't surprising because it lasted less than a second. But my instinct to turn toward the sound meant I was looking quickly at Paul and even more quickly back in the direction I'd been facing.

There, embedded into the molding around my window, was a very impressive-looking knife. It had been thrown with a great deal of force. And it had been thrown at my head.

"Alison!" my mother shouted. She took a step toward the ladder as Melissa also shouted for me.

"Mom!" Melissa yelled at the same time. She took a step toward me, saw I was all right, and stopped, looking like she didn't know what to do.

"I'm okay," I said. "It didn't hit me."

Paul, not constrained by gravity or the laws of physics, was immediately inches from my face. "Did anyone see where it came from?" he asked.

From across the room, I heard Josh's voice. It sounded hoarse. "What happened?" he said, running toward me.

I did the only thing that made sense. I climbed down the ladder to stop giving the person with the knife-throwing hobby a better target. I was in Josh's arms before both my feet were solidly on the floor. "I'm okay," I repeated. "Really. Not a scratch."

"Not for lack of trying," Paul said. Paul is a lovely man, but you don't want him around when people need to be comforted with encouraging words. I'd make a "Home on the Range" joke here, but I was pretty shook up from having a knife whiz by my head.

"Who was it?" Josh asked. It seemed a reasonable question.

"I saw it fly by," Liss said. She still looked stunned, but she was in information mode now and knew Paul could benefit from anything she could tell him. "It came from there." She pointed toward a spot about halfway between the window and the entrance to the movie room. "But there wasn't anybody there when I looked."

It seemed unlikely that Abby Lesniak had decided I was messing up her love life after all and taken a shot at killing me for it, so we had to think. Nobody had noticed a person walk-ing in or heard any footsteps. The knife had simply shown up and flown across the room, and when Melissa had looked back a second later, nobody was running for the exit.

"It doesn't make any sense," I said. But of course it did. Paul was already stroking his goatee. "But we know he's got a thing for knives."

"Keith Johnson," he said.

Chapter 30

There seemed to be no point in a search for Keith Johnson. The other times we'd tried to find the elusive—and seemingly murderous—ghost, we'd had to wait until he decided to show up again. Only luring him with Maxie's laptop had proved successful, and it was at best a long shot that such a thing would work again.

Besides, we had a spook show to put on, and I was not about to let a little thing like having a knife thrown at my head threaten that. I'm an innkeeper.

I took the offending blade out of my window molding as carefully as possible, noting that it would take some wood filler and a whole new paint job to hide the damage. On top of trying to end my life, Johnson had now created more home maintenance work for me. He was not going to be greeted warmly when he decided to materialize again.

There had been some talk of calling McElone about the attempt on my life, but she wouldn't even have been able to see Johnson if he'd decided to pop up right in front of her eyes. And it was a decent bet her handcuffs weren't going to be especially effective with him.

Paul had been uncharacteristically quiet since the knife had flown by my face. He seemed as deep in thought as I'd seen him, which was pretty deep. He did occasionally stop to confer, out of earshot from the rest of us, with his brother in a corner of the movie room near the ceiling. Richard was visibly agitated, gesturing more broadly than usual, but not speaking loudly enough for anyone else to hear. When Maxie got close enough to eavesdrop, the Harrison brothers stopped talking entirely and assumed identical arms-folded poses, pretending to watch the rest of us from their bird's-eye view.

Josh was sticking close to me, closer even than Mom and Melissa, which was no small feat. Anywhere I went, I felt like we were a unit, a hive. Presidents have had less personal security than I was getting.

It was starting to grate.

"Okay, everybody," I said. "I'm all right. Let's all take two steps back and give me a little room to breathe."

None of them moved. My father did back up a little bit, but he continued to hover within ten feet of me and carry a very large adjustable wrench, his best idea of a lethal weapon. Which, considering that I was in the room with someone who had been murdered with a steam iron, wasn't something I could necessarily dispute.

"Seriously," I said.

"I'm staying as close to you as I can," Josh said, his voice leaving no room for debate. "Someone tried to kill you, we don't know why, and I'm not going to be in another room if he tries again. Cope with it."

"I agree, but I think we know why," Melissa said. I stared at her. "No, Mom. We were getting close to the idea that Adrian Johnson killed her husband. The last time that happened, someone killed Richard. It's not just a coincidence that this happened right now."

As usual, my daughter made more sense than all the adults in the room, transparent or opaque. But I was focusing on the spook show, which was to start in half an hour. I looked around the room. "What am I forgetting?" I asked nobody in particular.

"The light thingy," Maxie offered from her current position, pretending to be lying on one of the sofas I keep in the room for movie nights and major spook shows. "That's not running yet."

I have a random light generator—you can get one at any party store—that sends patterns of dots in various colors around the walls and ceiling of the room. "Thanks, but it's not time for that yet," I told Maxie.

Everett, who had joined the party only a couple of minutes earlier once he got a psychic message or something from Maxie (or maybe just heard all the yelling), was in full camo and had a sidearm strapped to his right hip. Everett doesn't fool around.

"We should consider security measures for the gathering tonight, ghost lady," he said.

"We are all considering that, Everett," my mother told him. "Trust me."

Toward the back of the room, there was the sound of footsteps, and everyone in the area froze and turned to look.

Eduardo DiSica, the guest I had seen the least during the week, was standing at the entrance to the movie room and stopped abruptly when he saw Mom, Melissa, and me staring at him. I can only assume his startled expression would have been multiplied had he been able to see the other five people in the room gaping at him.

"Can I help you with something, Eduardo?" I asked.

"I thought the ghost show was going on tonight instead of this afternoon," he said meekly.

"It is," I assured him. "But not until eight."

"I wanted to get a good seat."

I smiled my best innkeeper smile at him. "Every seat is a good seat, Eduardo," I told my guest. "The show will take place all over the room."

"Oh. Okay. I'll tell Vanessa." He shuffled back out and into the front room, no doubt looking for his wife.

"See?" I said to my Secret Service detachment as soon as Eduardo was out of sight. "This is going to be a normal evening. For here. So let's focus on what we're doing for the guests and worry about the other stuff later."

My phone buzzed, and I saw Phyllis Coates's number in the caller ID. I picked up and didn't even have time to say hello. Phyllis wastes no time.

"I haven't heard from you since you started with this Johnson guy," she said. "What's the deal? You don't love me anymore?"

"I haven't found out anything worth telling you," I exaggerated. "You didn't want me to waste your time, did you?"

"You're a rotten liar, kid," Phyllis answered. "But I'm going to be nice to you anyway. I heard something about this story." This was news to me, as I had no idea Phyllis was digging into the murders other than my own faith that she'd pick up on what I'd told her. Phyllis is a bulldog.

Wasn't anybody going to let me just put on a spook show? "Okay, let's hear it," I said.

"Hey, listen, I don't have to burden you with this," Phyllis said. "I can call any one of a hundred hotel owners who also do some investigating and tell them all I've found out about this guy who drowned in a bathtub in Cranbury, a town I don't even cover."

"So how did you hear anything if you're not writing a story?" I could ask. Phyllis is a friend.

I stashed the stepladder in the closet at the far end of the movie room. "You got me thinking about it when you called, which I figured meant you wanted me to nose around, and I decided to ask a few questions. You want to know what I found out or not?"

"Sure. I'm sorry. It's been a rough week." I was having trouble remembering the last *easy* week, but that was a topic for another day.

Phyllis needed no further prompting. "So I hear there are rumors," she said. "I'm told Johnson's wife wasn't exactly playing the role of wife straight down the middle." Sometimes Phyllis speaks in code. Luckily, I've known her for many years and can usually decipher her.

"Adrian was cheating on her husband?" I said.

Josh froze while straightening a sofa. Melissa turned and stared at me, finger to her lips. Mom's eyes got big.

"Don't say that aloud," Paul admonished me. "We don't know where Keith Johnson is at this moment."

It was kind of late for that particular warning, but since Phyllis couldn't have seen or heard any of that and didn't know about the knife attack, she didn't pause. "Sounds like it. Talk is she was involved with Johnson's business partner."

"Adrian was sleeping with Hunter Evans?" I gasped. It just sneaked out, I swear.

Josh grabbed me, gently, by the arm and squinted his eyes as if in pain. "Please. Just think it," he said. "Don't say it."

Now they were getting me paranoid. I scanned the room for signs of Keith Johnson, but there were, as far as I could tell, none.

"That's the scuttlebutt around the police headquarters in Rumson," Phyllis said. "I know a few people there. I think you ought to look pretty carefully at this Evans guy for the murder. He gets to own the whole business instead of half, and he gets the wife. What's not to like?"

I could think of a good number of things about her scenario that I didn't like, but at least I had the presence of mind not to blurt out that Hunter Evans might have killed Keith Johnson to be with the dead man's wife. Give me a little credit.

"Do you know anything about the New Brunswick murder?" I asked her. Might as well go for broke.

"I'm assuming you don't mean the three shootings of drug dealers in the past four months," she said. "I'm guessing you mean the lawyer in the hotel who got beaned with an iron when he just happened to be working on . . . oh, yeah, the trial of Keith Johnson's murderer."

"*Alleged* murderer," I corrected.

"Yeah. Nope. You're on your own with that one."

I sighed, but Phyllis was just having fun.

"Except . . ."

She was getting back at me for my attitude and for making her work so hard on the two murders that she wasn't going to cover anyway. "Except what?" I asked.

"Except the cops have video of some blonde up in a guy's room that night stealing the iron out of his closet."

Video! Security footage! My first thought was that I'd never feel secure in a hotel room again. The second was what I said to Phyllis: "How do I get hold of that video?"

"You're a detective. You figure it out." And Phyllis hung up, probably laughing.

Chapter 31

"This is highly irregular," said Ramon Bornstein.

There was no time to drive to the Heldrich Hotel in New Brunswick and talk to its head of security, who as it turned out was Bornstein. So I'd called with only fifteen minutes until my guests would be expecting a spectacular (within my budget) spook show to remember as a highlight of their vacations. I had no time to fool around.

"I'm an investigator working in conjunction with the police," I said again. That was technically true, assuming your definition of *in conjunction* meant *at the same time as*. It was a fine line, and I was walking it. "I know you've already given them the footage, but I'm in a remote location, and I'd like to see it. Can you send it as a file?"

"I'd like to see some verification of your credentials," Bornstein said. "I can't simply send security footage to anyone and violate a guest's privacy."

"Seems to me you're already violating it by filming them in their rooms and not informing anybody," I countered. "Is that even legal?"

"It wouldn't be if we were doing that," Bornstein said with a snooty tone befitting the prices his hotel was charging for a room. "But we don't. The footage in question is of a public area, the hallway outside the guest room."

"Well, I'll know that when I see it," I suggested.

"And you'll see it when I have clearance from the police," Bornstein said.

Josh grabbed the phone from my hand. "This is Detective Barnett Kobielski of the New Brunswick Police Department," he said, his voice rougher than I'd heard it before. "I'm authorizing you to send this video footage to a Dropbox account on my authority. Is that enough for you?"

I gave my husband a warm hug, doing my best to avoid touching the phone and making a noise. But I did manage to hear Bornstein say, "Of course, Detective. As long as you are giving your okay."

"By the power vested in me," Josh said, which I thought was overkill but Bornstein probably thought was Kobielski being snide. "I need to get an edge on those county investigators, okay?"

"Sure, Detective." Now Bornstein sounded conspiratorial, as if he had a grudge with the county prosecutor's investigators too.

"Good. I'm giving the phone back to Ms. Kerby."

I decided to go for broke. "How'd the woman who stole the iron get a key to the murdered man's room?" I asked him. "Some crack security system you guys have." You can get people to talk if they're being defensive.

Sure enough, Bornstein sounded downright annoyed when he said, "You'd have to talk to the front desk attendant.

Apparently she was given keys to the wrong room and asked for a correction." An oldie but a goodie in this case. At least the murderer was consistent.

I gave Bornstein the code for my Dropbox account and disconnected the call. "Okay," I said. "Are we just about ready for a great spook show?"

"Is *that* what you call contact with the departed?" The voice was familiar, but it was coming from all the way across the room, in the entranceway. "That's so unfeeling."

All heads in the room turned toward the voice, which was accompanied by a person in shadows at the moment. But that didn't last, as she took two steps forward and was clearly visible.

"Madame Lorraine," I said. I hope my voice didn't betray how I was actually feeling. But it probably did.

"I have been sending you text messages," she said as she advanced on the group. "I have been very concerned about Paul Harrison."

Paul—and this *never* happened—burst out laughing. "Me?" he said when he could catch his "breath." "She's worried about *me*?"

I had mentioned to him about Madame Lorraine's pronouncements of his intense psychological pain, but like the rest of us, Paul had not taken them seriously. "I assure you, there's nothing to be concerned about," I told her.

"But there is," Madame Lorraine insisted even as my guests started to wander into the room. I had to get her out of here quickly or risk ruining the evening from my innkeeper's viewpoint. "I can feel it in this room."

"What can she feel in the room?" Vanessa DiSica asked her husband, Eduardo. "Can you feel anything?"

"It's a little warm," Eduardo volunteered.

"Please, have a seat wherever you like," I told the DiSicas. "We'll get started very soon." I turned toward Madame Lorraine. "Maybe if you'd like to come back tomorrow . . ."

She was having none of that. She turned directly away from where Paul and Richard were floating and clearly addressed the crown molding around the ceiling. "I know you are suffering, Mr. Harrison," she said. "I am here to relieve your pain."

Paul was giggling so intensely at this point that if he were alive, he would undoubtedly have had real pain, probably around his midsection. "Oh, she is hilarious," he managed.

"Don't be so disrespectful," Richard admonished his younger brother. But he didn't dare make eye contact with Paul.

"Gimme your phone," Maxie urged Melissa. "I want video of this for my Facebook page." Despite having been dead for years, Maxie had never deleted her Facebook page. She liked to post things on it and see what theories people who viewed them might have about their origins.

Melissa held onto her phone without comment.

"Madame Lorraine," my mother attempted, "it's really not necessary right now. Paul is all right. Why don't we talk about this in the kitchen?" For Mom, everything that is important happens in the kitchen.

Penny Desmond walked in from the hallway side, gave Madame Lorraine a rather puzzled look, and took a seat on one of the sofas, exactly the seat I would have chosen if I were a guest here. The sofas are incredibly comfortable. On movie nights guests often fall asleep on them, and I don't even get offended.

"Good evening, Penny." I'm a terrific host. It says so on many of the evaluation cards I get back from Senior Plus Tours. Some, anyway.

"Hi, Alison." She looked at Madame Lorraine but did not ask. Penny was exceedingly polite. If she were forty years younger and dead, she would have been a good match for Paul.

"I'm staying right here until I get a sense that Paul Harrison is no longer distressed," Madame Lorraine told Mom.

"And how will you get that?"

Madame Lorraine regarded my mother with something between pity and scorn. That was enough to ruin her in my eyes. "It's simply a feeling one experiences," she said to Mom in a condescending tone. "I will just know."

"Of course you will," Mom said. Melissa moved close to her grandmother's side with a fierce look of protection in her eye. She took Mom's arm and led her away from Madame Lorraine, which was best.

It occurred to me that I didn't need to remove Madame Lorraine so much as rustle her to a far corner of the room where she could talk to the drywall to her heart's content and not disrupt the spook show. I walked over to her. "Actually, Madame Lorraine, Paul is over there by the light generator."

"But I can feel his presence here." Clearly I was the amateur and Madame Lorraine the professional in the ghost business. But I was the innkeeper, and I was going to make sure she was on the move.

"I'm willing to bet you'll feel it stronger over there." I looked up at the blank space on the wall where I was intending to divert her attention. "Right, Paul?"

Paul, at the sound of his name, looked over. He'd stopped dissolving into hysterics, which was helpful, but hadn't been paying attention, which wasn't. "What?" he asked. He floated over closer to us.

Proving the intensely authentic medium we all knew she was, Madame Lorraine looked blankly at the wall. "Yes, I am feeling his presence fade," she said as Paul hovered within four feet of her. "Perhaps that is the place to be." She walked over to the wall I'd indicated.

That was perfect timing because Abby Lesniak was just walking into the movie room looking relaxed and content, if not ecstatic. She nodded her hellos to everyone she could see and sat a little removed from the group in one of the easy chairs.

I figured we were already a few minutes late for the start of the show due to all the distractions. There was no point in waiting any longer. I signaled to Maxie, who said to Paul, "Let's go." My father joined them in the center of the room, several feet above the heads of the seated guests. Everett hovered close by in anticipation of his military drill should that be called for in the program (we're never all that set ahead of time). Richard, with an air of embarrassment at the spectacle he was forced to endure, backed up to the outside wall a little too much. He was only partly visible by the time he'd crossed his arms to look disapproving.

Melissa and Mom walked to respective sides of the room, knowing they wouldn't necessarily be called upon as part of the entertainment but there in case someone (okay, Maxie) improvised and they were needed. I walked to the front of the room just under the big TV, which was not going to be used tonight.

Josh took a stance directly behind me and very close. He never participated in the spook shows. This was my husband acting as my security detail. I can't say I objected.

The general din in the room lowered to a mumble, and I was just about to start when Greg Lewis walked in carrying a boom box in one hand and a bouquet of Mylar balloons in the other. He looked like John Cusack in *Say Anything* if he were visiting someone in the hospital just after a baby was born.

"Watch this," Melissa said quietly.

Greg wasted no time and did not respond when I said, "Good evening, Mr. Lewis." He marched straight through the room after pushing a button on the boom box. Melissa nodded in a conspiratorial fashion to him, and music, featuring Mr. Lewis himself as vocalist (and, one assumed, composer and band), began to play through the speakers he carried.

The song was clearly called "Abigail," and he directed it right at Abby Lesniak, who looked absolutely stunned. She opened and closed her mouth a few times but made no sounds. Her eyes grew misty.

"Abby." Mr. Lewis turned the music down, not off, and stood directly in front of her easy chair. "I'm sorry I didn't say anything sooner, but I've been trying to figure out the right way to do it. All week I've been thinking about you, and now it's the last night and this is my last chance. I couldn't let it go by."

Abby remained unable to speak, but she took his hand after he put the boom box down on the easy chair next to her.

"You've been the best part of this vacation for me," Mr. Lewis went on. "I know I haven't approached you very often, but that's because I'm shy."

"Obviously," Eduardo DiSica said, and everyone laughed.

Everyone except Greg Lewis. He never took his eyes away from Abby's. "Do you think we could get to know each other better in the time we have left?" he asked her.

There were hoots and cries of "whooo!" from the group. People of any age can act like silly kids. Never doubt that.

Abby finally seemed to have mastered her emotions again. She put her other hand on top of Greg's and said quietly, "I'd like that." He sat down next to her, and the collected group applauded.

Finally, it seemed it was my time to begin the ultimate spook show of the week. I cleared my throat and said as the collected audience (minus Madame Lorraine, who was still in deep conversation with a blank wall) turned its attention back to me, "Good evening, everybody."

And that was as far as I got.

From the side adjacent to the entrance to the house came three uninvited guests. For a moment, I stiffened as I saw Paul tense up, perhaps thinking this was Keith Johnson's new attempt on my life.

Instead it was a reunion of suspects in Keith's murder. Into the movie room strode Adrian Van Doren Johnson followed by her stepchildren, Braden and Erika. I breathed a small sigh of relief in noticing that no one was brandishing a weapon of any sort. In my experience, that was how these things usually ended up going.

"Twenty-five thousand dollars," Adrian said as soon as she was close enough to be heard.

"Oh, for crying out loud," I heard myself say. "Can't I just start the show?"

Chapter 32

My five guests and five ghosts all turned toward Adrian when she spoke, as did the two living blood relatives in my own entourage. Josh just took a step forward and stood slightly in front of me, not blocking me out of view but certainly making me a harder target to hit.

"Twenty-five thousand?" I parroted back to Adrian. I remembered something about her offering me bunches of money, but that seemed like a long time ago now.

"I want you to drop the investigation into Keith's death," she reminded me. "My children and I are raising our offer to twenty-five thousand dollars and not a penny more."

"I'd take it," Eduardo DiSica said, seemingly to himself.

I glanced over at Paul, who was moving toward Adrian. "Take the money if you like," he suggested. "How will she know if I'm investigating?" It was a decent point, but not when I thought it through. I'd be the visible member of the team, and a ticked-off murderess is one thing; a ticked-off murderess who just gave you a large sum of money and didn't get what she wanted would be worse.

"I don't think I can do that," I said. "Believe me, I'm sorry I can't take your money. Now if you don't mind—"

"Thirty thousand," Braden piped up.

"Wait. What happened to 'not a penny more'?"

Maxie swooped down from the ceiling. "Take the money. You could use a new laptop and fix your ceiling, and you could buy me a car."

That was new. I looked at her. "A *car*?"

She waved a hand. "We'll talk later."

"What about a car?" Erika asked. It was, at least from her perspective, a reasonable question. I didn't answer it.

"It's not that I don't *want* the money," I told Braden. "Believe me, it would do me a great deal of good. But there's only so much that's within my power. Frankly, I find it interesting that you think my stopping is worth that much. The last time you'd just talked to Hunter Evans. Who have you spoken to this time?" I looked at Adrian when I said that because I was fairly certain she was the source of all this bizarre bribery.

Adrian twitched the corner of her mouth. Left side, for those keeping score at home. "I don't know what you're talking about," she said.

Not one of the guests so much as blinked. They clearly thought this was part of the spook show. They were probably wondering when the ghosts would get involved. So I decided to indulge them. It's what a good host does.

"I think there's a reason you want me to stop investigating, and it's the most obvious one a person could imagine," I said, advancing on Adrian as if I were actually confident in my knowledge or my safety. Josh stayed at my side the whole way. "I think you're the one who killed Keith Johnson so you could inherit his money and continue your love affair with his business partner, Hunter Evans. Best of both worlds. What about that? Were you going to kill Hunter's wife too?"

I got precisely the reaction I expected, and in anticipation of it, I scanned the upper reaches of my movie room. I caught Paul's eye, but he was already lowering himself, focusing on the space around Adrian. He knew what I was trying to do.

Sure enough, Keith Johnson rose up from the basement dramatically, face angry, holding out his right index finger and pointing at me. All he needed was a cape and he could have won a Dracula look-alike contest.

My father took up a defensive position between Johnson and me. Maxie, now with an expression of complete seriousness, swooped down behind him with Everett, in camouflage fatigues, moving in from the left flank.

"I think Keith found out about your romance with Hunter Evans and was going to divorce you and cut you out of his will," I said, although I had absolutely no evidence of any of that and in fact didn't even believe it to be true. The idea was to irritate Johnson into doing something rash that hopefully didn't include killing me. "I think you decided to do something about it before he could take you back to your middle-class life, and you went into his room at the Cranbury Bog and drowned him in his bathtub. How did you get him to lie down in that water, Adrian?"

I saw Melissa lunge a little toward Johnson, whose face was practically apoplectic, but my mother firmly grasped her shoulders and wouldn't let her advance. Mom shook her head in my direction, but the die was cast; I had to follow through on this plan even though I'd just thought it up.

"You have no idea what you're saying," Adrian growled at me.

But her response was nothing compared to her dead husband's. "How *dare* you!" Keith Johnson bellowed. But, significantly, he didn't deny anything I'd just suggested.

He did, however, reach into the suit jacket he was wearing.

Paul shouted, "Duck!" So I dove for the floor and lay facedown for a few seconds. Then I rolled over to see what was going on.

"What in the name of—" Adrian looked positively lost for a response. She looked down at me. "You really are insane."

"She's crazy," Erika echoed. Erika didn't have too many original thoughts, but she was happy to repeat those of other people.

But then she and the guests got the spook show everyone except the Johnson family members had been expecting, and they seemed very pleased with it. The drapes on all the windows (there are six in the movie room, which makes it hard to darken the space for movies during the day) flapped wildly. The chandelier and two other light fixtures that included ceiling fans (which worried me) started to sway. The lights went out briefly, came back on, went out again, and then came on only in the front part of the room.

Madame Lorraine turned around when her view of the blank wall was dimmed and shouted, "Hey!"

The light generator I'd positioned on the floor came on, making green and blue dots of light circulate on the walls and ceiling, not to mention on the people in the room. Vanessa

DiSica let out an "Ooh!" and her husband seemed fascinated with watching one particular dot's journey. He craned his neck when it flew directly over his head and ended up circling around toward the other side of the room.

One runner rug I have in the aisle between two rows of chairs partially rolled itself up and came to a rest halfway toward the front of the room.

Melissa watched with some amusement as I raised myself up off the floor and stood facing Adrian again. I felt foolish, but Paul had rather emphatically told me to duck, you'll recall.

"What is this all about?" Braden Johnson demanded.

"Didn't you read the sign on the way into the house?" Mom asked him. "The place is haunted. And the ghosts don't care for the way you're treating my daughter."

"Oh, please," said Madame Lorraine.

"That's not entirely true," I said, looking at Adrian with what I hoped appeared to be defiance. "The fact is, they don't care for the way your dead husband was treating me, and they're handling the situation."

Sure enough, Keith Johnson had been contained. Paul was holding him by one arm and Everett the other, the three of them hovering two feet off the floor. Maxie, a satisfied look on her face, was wiping her long, sharp fingernails with a napkin from my snack bar area. I noticed a few scratches on Johnson's right cheek. Who knew that was even possible?

The guests, who had not seen any of the action on the part of the ghosts, applauded. They are such lovely people. I like my job a lot.

"What are you talking about?" Adrian demanded. "Keith is dead."

"Yes, and you killed him. I'm guessing from the wet jeans outside the room that you got in there and sat on top of him until he drowned."

She gave me the one line that always proves a person is guilty. "You have no proof."

At Paul's urging, even as he tried to quiet the angry Keith Johnson, I told her, "I will have the testimony of Hunter Evans, who will say you were having an affair with him because he wants to stay out of jail and he can get immunity by rolling over on you. Nobody saw you at the inn, at least nobody who will testify, but there was a wet pair of jeans found at the base of the window outside Keith's room. You're about the same size as Cassidy. The police didn't find the jeans because Robin Witherspoon removed them thinking Erika had killed her father for Hunter Evans. But it was you. You were staying in the next room with Hunter Evans and had a whole bag packed, didn't you? And if that's not enough, I will get the confession of the victim himself, although that admittedly won't be admissible in court."

"Never!" Keith shouted. "I won't ever tell you that! She didn't kill me! Cassidy killed me!"

One thing you have to like about liars: they stick to their story no matter how stupid or disproven it might be.

"What are you talking about?" Braden shouted. "You think you can get a confession from a dead man? Are you some fake boardwalk medium or something?"

"Hey," said Madame Lorraine, who had given up on the wall and walked over to watch the drama play out.

"That's nothing," Adrian said with her usual air of superiority restored. "Cassidy's trial will go on as it has been and she'll be convicted. You have no evidence that can prove anybody but she killed Keith."

"See?" Johnson yelled. It was not terribly convincing.

"You get the money from Keith's will, almost all of it, right?" I said. "You killed your husband, and now you get his partner who'll own his whole business, the inheritance from Keith, and the money from Cassidy, who'll be in jail and prohibited by law from profiting from her crime even though she didn't kill Keith. Nice plan, Adrian."

"I did nothing of the sort," Adrian said. "You are fabricating the whole scenario." I'll bet she didn't talk that way when her husband was a lineman for Public Service Electric and Gas.

"How about this," I shot back as Braden took a menacing step forward and stopped when Josh moved toward him. "Robin Witherspoon saw you walking out of Keith's room before Cassidy got there, and you were only wearing a long men's shirt." Now that was a complete and total lie, but it was a calculated one.

And it got the response I had hoped for. "That's impossible," Adrian said. "I was never in that hallway. I walked out through the patio doors and into Hunter's room." Then she realized what she had said and stopped immobile in her tracks.

"Game, set, and match," Mom said, beaming. She looked at me. "You're so smart."

"It won't be admissible," Richard warned from his corner. "It will be hearsay. She'd have to confess to the police, and she won't."

"Because she didn't do it!" Keith was inexplicably tied to the falsehood that the woman he loved hadn't actually murdered him when he undoubtedly knew for a fact that she did. Love isn't just blind; sometimes it's also stupid.

I reached into my pocket and took out the voice recorder, which I hadn't planned on using until the lights had gone out. "The police and the county prosecutor will definitely be interested in hearing this," I said.

"They won't get the chance." The voice came from the direction of the hallway. I counted up the people in the room and couldn't think of anyone else who might have walked in, and if there had been the sound of a car driving up to the back door, I hadn't noticed it.

So I was more than a little disappointed when Cassidy Van Doren walked into the movie room. And I was even more unhappy when I saw she was carrying a gun.

"They come here," I said quietly to myself. "They all come here. How do they find me?"

Chapter 33

"Give me that recorder," Cassidy said as she approached me.

Josh, trying to stand between us, was dangerously positioned in the path of that pistol. I tried to push him out of the way, but he would not be moved.

"My mom just proved that you didn't kill your stepfather," Melissa said to Cassidy. "You don't understand."

"I understand perfectly. Just give me the recorder, and this will be over." I didn't care for the sound of that.

Paul threw up his hands in a gesture of realization. "There was only one person both Keith Johnson and Cassidy Van Doren loved enough to protect," he said. "Cassidy is willingly taking the blame for Keith's murder so she can keep her mother out of jail."

"I'll find something to hit her with," Maxie said, but I shook my head negatively. The last time she'd helped me like that I'd almost gotten shot and spent the night in the hospital. The ceiling in my den had been damaged to the tune of thousands of dollars my insurance company didn't see as covered by their policy. They have some prejudice against gunshot wounds to the ceiling.

"This is one crazy show," Eduardo DiSica told his wife. "She really did save the best for last."

"You can't have the recorder," I said to Cassidy. "It's evidence in your trial. And it points to your mother killing your stepfather and your attorney."

Cassidy actually stopped moving for a moment and blinked twice. It became evident she was trying to remember. "The Harrison guy?" she asked.

Richard looked pained.

"I did not kill a lawyer," Adrian said.

I wasn't going to mention the gun in Cassidy's hand because, frankly, I feel it's better not to draw attention to such things. If Cassidy was just brandishing it as, say, a cute accessory to her outfit, who was I to question her taste? But the way she was pointing it at Josh (who wasn't giving her a clear shot at me) indicated this was not a fashion choice.

"The recorder," Cassidy said. "*Now*." She held out her left hand, which was not pointing a gun in my direction.

"I don't think so," I told her. "Why would you want to destroy evidence against the woman who shot your stepfather and set you up for it?"

"None of your business," Cassidy said. She wasn't much of an ad-libber.

"It is her business," Mom said. My mother chooses the oddest times to stick up for me. "She's supposed to find out who killed everybody, and you didn't kill your stepfather. Why do you want everybody to think you did?"

"She *did*!" Keith Johnson cried, but he seemingly couldn't move with the ghosts holding him in place, and we'd all heard that before, so nobody paid any attention to him.

"Because that's how it works," Cassidy said.

Somehow that made sense. This was a plan; it had been decided upon in advance. In addition to not having given her the voice recorder, I also hadn't turned it off, so it was for the record that I said, "So that's it. You're protecting your mother by going to jail for the rest of your life for a murder you didn't commit?"

"It doesn't matter," Cassidy answered. "I was going anyway."

"Going?" Josh repeated. "To jail? Why?"

"Because she's the one who killed Richard," Paul said. "She was protecting her mother then too. I'm willing to bet—"

"Hang on." Maxie flew through the ceiling and returned a few seconds later in the trench coat. Her laptop came out when the coat vanished, and the guests applauded the effect. Adrian, Braden, and Erika looked puzzled. Cassidy wasn't watching; she was fixed directly on Josh and me. "Sure enough."

She turned the laptop toward us so we could see the screen. And there, in a grainy but certainly visible hotel security video frame, was Cassidy Van Doren in a blonde wig being escorted into a hotel room by a short, ordinary man shot from behind whom I could only assume was Tom Zink. "That's her," Maxie said, just in case we hadn't caught the resemblance.

"Cassie," Braden, who hadn't heard Maxie speak, breathed. He didn't sound shocked that his stepsister had killed her attorney or that a laptop computer had just floated into the room. He sounded appalled that Cassidy had been careless enough to get caught.

"That whole scene on the highway coming here was just to throw us off," I said, thinking aloud. "You never were sideswiped by an SUV, were you? You drove your own car down a ravine and broke two of your ribs . . . for what?" And then it hit me. Paul looked at me funny. I looked back at Cassidy. "You really *were* blackmailing your stepfather, weren't you?"

Cassidy did not so much as move a facial muscle. "I have no idea what you're talking about."

"I *told* you!" Keith Johnson shouted. The one time he'd told me the truth and I hadn't believed him.

I advanced a hair on Cassidy, who I remembered was still holding a gun and demanding my voice recorder. Maybe advancing was a bad move. "You knew about his shady business dealings."

"Wait, what?" Johnson said.

"You knew your stepfather was taking money from clients to keep your mother in luxury and not paying them back. You knew he was running a pyramid scheme he could never sustain. And when you confronted him with it, he agreed to funnel money to you to keep you quiet. So how did the feds find out?"

"I have no idea what you're talking about." Cassidy was stuck in one mode.

"It had nothing to do with her," Keith said bitterly. "I paid her all that money and they found out anyway." He looked askance at Adrian. "I think it was Hunter's wife who talked."

"That's not all of it," Paul said. "Cassidy stole the iron from Thomas Zink's room and then went to Richard's and . . ." His voice trailed off when he looked at his brother.

Richard's eyes were wide when he wasn't blinking uncontrollably. His mouth hung open. Sounds were coming out of it, but they weren't coherent. He looked directly at Cassidy.

"Oh, Richard," Paul said. "I'm so sorry."

"It can't be," Richard said quietly.

"That's enough," Cassidy barked. "Give me the voice recorder."

"What are you going to do?" I asked, trying to step out of Josh's protection so I could at least face my attacker. "Shoot me?"

"That's what the gun is for." Cassidy definitely had a mean streak. I was feeling a little sweat on the back of my neck.

"There are eight other people in this room who'll see you do it," I reminded her. "Not to mention your mother and your stepbrother and stepsister. How will you deal with that?"

Cassidy didn't miss a beat. "I guess I'll have to shoot all of them too," she said. "Except my mom and my stepbrother."

"Ooh," said Penny Desmond. She didn't sound the least bit worried despite Cassidy's pronouncement that she was going to shoot everyone in the room. And Erika didn't seem to notice that she had been included in that group. She didn't react at all.

"I don't really see that working out for you," I told the woman with the pistol. "They'll figure out it was you."

"She's going to jail anyway," Adrian countered. "So she'll go to jail more. What's the difference?"

I regarded the widow Johnson for a moment. "I don't get it. How come everybody's so crazy about her? She's really not likable at all."

"How dare you," Keith Johnson said.

"For the love of . . . she *killed* you!" Maxie yelled at him as she put the laptop on a side table.

Keith, for once, shut up.

Greg Lewis and Abby Lesniak were sitting on the sofa, snuggled against each other. They didn't seem to have noticed anything that was going on.

"She's my *mother*," Cassidy said. "And I'm not going to let her spend the rest of her life in prison."

That made even less sense than the murderers I've gotten used to over the years, which is a sentence most people will never say. Sometimes I envy most people.

"So when Richard was closing in on Adrian as the woman who killed Keith Johnson, you decided—or did your mother ask you—to steal a hotel iron and murder him?" I was confronting Cassidy directly. "Couldn't you just fire the lawyer?"

"It just can't be," Richard repeated to no one in particular.

"My *stepfather* wouldn't allow that," Cassidy said. "He'd left instructions to hire that guy if there was any trouble. He thought it would be about the money that was getting bounced around, but it turned out to be him getting drowned by his own wife in a bathtub."

"Why *was* Mr. Johnson funneling money to you?" Melissa asked Cassidy. "I didn't think he liked you very much."

"I don't," Keith Johnson said. Nobody paid attention to that either.

"Blackmail," I guessed. "Cassidy wanted to get Keith out of her mother's life and knew something about him or his business. She tried to use it for leverage, and Keith, assuming everyone had a price, just sent money her way. But it didn't work."

"Stupid girl," Keith said.

"Enough of this," Cassidy said. She pointed the barrel of the gun at Josh. "Get out of the way."

"No," my husband said, but I was already trying to push in front of him. I'd spent too long looking for a good man and had gone through a Swine to get to him. The last thing I'd do—perhaps literally—was let him get shot.

"I need that voice recorder," Cassidy said louder.

"And the laptop," Vanessa DiSica said, pointing. "That's what had your picture on it."

Cassidy turned. "What?" she asked.

Josh moved quickly toward her, but Cassidy was just as fast at pivoting and training the pistol on him again. "Don't." Josh stopped after taking one step.

"If you're going to jail and you're sure you'll get caught, why bother to shoot anyone here?" My daughter, sensible budding teenager that she is, was trying to reason with the homicidal maniac; it was almost cute. "Just confess to the murders and go to jail. You didn't have to kill anyone else."

"Because there's always the chance of being acquitted, a mistrial, or multiple appeals," Richard said quietly. "No sense in confessing and being sentenced when she could stay out of jail for years, if not decades."

"Look, Everett's holding this guy's arms, but somebody should be able to clobber the girl with the gun," Maxie said. "None of the other nut jobs have a weapon."

"I'm still holding him too," Paul noted.

"I'll look for something," Dad told them. "I might have a bigger pipe wrench in the basement." He was through the floor before I could tell him he already had a wrench and that I'd moved the bigger pipe wrench into the kitchen to do a repair under the sink.

That seemed to leave things to Everett, who looked at Maxie. "I might be able to hold her for a moment, but I don't know that I can keep a grip that long," he said.

"Don't hold her; *hit* her!" his wife told him.

But Cassidy and her family, of course, heard none of this. She sneered at Melissa—which is a punishable offense in my judicial code all by itself—and shook her head seemingly in wonder at the ridiculous suggestion that had been made. "Everyone here heard what was said about my mother," she told Liss. "They'll testify to it, and she will be charged."

Everett was scanning the room, presumably for a suitable blunt instrument to immobilize Cassidy. He rushed out of the room without comment, no doubt looking for something familiar to him like his service weapon, which I'm not even sure is real.

"No one will tell, I'm sure," Melissa said. She was stalling. "I'm sure everyone here would promise."

"Oh, no," Eduardo said. "I'd tell in a second." The guests were enjoying what they saw as their ultimate spook show just a little too much.

Cassidy actually gestured toward him with the gun. "See?" she said to Melissa. She turned back toward Josh. "Get out of the way. I need that voice recorder."

I saw an opening. "Because it proves you killed Richard Harrison," I said.

Richard was shaking his head. "No," he practically whimpered.

I'd faced the barrel of a gun too many times in the past few years after having gone all those years before without it happening once. It has gone from something that terrified me from head to foot into something that really annoys the living hell out of me. It's not that I don't care if I get shot; it's that the utter lack of imagination in holding me in check with a gun is offensive to my intelligence.

"That's not it," Cassidy said. "I told you. He was just an annoyance."

I heard Richard make a noise like something caught him in the throat.

My father rose through the floor holding a rubber mallet inside his jacket. "This?" he asked.

But I had other plans. I shook my head, and Dad stopped where he was. "What?"

"An annoyance? That man was doing all he could to help you, and he was an annoyance?" I didn't dare steal a glance at Richard. "He loved you."

Cassidy Van Doren made what was perhaps the second biggest mistake of her life. She laughed. "He *loved* me?" She looked at Braden. "Did you hear that?" The two of them almost doubled over in hysterics.

I knew that would do it. Richard, bellowing with a rage I'll bet even Paul wouldn't have thought possible, launched himself at Cassidy and caught her at the legs. She fell backward at the impact and landed on her back, the gun flying out of her hand. I was afraid it would go off, but Penny Desmond, the closest person to Cassidy when she fell, caught it neatly and held it out toward me. "Is this what I'm supposed to do?" she asked.

"Yes, Penny. That is exactly what you were supposed to do. Thank you." I grabbed the gun and turned it around to point the barrel at the prone Cassidy, who might not have known Richard was next to her sobbing. The only reason she could have been aware was that he was also punching the floor in frustration, and her face was in the way. She probably didn't feel it because his fist went all the way through the floor. It takes great focus for a ghost to affect something in the physical world like that. Richard was pretty steamed.

Cassidy didn't appear to be moving anytime soon, so I pivoted to point the gun at her mother and stepsiblings.

But Adrian, Braden, and Erika had all run for the door. I heard a car starting up outside and knew it was far too late to catch them. So I did something even better.

I called McElone.

"That was wonderful," Eduardo DiSica said after the guests had finished applauding. "You really topped yourself."

The only guests not obviously thrilled with the "performance" were Greg Lewis and Abby Lesniak, but that was only because they couldn't possibly have broken eye contact the whole time the melodrama was playing out in front of them. I doubt they had any idea what had just taken place.

"It was great," Abby said.

"Great," Greg echoed.

But then I felt my daughter's arms around my waist and my husband's around my shoulders, and my mother was standing nearby because I felt her warm hand on my back. My father, rubber mallet in hand, was hovering over Mom, and Paul was attending to his brother, who sat stunned and no longer violent on the floor next to Cassidy, who was breathing and uninjured to the naked eye but not moving.

"What are we gonna do with this guy?" Maxie asked Everett, who had returned no doubt from the kitchen holding the baseball bat I keep in the closet. It's a long story. She gestured toward Keith Johnson, who no longer seemed to be straining against her grip.

"Is there jail for people like us?" Everett asked. "He did try to kill the ghost lady." That's me.

"I didn't!" Johnson insisted. "I was just trying to scare her, honest!" Given the level of honesty we'd gotten from him, I saw no reason to believe that.

"Paul," I said. He looked up from Richard, who struggled to get into a standing position and then floated a few inches above the prone Cassidy. "Do you remember when all those ghosts were here after we held that fake séance?"

"A fake séance?" Madame Lorraine was appalled.

"The thing about donating ectoplasm to create a kind of cage, a solitary confinement, for a person like me?" Paul shuddered a bit even thinking about it.

"That's what I had in mind." I nodded my head toward Keith Johnson.

Johnson's eyes looked absolutely terrified. "No. Really. I didn't want to hurt anybody. Please!"

I had never intended to condemn him to something so permanent and awful, and I doubt Paul even knew how to implement it. But keeping Keith Johnson away had become a serious priority. "There's one other way," I said.

"Anything!" Johnson put his hands together as if in prayer. Granted, they were behind him because Maxie was still holding him, but it was the gesture that mattered. I thought I was a fairly poor deity to choose but didn't see how I could argue.

"You need to leave this house, this town, this *state* and never come back," I said. "If you're spotted by any ghost in this area anytime ever, they'll know what to do. Paul will see to it."

Johnson was already nodding before Paul could put on a look of complete conviction on his face.

"Absolutely! I promise. I'll leave now!" He looked at Maxie, who was still holding him in place. "Just let me go!"

Maxie looked at me. I walked up close to Johnson and stared into his eyes. "You have to *mean* it," I said. "You can't *ever* come back." And in his case, *ever* was a long time.

His voice wavered. "Not even to see Adrian?" Some guys really don't ever learn.

"Lock him up," I said to Paul, who was about to look confused.

"No!" Johnson knelt in midair and really accentuated his attempt at pathos, which came across more as desperation. "I'll go. Really. Forever."

I looked at Paul. "How many ghosts do you have contact with in this area?" I asked.

He had no idea. "Thousands," he said.

"You get it?" I said to Johnson.

He nodded. I looked at Maxie. "Let him go. If he doesn't leave the house immediately, you all know what to do."

Maxie let go of Keith Johnson's hands, and he exited straight through the wall of the movie room toward the beach. I let out a sigh. "That's that," I said to myself.

The guests applauded and stood up.

"Best yet," Eduardo DiSica told me as he and Vanessa walked out.

She agreed. "I thought it was amazing. That girl on the floor really looks like she's knocked out."

Oh, yeah, Cassidy. After the guests left, I asked Dad to find some rope, and we tied her up. McElone would be here in a minute, but she'd be happier if we delivered our package outside. The lieutenant doesn't care much to come inside where the ghosts are.

I got hugs from Mom, Melissa, and mostly Josh and warm sensations from Dad and Paul as they touched me. Maxie beckoned Everett to join her on the roof and watch to see if Johnson was really leaving and, if so, whether he was swimming to England. They rose through the ceiling.

I was about to help Cassidy to her feet for her perp walk when I looked over at the corner of the room. There stood Madame Lorraine, facing the center of the action and looking somewhat awed. She walked slowly toward me and stopped.

"You really are a great performer," she said. "They believed everything you said."

I smiled. "Some of us got it and some of us ain't," I told Madame Lorraine. "You know."

Chapter 34

"Adrian Johnson and her two stepchildren were arrested on the Garden State Parkway near Exit 100B, maybe a half hour after you called me." Detective Lieutenant Anita McElone and I were sitting on my front porch, which is as far as McElone will go toward my house unless absolutely necessary. "Once we had an APB out on them, the troopers didn't need much more. They were heading north, probably to the house in Upper Saddle River and then maybe to skip out of the state."

"But they only made it to Asbury Park." I was sipping a lemonade. McElone was being her usual stoic self and drinking nothing. It wasn't that hot yet, but it was still stubbornness on her part.

"And then they started turning on each other like a bag of snakes," McElone said. "Everybody blamed everybody else, but it sure wasn't their fault, that was for certain. The prosecutors will sort it out, but almost everybody's going to jail, I would bet."

"I don't get what Erika and Braden got out of this deal," I said. "They seemed like the odd, um, couple out."

"Seems the Ponzi scheme old Keith was running wasn't something he could do alone," McElone told me. "He needed some inside help from his son the Wall Street stockbroker."

"And Erika?"

McElone came very close to smiling. "She was the only one who didn't just adore her stepmom," she said. "She didn't want Adrian to go to jail because that would have jeopardized Erika's own arrangement with Keith, which included him buying her a boutique in Manhattan with the pyramid money."

"But she doesn't have a boutique in Manhattan." I thought it was important to point that out.

"If you look deep enough, you'll find a lease signed by Keith Johnson the day before he died. For a place that was going to be called Eriqua. I am not kidding. Once the investors had done enough of an audit after Keith died, it became a Starbucks."

The past night had included a quick visit from McElone and four of her best blue-uniformed friends, who had taken Cassidy Van Doren away (I was guessing this time without bail) and questioned everyone who had been in the room, yielding what I expected were somewhat confusing results. Half the group thought the whole thing was a swell show. Who was I to tell them otherwise? Evaluation forms would be filled out today, after all.

Mom and Dad, as ever, had witnessed the mayhem without comment and then gone home, Mom driving her Dodge Viper at five miles below the speed limit the whole way. Even if Cassidy Van Doren *had* been menaced by someone on the road, it would not have been my mother. She's more of an obstacle than a threat.

Josh had gone to work this morning as usual and Melissa, first vacation day of the summer, was sleeping in. I'd already fielded a phone call from Phyllis, who wasn't going to write an article about murders that didn't take place in her coverage area but scolded me for not reporting back to her immediately. I grinned because that's how you know she's Phyllis.

McElone had come by to get her last shot at the guests before they all went home, which they would do in a few hours when the Senior Tours Plus van would roll up to my door. They all seemed thrilled with the previous night's festivities (as they saw it), and I'd noticed Greg Lewis and Abby Lesniak going out for a late bite at an all-night diner (as most of them are in New Jersey) some miles down the road. I'd been in bed long before they got back.

Now with her questioning all done, McElone was taking a moment—rare for her—to discuss the case after the fact. And I could tell it was making her uncomfortable. If there's one thing McElone can't stand, it's not being able to do everything herself.

"How much ghosty stuff was involved in this?" she asked me. "You know I can't use any of that in my report."

"Almost everything is on that voice recorder I gave you," I reminded her. "There's nothing ghost-adjacent on there, although you'll hear breaks where I'm talking to someone who isn't exactly there. I'd think you'd get a lot from the confessions. Has Cassidy talked yet?"

McElone shook her head. "She lawyered up. Apparently it's gotten to be a habit with her."

"Just don't let her near this guy with any ironing instruments," I said.

McElone grimaced, which is as close to a smile as I'll ever get out of her. "I don't think that's going to happen."

She left shortly after, so I went inside to see if any of the guests needed help with packing or moving luggage. The van driver, a lovely guy with enormous arms, usually handles that, but some of the guests—usually the men—feel it's a sign of weakness to ask someone for help.

Melissa, now awake, was in the den pouring an iced coffee (that is, coffee from the urn over ice I'd left out in a bucket) for herself. She is infinitely more cheerful when she doesn't have to wake up early, but her face was still telling me not to engage her in conversation just yet. I moved on.

Nobody was in the movie room, but I found Paul and Richard in the library of all places. "Catching up on your reading?" I asked.

Paul gave me a look much like Melissa's, which indicated he and Richard were acting like close brothers again, and I kept walking. But it made me wonder: Was Paul planning on leaving again? Was he going somewhere with Richard? Would we have to go through that drama one more time?

Penny Desmond was looking out through the French doors at the deck, the beach, and the ocean. A lot of guests do this on the last morning, thinking about how they'll be back in their homes soon and away from the beauty of the shore. It's one of the reasons I decided to come back to Harbor

Haven and buy the ridiculously large Victorian that became the guesthouse.

"Maybe you'll come back someday," I said to Penny when I got close enough to do so without shouting.

"Oh, I don't know," she answered. "I've never been much for the beach. Sand between your toes, having to shower off whenever you come in, salt all over from the ocean. Not for me. I like a nice little town to walk around in. You have a good one here, but I have pretty much the same thing at home without all the sand."

I had to ask. "Then why did you come here for vacation?"

She looked at me as if it were obvious. "The ghosts," she said. "They were fantastic."

My phone buzzed, and when I saw Tony Mandorisi's name in the caller ID, I picked up immediately. Tony doesn't call that often; he lets Jeannie be the social liaison. "What's up?" I asked.

"I've got a guy."

That was a stumper. "Does Jeannie know?" I asked.

"Don't be hilarious, Alison. A guy. To fix your ceiling and put in a beam."

"You can have all the guys you want, Tony." I noticed Penny giving me an amused look. "But I don't have the money to pay your guys for that big a job, and you and I know I can't do it myself. We've talked about this."

"This guy works cheap," Tony said. "He's my brother."

And I will tell you, because I know you'll never mention it to Tony or Jeannie, my first thought was, *Oh, please, no. Not another brother.*

"How cheap?" I asked. You have to be practical.

"We'll talk about it, but trust me, you can afford it. I'll call you later."

I gave up seeking people out for a while because that wasn't working well for me today. I didn't need to clean any of the guest rooms because they were still in them, but then I saw Abby and Greg walking down the stairs without luggage, looking absolutely euphoric. I hadn't done anything to help them and that had worked like a charm.

"You look very happy," I told them in case they hadn't figured that out.

"We are," Greg Lewis said. "I just wish I hadn't waited so long to say something."

Abby patted his arm. "You have plenty of time now," she said.

"What took you so long?" I asked. "Just shy?" Greg could have saved me a lot of innkeeper angst if he'd approached Abby, say, the day after they'd arrived.

"No, not just shy. I was getting everything together so it would be perfect, and that took time. I had to write the song and record it out on the beach so I could get the sound of the surf, and I was experimenting with my own balloons before I gave up and went to that store you told me about. That worked out well."

Experimenting with . . . "Were you making a stretching noise in the extra guest room that night?" I asked. Greg looked guilty. "Why did you go in there? *How* did you go in there? The room was locked."

"I just needed a little private space, and my room wasn't big enough," he explained. "And I got in . . . well, I picked the lock. I'm a locksmith. There's nothing in the house I couldn't have opened if I'd wanted to."

That was sort of creepy. "But you didn't, right? I mean, open any other doors."

Greg looked offended. "No! Of course not! Just that one time, and then I never did it again. I just needed the extra space in there."

I told them I was glad they'd met at my house and wished them well. The van was pulling up, and the guests were starting to drift toward the front door. I'd be needed to host them out (say good-bye) in a minute or two.

Maxie dropped down and looked at me. "You know, Paul's talking to Richard about leaving again," she said.

I'd figured that. Richard was still rocked emotionally by the revelations of the night before and would no doubt want to bolt this area as quickly as possible. And since Paul had come back only because his brother needed help, there was no reason for him to stick around either.

"Paul's a big boy," I told her. "He can do what he wants to do." As long as it was stay around my house and be my conscience. He was the Jiminy Cricket of ghosts.

Maxie shrugged. "Whatevs."

Melissa, aware the guests would be leaving soon, came to the front room to help me see them off. She is comanager of the guesthouse and knows exactly what that means. It means she does a lot of work and doesn't get paid.

The van arrived exactly on time as it always does, and everybody got their luggage and themselves aboard. Many fond farewells, all of them sincere, were offered. But as always, it was something of a relief when the van pulled away and I knew I'd have two days before it showed up with new guests to entertain again.

I turned back toward the house and saw Richard phasing through the front door. He wasn't carrying any luggage, of course, but I could tell by his expression and the flow of his movement that he was leaving the guesthouse for parts unknown.

Paul was right behind him.

For all my show about how it was Paul's decision to stay or go, that moment made me want to yell to him not to leave, that he was my friend and I needed him here. But I didn't because I'm an adult and because I respect the choices others make even if they don't match my own.

Besides, Melissa said it. "You're not leaving, are you, Paul?"

Paul looked at Liss, then at Richard, then at me, and then back at Richard again. "No," he said. "What gave you that idea?"

It was mostly Maxie. I didn't say that either, but Liss didn't pick it up for me this time. "Well, Richard . . ." I began.

Richard turned—he had passed us already—and looked at me. "Yes," he said. "I am leaving. I don't know where I'll be, but I need a break from this place." He looked at the house. "No offense."

"We understand," Melissa told him. "You've been through a lot." That girl has a future in diplomacy. Or any other field.

Richard looked away to avoid eye contact. "I wanted to . . . thank you. For the help you've given me these past few days. I realize it was done with the best possible intentions." The man's warmest thoughts could have kept the ice in my freezer solid. Of course, it was in a freezer, but you get the idea.

"But I still think Paul should come with me," Richard went on. He looked at his brother. "You were doing all that traveling, and there's still a lot of world to see."

Paul smiled that crooked smile of his. "I have plenty of time," he said. "Keep me informed about your whereabouts, Richard. I'll be in contact every night." He looked up at the sky, which was his sign for the Ghosternet.

"I will do that." And with that, Richard leapt into the sky and vanished in the distance.

We turned back and moved toward the house. "So you don't need to see the world anymore?" I asked Paul.

"I still intend to do so, but with all eternity ahead of me, I don't see a great rush," he answered. "One thing I've learned is that it's good to have a home base. And it's nice to have people you see every day."

"Stop it," Melissa said. "You'll make me cry."

We all laughed at that and went inside. I had every intention of sitting down in a nice soft easy chair for at least two days—after I cleaned the guest rooms, changed all the sheets, and took a look at that beam in the den again. Maybe Tony was right.

You can't let old wounds stay open forever.

Read an excerpt from

BONES BEHIND THE WHEEL

the next

HAUNTED GUESTHOUSE MYSTERY

by E. J. COPPERMAN

available soon in hardcover from
Crooked Lane Books

CROOKED
LANE

NEW YORK

Chapter 1

"This is no walk on the beach."

Against all evidence to the contrary, I had to agree. Katrina Breslin and I were, in fact, on the sand behind my massive Victorian home/business and we *were*, indeed, traveling by foot, but you couldn't possibly have mistaken what we were doing for a nice, relaxing walk on the beach.

"We just need to get a little farther down toward the ocean and the other houses," I suggested, pointing south. "There isn't quite so much heavy equipment down there."

The state of New Jersey in its infinite wisdom (and this might be the time to remind you that the National Language of New Jersey is Sarcasm) had decided to do some—it said—necessary excavation on parts of the shore in Harbor Haven, the town where I live and run a guesthouse. The state had noted that Superstorm Sandy (we're not allowed to call it a *hurricane*) had done considerable damage to the area just a few years back and erosion had also taken a toll, so bolstering the dunes was necessary, and apparently that was done by moving huge amounts of sand around in what appeared to be a completely random pattern. I didn't see how using bulldozers and other huge machines to move sand from one place to another was going to protect anything, but oddly, I had not been consulted. I had been nice enough to let the foreman, Bill Harrelson, and his crew use my bathrooms while they were here, with the provision that they make sure to keep them clean and not abuse the privilege, which they had not. They'd been conscientious visitors.

If I'm going to be fair—and there is no reason to expect that I will—it made sense for the work, if it was really going to be done, to take place now. November is hardly peak tourist season on the Jersey Shore, although Senior Plus Tours, the company that steers a number of guests in my direction each month, had still sent three this week. They weren't here so much for the lovely beaches (now being bulldozed) or the amusement piers (closed for the season except, for some reason, on Thanksgiving).

They were here for the ghosts.

Perhaps I should explain.

A little over four years ago, I was a newly divorced single mother who had just won a lawsuit against a previous employer whose hands hadn't remembered his marriage vows and whose ears had been deaf to my refusals until I decked him. Sorry, until he slipped on some spilled copier toner and bumped his head on my fist. That's what it said in the depositions.

I decided to take charge of the changes in my life instead of letting them be imposed upon me, so I moved back to Harbor Haven, where I'd grown up, and bought the Victorian, not in spite of but because of its having far too many rooms for me and my then-nine-year-old daughter Melissa to

inhabit. I wanted to own and run a guesthouse in my hometown and got a deal on the place because it needed a *lot* of
repairs and renovation.

In the midst of doing those—my father had been an inde-
pendent contractor and had taught me how to do home repair
work so I wouldn't be taken in by contractors less scrupulous
than he was—I met with an "accident" and was hit on the
head with a bucket of drywall compound, which I can tell you
hurt quite a bit.

When I regained what few senses I had, I could see two
people who I'd have sworn had not been there pre-bucket. As
it turned out, they were Paul Harrison and Maxie Malone,
and they had recently *kicked* the bucket in what was now my
new house. They were ghosts (go figure) who wanted to know
who had killed them (which, in retrospect, was probably reasonable) and wanted me to help them find out (which was
not, even in retrospect).

That's a story told elsewhere, but suffice it to say we found
Paul and Maxie's murderer, and I think all of us expected
that would propel them to some other area of the afterlife,
what with the "unfinished business" on this planet completed.
But no. Paul and Maxie were still here in the guesthouse four
years and change later.

We had worked out an arrangement: Paul had been a private investigator just getting started when he and Maxie had
met their end (if you want to call it that), and he still wanted
to investigate things. Problem was, he needed someone in the
living world to go other places and ask the questions, because
the vast majority of people couldn't see or hear him and at

the time he was unable to move past my property line. He has since overcome that last restriction, but only a select few, including Melissa and my mother, can see the ghosts. Liss and Mom always could and had chosen not to tell me about it because they thought I'd feel bad. That was something of a miscalculation on their part, but I will admit I probably would have at least taken my daughter to a psychotherapist if I'd heard she could see the spirits of the undead and was fine with it.

Paul wanted me to get a private investigator license so I could help him with what he saw as his detective agency. I had discovered that some guests actually *want* to be in a house with ghosts and that that could help my business. So I agreed to do as Paul asked if he and Maxie would put on "spook shows" for the guests twice a day. Senior Plus provided the guests who wanted some interaction with the deceased, and I did the occasional work with Paul, which so far had not once worked out profitably for me. But we make the bargains we make and move on.

So now I was a newly remarried single mother and inn-keeper/extremely part-time private detective, walking on the beach with one of my guests who had observed that what we were doing was certainly no walk on the beach.

Katrina looked down the beach in the direction I'd indicated. "I don't think it's that much better down there, Alison," she said.

She had a point. The earth-moving equipment was located in every location as far as the eye could see, and when you're on the shore, you can see pretty far. There aren't any private houses near mine because much of the beachfront has been bought up by businesses, and some of it is just municipal territory to lure the tourists, which I appreciate. The previous owners of my house (with the exception of Maxie, who had occupied the place briefly before her demise) had held fast against the commercialization of the beach, although I imagine the seven bedrooms in the house hadn't been put there just because they'd decided to have a large family.

"Maybe it's just not a good idea to stroll out here," Katrina said. You could hear the unspoken *today* at the end of her sentence, because she clearly knew this wasn't getting any better before she ended her vacation and went home in three days.

"I'm so sorry," I told her. "The town didn't tell us the dates they'd be working on our property specifically, so I couldn't warn you too much in advance."

Katrina turned toward the guesthouse and started in that direction, so I followed her. "It's not a big deal," she said. "I wasn't expecting to go swimming or anything." That was fortunate, because the heavy cardigan she was wearing would no doubt have weighed her down once it was saturated. "I came to get away from my life for a while and maybe see some ghosts." She smiled.

Of course, Katrina and the other guests, a couple named Adam and Steve Cosgrove, had not seen and would not see Paul and Maxie. They wouldn't see Maxie's husband, Everett, or my father when he dropped by with my mother, who was thankfully not yet a ghost. They'd see what we wanted them to see of the *results* the ghosts have, which consist mainly of carefully planned objects flying by and effects (pretty cheesy ones) we put together for entertainment purposes. We never scare the guests, largely because Paul and Maxie et al. are not scary people. We've discovered that people are pretty much who they are, and death doesn't change that so much as make them considerably less tangible.

"Have you been enjoying the shows so far?" I asked. It's always good to get feedback from a guest during the stay if you can, because if there's something that's bothering him or her, you can fix it rather than read it on a guest evaluation form after they leave.

"Yeah, more than I thought I would, to tell you the truth." Katrina stopped for a moment to regard me with an amused smile. "That Maxie is a riot."

It's not the word I would have chosen—Maxie and I have a complicated relationship based on mutual irritation—but the customer is always right, and Maxie's heart (if she still had one) was in the right place. I was pretty sure. I'd check at the Harbor Haven Cemetery.

"She has a style," I allowed, and started walking again toward the house, letting Katrina follow this time.

We reached the edge of my property, and I stopped—for lack of a better word—dead in my tracks.

The excavation being done in what was basically my backyard had been carefully described to me by the construction firm the town had hired to handle the erosion issues. It was going to take six days, I'd been told, and would inconvenience me only by having the huge bulldozers and other beasts of sand-moving parked behind my house. The actual amount of earth displaced (that was their word) this far from the ocean would be "minimal."

So the enormous hole now occupying about a quarter of my backyard was something of a surprise.

It hadn't been visible when we were approaching because of the ginormous excavator that I thought had been idly parked on the spot but now was clearly digging something out of the crater it had dug in the sand. *My* sand. (I can show you the deed.)

I stood there stunned for a moment while Katrina, stopping at my side, said, "Wow."

No kidding.

I opened and closed my mouth a couple of times, something I often do with sound coming out. That didn't seem completely possible at the moment. This violation of my property was enormous and clearly going to take a *while* to restore. I hadn't been this angry since any time ever that I'd seen my ex-husband, The Swine. (It's not the name on his birth certificate, but it's much more descriptive of the man he had become.)

When I could start breathing normally, or close to it, again, I noticed Bill Harrelson, the foreman for my section of the project, trudging from the side of my house toward the Grand Canyon that had suddenly been deposited where a placid beach had been before. I reminded myself there was a guest present (you need to watch your language under such circumstances) and headed for him.

"Bill," I managed. There were so many other words that could have been.

He held up his hands, palms out, feigning innocence. "Hang on, Alison," he said.

"Hang on? You told me you were parking some equipment, and now I have a bottomless pit in my backyard. You want me to hang on? I might trip and end up on the molten core of the Earth."

"I don't know what happened either," Bill protested. "I just got a text to come back here. Let me see what's going on."

Okay, so I could hang on. For a minute. Tops.

Bill walked to the side of the extractor, whose arm was extended deep into the crater. Katrina looked over at me. "Good thing it's not the summer, huh?" she said.

Now, I liked Katrina. Truly. She had seemed, in the short time I'd known her, to be a very nice and level-headed person. So I made a concerted effort not to scream at her. I'm a good hostess.

"Yes," I said. It wasn't terribly original, but it avoided snarling. That was something.

"I mean, it would really have hurt your business then, I'm guessing," Katrina continued. She was clearly operating under the assumption that I had not understood her point.

"Yup." I saw Bill talking earnestly with the extractor operator and then, shaking his head, walking around to the front of the big machine and looking down into the pit, which was something I didn't think you were supposed to do unless you were in a Vincent Price movie. And even then it generally didn't turn out all that well for the person leaning over the edge.

"Because a lot of people come here for the beach." Katrina, no doubt spurred on by my terseness, was now explaining the appeal of the Jersey Shore to me. I needed to let her off the hook but I was busy watching Bill, who didn't exactly recoil from what he saw in the hole but did seem to move back a couple of feet instinctively. "You know, not just for the ghosts."

"I know, Katrina. Sorry, but I have to see if there's a problem. Excuse me, okay?" Like most people, I did not wait for a response and walked past Katrina toward Bill, who took what appeared to be another incredulous look down into the gaping hole (whose repair bill I was already mentally sending to the state) and then stood up straight again, a look on his face that indicated wonder and some unease.

"What's the problem, Bill?" I asked. As I walked to his side, I could see more of the crater and the arm of the excavator digging into it. The machine had clearly unearthed material other than sand, material its operator hadn't been expecting, because the claw appeared to be dragging something out of the ground. Something metal and large.

Bill wheeled to face me, a sign that he hadn't known I was lurking behind him. "Alison!" I gave him a moment—that was certainly my name, and I didn't see any reason to dispute it. "There's something down there."

"Yeah, I get that. What is it and why did your guys start digging here? I'm not on the list for major excavation." The lawsuit I was planning could lead to another renovation of the guesthouse, maybe add an outdoor swimming pool. Because there are, believe it or not, some strange people who like to come to the beach and then swim in a pool. I know.

"One of the guys had a divining rod and read some metal vibrations," Bill said. "He thought it might be a rare coin or something."

I glanced down toward the tremendous maw they'd opened up but didn't get any closer. I have this thing about not falling into bottomless pits. "That's bigger than a coin."

"Yeah. It's a Continental."

Of course it was. What was a Continental? "A what?"

"A Continental." He saw the confusion in my eyes. "A *Lincoln Continental*."

I confess; it took me a second. "It's a car?"

Bill nodded fervently. "Yeah. By the look of it, I'd say midseventies, maybe. A Continental sedan. Green."

Well, the color made all the difference. "What's it doing down there?" I asked. It seemed like a logical question. Forget that Bill's crew had been scavenging for change on my beach like some tinfoil hat prospector and they'd chose to dig for a quarter with a shovel the size of, well, a Lincoln Continental. "Why is there a car buried in my backyard?"

He spread out his hands, palms out. "I wish I knew. But . . ."

I didn't hear what he said next because the man operating the excavator decided to start it up. You sort of get used to the noise from the construction equipment after a day or . . . never . . . but usually you're not as close to the big machines as I was right now. The scoop on the front of the rig moved, down, digging under the frame of what I guessed was the car's rear end. Bill motioned me away from the pit, and I was happy to walk back in the direction of the ocean, whose roar was considerably more soothing than that of the Caterpillar equipment causing yet more damage to property that was described in detail in my deed.

Katrina, whom I'd left perhaps fifty feet away, was

watching the earth-moving machine quite closely with an expression on her face indicating she'd seen something incredibly wondrous. It's not that I get to see tremendous trucks carve out part of my property every day, but her look was more in the area of having seen a genie create a palace of gold using some straw and a used fez.

Then I realized she was taking in the spectacle that was Bill Harrelson.

Bill wasn't really my type, but that was okay because I was married and needed only one man in my type. But to Katrina, Bill was clearly a type in and of himself. I considered standing back but remembered I wanted an explanation about the vintage sedan now being brought out of my property, so I stopped as soon as I thought speech would be plausible and looked at Bill.

"But what?" I said.

Luckily Bill wasn't in the mood to play coy. He'd been shaken by what he'd seen in the hole, and now it was coming out to be seen by all. So he had to come clean right away. "There's something inside the Continental, I'm pretty sure," he said.

I didn't like the way he said the word *something*, but I didn't get to ask right away because Katrina, stars in her eyes, was nudging me in the side. "I haven't been introduced," she said.

She would continue to not be introduced for a moment, though. I didn't like Bill's ominous tone. "What's in the car?" I asked him.

"It looked a lot like a skeleton," he said.